Praise for *She Wouldn't Change a Thing*

"Adlakha's debut is a truly compelling read, making the reader consider what they would do if offered a second chance, how they might deal with an impossible choice, and what is most important in life. The characters are relatable, the story is gripping, and the blend of domestic fiction with a hint of science fiction is just plain great." —*Booklist* (starred review)

"For me, a mind-bending story only works if its characters are real and relatable. Sarah Adlakha gets it exactly right in *She Wouldn't Change a Thing*. Her protagonist, faced with impossible, life-altering choices, will keep the reader awake at night wondering, 'What would I do?'"

—Diane Chamberlain, *New York Times* bestselling author of *Big Lies in a Small Town*

"A thrilling, breathtaking, heartbreaking story. In this dazzling debut novel, Sarah Adlakha has crafted a world where the magical not only seems possible, but probable, and where the complicated, complex characters, and the often untenable decisions they're forced to make, will haunt you long after the last sentence."

—Rita Woods, author of *Remembrance*

"Book clubs rejoice! *She Wouldn't Change a Thing* is your next selection. It begins as devastatingly realistic, and evolves into simply . . . devastating. Haunting, thought-provoking, and endlessly discussable, this touching and evocative book will linger long after you turn the final page. What would you do with a second chance at your life? Are you sure? Read this—and then decide." —Hank Phillippi Ryan, *USA Today* bestselling author of *Her Perfect Life*

"With searing precision and eerie intensity, Adlakha delivers a dazzling braided narrative of the inevitability of our choices and the sacrifices we make for love. *She Wouldn't Change a Thing* is a story that will break your heart into smithereens, infuse your spirit with hope, and stay with you long after you've turned the final page." —Emily Colin, *New York Times* bestselling author of *The Memory Thief*

"*She Wouldn't Change a Thing* is a complex, intelligent psychological thriller whose unexpected twists and turns gripped me from start to finish. With skillful storytelling, Sarah Adlakha dives into the life of a mother who is forced to decide between her family and her morality, leaving the reader wondering if everything would be different with a single choice. A captivating debut that makes us question our very reality."

—Serena Burdick, bestselling author of *The Girls with No Names*

"Adlakha takes the classic 'what if?' tale and grounds it in a premise that is so outrageous, yet so solidly believable, I blew through it in twenty-four hours, because I *had* to know what happened next. A powerful and rare treatise on fate, love, morality, and spirituality that will make you question everything—including yourself. This book absolutely blew my mind."

—Colleen Oakley, *USA Today* bestselling author of *The Invisible Husband of Frick Island*

Forge Books by Sarah Adlakha

She Wouldn't Change a Thing
Midnight on the Marne

she

wouldn't

change a

thing

SARAH ADLAKHA

A TOM DOHERTY ASSOCIATES BOOK
New York

This is a work of fiction. All of the characters, organizations, and events portrayed in this novel are either products of the author's imagination or are used fictitiously.

A Forge Book
Published by Tom Doherty Associates
120 Broadway
New York, NY 10271

www.tor-forge.com

Forge® is a registered trademark of Macmillan Publishing Group, LLC.

The Library of Congress has cataloged the hardcover edition as follows:

Names: Adlakha, Sarah, author.
Title: She wouldn't change a thing / Sarah Adlakha.
Description: First edition. | New York : Forge, 2021. | A Tom Doherty
    Associates book.
Identifiers: LCCN 2021009150 (print) | LCCN 2021009151 (ebook) |
    ISBN 9781250774552 (hardcover) | ISBN 9781250774569 (ebook)
Subjects: LCSH: Time travel—Fiction. | GSAFD: Fantasy fiction.
Classification: LCC PS3601.D5485 S54 2021 (print) |
    LCC PS3601.D5485 (ebook) | DDC 813/.6—dc23
LC record available at https://lccn.loc.gov/2021009150
LC ebook record available at https://lccn.loc.gov/2021009151

ISBN 978-1-250-77457-6 (trade paperback)

Our books may be purchased in bulk for promotional, educational, or business
use. Please contact your local bookseller or the Macmillan Corporate and
Premium Sales Department at 1-800-221-7945, extension 5442, or by email
at MacmillanSpecialMarkets@macmillan.com.

First Forge Paperback Edition: 2022

Printed in the United States of America

10 9 8 7 6 5 4 3 2 1

For Sati, Mari,

Vidy, and Jiya.

The ones I could

never let go.

We are not human beings having a spiritual experience. We are spiritual beings having a human experience.

—Pierre Teilhard de Chardin

PART I

maria

Bienville, Mississippi, 2010

LAUGHTER.

It was the laughter she would remember, years later, when she thought about that moment, even though she couldn't hear it. They were too far away, or perhaps *she* was too far away, tucked beneath the canopy and sheltered from the sun, listening to the waves roll onto the shore as they tried to lull her to sleep in chorus with the gulls that soared overhead. Her family danced along the beach, her husband crashing through the surf with a daughter tucked under each arm, their laughter searching for her over the expanse of sand. It was useless; it never found her; and as the image of her family faded from her mind, panic took its place.

7:30 A.M.

That couldn't be right. Her alarm was set for 6:30 and it hadn't gone off yet. She reached across the bed for her husband, but the sheets were abandoned and cold. Why didn't he wake her up? She rubbed her eyes and took another look at the clock.

7:31 A.M.

The shower was running in the bathroom. She thought she'd

managed to rein in her frustration, but the door slammed against the wall when she pushed it open.

"Why didn't you wake me up?"

Her husband wiped away the droplets of water from the shower door and smiled at her. "I thought you were taking the day off," he said. "So I let you sleep in."

A thousand things were spinning through her head—kids, school, work, hair, clothes, teeth—but she couldn't stop hearing, *I thought you were taking the day off.* When had she ever just *taken a day off*?

Her husband's smile faded back into oblivion behind the fog of the tempered shower glass as Maria got to work with a toothbrush in one hand and a hairbrush in the other. She was thankful she could no longer see him. It was impossible to stay mad at Will when she could see his face.

By the time she got her teeth brushed and her hair wrangled into a ponytail, there were a dozen spiky grays sticking out of her head at all angles, but there was no use trying to tame them. There was no time for hair spray; no time for makeup, though she could have used a gallon of concealer for the bags around her eyes; no time for the cocoa butter belly lotion that was supposed to have prevented the stretch marks that were already streaked across her belly. No one expected these things from her anymore. Makeup and hair spray were for single women or newlyweds, not a pregnant mother of two with a full-time job and a husband whose work hours stretched long into the night.

"Did you wake the girls up?" she asked, but she was already on her way out the door. She could hear her husband mumbling something about letting all of them sleep in, as she waddled down the hallway like a beleaguered penguin. This pregnancy was nothing like the other two, though she couldn't say why. There were no complications, and chromosomally their unborn son was perfect; they had the results of genetic testing to prove it. But there was an uneasiness that had clung to her throughout this pregnancy, like she hadn't appreciated what she'd been given and was pushing her luck thinking she could pull this off at her age. Forty felt too old.

Emily was already awake. She sat like a statue in her toddler bed, and Maria could smell the urine before she even reached her daughter's side. She pulled back the waistband of the soaked pajama bottoms, knowing what she'd find.

"Why aren't you wearing your Pull-Ups, baby?"

"I'm sorry, Mommy." Emily's lip trembled as tears filled her mahogany-colored eyes. Maria wanted to feel sorry for her, but it was the third time in three days that her daughter had taken off her bedtime Pull-Ups, and there was no time for pity. "I'm a big girl. I don't wear diapers."

"Okay." Maria kissed the top of her daughter's head as she pulled her off the bed with more force than she'd intended. "Don't cry. It was just an accident." The urine spot on the mattress was bigger than seemed possible and was an unpleasant reminder that she'd forgotten to put on the waterproof mattress cover when she'd changed the sheets the previous night. Just one more thing to deal with after work.

She was wiping the urine off her daughter when Will walked into the bathroom. He was going on about a car servicing appointment that was scheduled for that afternoon.

"Three o'clock," he said. "And you can get a rental if you can't stay. Just let them know when you get there."

"Three?" she mumbled. "That's not great timing." Did she already know about this? It seemed like something she would have put in her calendar, but her memory was unreliable these days. Pregnancy brain. That's what people called it, but she didn't remember battling with her mind like this during her previous pregnancies. Maybe she'd already cleared out her afternoon schedule and had just forgotten.

"It's okay if you can't make it," Will continued. "I can do it early next week, after I get back from the conference."

"No, it's fine. I can do it." Maria shrugged it off, as if one more thing on her plate wouldn't break her, as if she wasn't about to crumple under the weight of her responsibilities, as if she hadn't forgotten that her husband would be gone to a medical conference for the next two days. "Can you help me get Charlotte ready?" she said, filling the sink with water and tossing the wipes into the toilet before remembering they weren't flushable.

"Sorry, hon," Will said. "I can't this morning. I have an eight o'clock patient scheduled."

Maria paused for two seconds, time she didn't have to spare, amazed at how effortlessly her husband could pawn off the responsibility of their kids onto her. Was this the nature of all men?

"I have an eight o'clock patient, too," she said, but Will was too smart to follow her down that road. It was an ill-fated path. So instead of reminding her that his eight o'clock patient was sitting in the operating room with a team of medical staff who were all anticipating his arrival, whereas her eight o'clock patient was sitting in a cozy waiting room with music and coffee—maybe even doughnuts if her secretary had thought to pick some up—he leaned down and kissed her belly.

"Yuck."

They both turned at the same time to see their five-year-old standing in the doorway, pointing toward the sink, where Maria was dipping her little sister's backside into the water.

"I'm not brushing my teeth there."

Will laughed and leaned over to land a kiss on Charlotte's head before he walked out the door. "I don't blame you, baby."

"Not helpful," Maria called out to him as he disappeared down the hallway. She could hear him laughing as he descended the stairs and she felt the tension briefly lift from her chest. Her husband's laughter always did that to her, eased her worries, though she still felt envious that he would get to drive to work in silence. Just once, she wanted to experience that. She wanted to know what it felt like to leave her husband behind to fight the battles she fought every morning.

Charlotte's hair was a mess of tangles, and Maria didn't realize she was talking about cutting it all off until her three-year-old offered to help. "I can cut really good," Emily said, looking up at Maria with pleading eyes.

"I know you can, baby, but you're not cutting your sister's hair."

Maria tossed the brush onto the counter and gathered Charlotte's hair into a tangled mess that somewhat resembled a ponytail.

"Why not?" Emily whined.

"Because you'll cut my ear off!" Charlotte screamed, covering her ears with her hands, backing away from her sister, and almost falling into the bathtub. "And then I'll bleed to death!"

"Mommy, I won't do that!" Emily was scrounging through the bathroom drawers in search of a pair of scissors, pulling out empty toothpaste tubes and broken headbands and long-lost hair bows, while Maria trailed behind her with the brush.

"Enough!" she yelled, slamming one of the drawers shut to get their attention. "No one's cutting anyone's hair. Or ears. Or anything else. We have to be out of this house in five minutes, so downstairs now."

She caught Charlotte rolling her eyes before she turned off the light and wondered where a kindergartner would pick up that habit.

The dishes hadn't been run the previous night, so Maria picked out two of the least filthy plastic bowls she could find and wiped them down with a damp paper towel before dropping them onto the counter. She was trying to remember the last time she'd been grocery shopping—the pantry shelves were almost barren—when Charlotte startled her from behind.

"Annabelle's mommy makes her a proper breakfast every morning."

"Is that so?" Maria could feel her eyes rolling, before she stopped herself halfway through. At least now she knew where her daughter picked it up.

"Yes," Charlotte replied. "Eggs and bacon and toast. And always fruit."

"Annabelle's going to have cholesterol problems by the time she's ten," Maria mumbled, ripping open a package of Pop-Tarts and throwing one into each bowl before handing them to her daughters. "And I give you fruit. These are *blueberry* Pop-Tarts. Now go hop into the car and I'll help buckle you up in just a minute."

"But I need lunch, Mommy." Charlotte spun around as she spoke, dropping her Pop-Tart onto the floor. Maria picked it up and brushed it off before placing it back in the bowl. The crumbs on the floor would have to wait until after work.

"There's money in your lunch account, sweetie. Just get a school lunch today."

"But there's a field trip. Mrs. Nelson said to pack a lunch. And you need to sign the paper."

"What?" Maria snatched Charlotte's backpack off the kitchen counter and dug through the pile of loose papers and food wrappers and sweatshirts that hadn't been cleaned out in weeks. "Why didn't you tell me about this last night?"

"It's in my take-home folder. You're supposed to look in my take-home folder every night."

The unsigned permission slip was at the front of a stack of neglected papers that must have been sent home daily for the past few weeks. It was decorated with sticky tabs and highlighter marks showing Maria exactly where her signature was required, along with a reminder stapled to the top, also colorfully highlighted, that the children would need a sack lunch.

She pulled the bread off the shelf in the refrigerator and mumbled a profanity under her breath that she hoped her daughters didn't hear. There were only two pieces left, besides the end pieces, which she tossed into the garbage, and as she was slathering peanut butter across the bread, Charlotte gasped.

"Mommy! No peanut butter!"

Maria jumped, almost dropping the knife into the sink, and turned to her daughter. "I thought you liked peanut butter."

"Jackson can't have peanuts, so nobody can bring peanut butter for snack or lunch."

Maria thought about all the boxes of peanut butter crackers she'd sent to school with Charlotte over the last few months and wondered where they all went. There was probably a letter in the take-home folder informing the parents about Jackson's peanut allergy, and she expected Mrs. Nelson found her quite obnoxious. Or hopefully just oblivious. She could feel Charlotte's eyes following her as she reached into the garbage and pulled out the end pieces of bread.

"I'm not eating that!" Charlotte screeched.

"They're still in the bag," Maria replied. "They haven't touched anything in the garbage. They're fine."

"Ew!" Emily scrunched up her nose and looked at her sister. "You have to eat garbage."

"I'm not eating that, Mommy!"

"I have nothing else." Maria waved her hand up and down the length of the open refrigerator in front of them. "We're almost on Empty here, sweetie. It's this or nothing."

"Nothing," Charlotte said, with her hands crossed firmly across her chest.

"I can't send you to school with nothing." Maria held the two end pieces in one hand and rifled through the back of the refrigerator for something to put on them, eventually pulling out an old jar of jelly. She wondered if jelly ever expired. "Strawberry?"

By the time the trio made their way out the door, Maria was already fifteen minutes late for her first patient of the day and both of her daughters were mad at her about something, though she couldn't remember what. She was too busy running through a checklist in her mind of what she needed to get done before the weekend: groceries, laundry, dishes, bills, and the baby who was due any day now. She couldn't forget about him, and while she'd never been one to shy away from a challenge, she couldn't even begin to imagine how she was going to pull this off.

Her husband had offered to hire a nanny to get the kids to and from school and to fix dinner for them on weeknights, maybe even run some laundry and straighten up the house. But what kind of a mother couldn't do those things for her own children? Something would have to give. She couldn't hold it together forever, and if she didn't make some changes soon, Maria knew the dam was going to break and there'd be no salvaging what was waiting downstream.

CHAPTER TWO

S ORRY I'M LATE."
Maria bustled through the front door of her psychiatry
clinic, the chilled April wind clinging to her like an uninvited
guest and following her into the office. Rachel was sitting at her
desk, clicking away at her computer, while the melody of soft jazz
and the aroma of freshly brewed coffee filled the air around them
with a warmth that instantly melted away Maria's anxieties.

"That smells so good," she said. "I can't wait to drink real coffee again."

"Soon," her secretary said. "And you're not late. Your eight
o'clock canceled this morning and you don't have another patient
scheduled until nine."

Maria hesitated, wanting to tell Rachel how helpful that information would have been half an hour earlier, but instead she
just smiled and shrugged off the maternity coat she was no longer
able to button. Her secretary was more forgetful these days, too,
though her reasons were different than Maria's.

As she entered her private office, Maria threw her coat onto an
empty chair and sat down to scroll through the list of patients she
had scheduled for the day. Her last patient was scheduled for two
o'clock, giving her just enough time to get to the car appointment
her husband had been talking about, the one that had long since
slipped her mind. Her nine o'clock was a new patient, and she

was scanning through the limited information they had about her when Rachel walked in.

"Here you go." The thick southern drawl of Rachel's words and the scent of her imitation Armani perfume lingered in the air as she leaned over to place a cup of decaffeinated coffee in front of Maria. Her auburn hair was perfectly rolled and sprayed into place, and her makeup was impeccable. Maria felt like a troll next to her.

"Thanks."

She could feel Rachel's eyes lingering on her swollen belly. It was always an odd dance between them when it came to Maria's pregnancy. Six months earlier, Rachel had found her ten-month-old son lying lifeless in his crib. Maria could still hear the screams that rang through the phone that morning when Rachel's neighbor informed her that the unthinkable had happened.

"No problem," Rachel replied, her eyes unwavering. "How's the little guy doing?"

"He's good," Maria said, patting her belly. At the time of Jonathan's death, she'd been just three months pregnant and had barely managed to share the news with her husband. Out of respect for Rachel, she'd kept the baby a secret until she'd started to show, and she was always far too overwhelmed with guilt to ever celebrate the news they were having a boy.

The chime of the front door saved her from another awkward conversation, and as Rachel retreated to the front office, Maria finished scanning over her notes.

Sylvia Woolf. Twenty-three-year-old woman complaining of new onset depression. No referral from a primary care physician. No insurance on file. Cash paying patient.

Sylvia was the embodiment of major depressive disorder. If there were an illustration to go along with the definition of the word *depression*, it would have been her picture. She was forgettable, the kind of person who was described with words like *average* and *ordinary*, because no one could remember the color of her hair or how tall she stood or if she had an accent.

"So, what brings you in today?" Maria asked, smiling as she settled herself into the chair behind her desk. Sylvia's hair hung like a limp, washed-out shower curtain, and her vacant, expressionless eyes were lost in the swirling pattern of the throw rug on Maria's office floor. She was too busy picking at her cuticles and gnawing on her fingernails to notice her doctor watching her, and Maria couldn't help but wonder if she was getting a glimpse into her future with teenage daughters. She was so wrapped up in her own thoughts that she jumped when Sylvia spoke.

"I need to talk to you about something."

"Okay," Maria said, shifting in her chair before uncrossing and recrossing her legs. "What would you like to talk about?"

"I'm not here because I'm depressed. I'm here because I need to talk to you about something." Sylvia's attention was no longer stuck on the rug between them. Her posture had straightened, her nail-picking had ceased, and the confidence that was so obviously lacking when she first sat down was now almost physical between them. She looked like a different woman. "You're probably going to think I'm crazy when I say this, but I need you to promise me that you won't have me locked up in a psych hospital."

"I don't . . . I mean, I can't promise that . . ." After a deep breath, Maria cleared her throat and leaned back in her chair, grasping for an air of professionalism. "It's harder than you think to get admitted to a psych hospital these days. Insurance companies won't pay unless you threaten to kill yourself, or someone else, and it doesn't do much good in the long run."

"I'm not going to hurt anyone," Sylvia replied. "And I'm not depressed. I'm here because God brought me back for a special purpose."

"What do you mean?"

"I mean I've been through all of this before," Sylvia continued. "I've already lived this life, and I was brought back here by God to fulfill a very special purpose."

It was an unexpected turn, a setback Maria hadn't anticipated, as Sylvia drove their conversation down a path riddled with religious delusions. "Are you saying that God brought you back from the future?"

"Exactly," Sylvia replied. "I know this sounds crazy, and you probably think I belong in the hospital, but I need you to hear me out and just try to consider the possibility. You have no idea how difficult it is to prove that you've come back from the future. It seems like it should be easy, right? But no matter what I tell you is going to happen, we'll have to wait for it to happen before you'll believe me."

Sylvia's pause was filled with expectation, so Maria nodded accordingly, but diagnoses were streaming through her head like the credits of a movie.

"So I have no way to prove myself to you," she continued, "but I know about things that are going to happen to people."

"Sometimes life can get pretty confusing," Maria said, echoing the same worn-out words she'd been using for years. Psychosis would be the official diagnosis on paper for now, but she would have to follow Sylvia closely to rule out specific causes. She was so busy jotting down her thoughts—*Rule out bipolar disorder, schizophrenia, schizoaffective disorder*—that Sylvia's voice startled her again.

"I'm not confused," she said. "Not anymore. The dreams finally make sense, but I just couldn't do it."

"Do what?"

"Save those people from that tornado."

Maria nodded. There it was. The catalyst to Sylvia's delusions. There was nothing like a tornado to drag them out of hiding. If there was anything that could act as tinder to ignite religious delusions, it was a natural disaster, and there was no shortage of coverage on the F5 tornado that had swept through their area and left seventeen people dead. Add to that the unending news coverage to satisfy a nation full of people who were fascinated by death and you had the perfect recipe for a forest fire.

"It's hard, isn't it?" Maria said. "When the news is constantly replaying those horrible images over and over. Sometimes, when people have bad depression, the things that happen around them, that have absolutely nothing to do with them, start to feel very personal. And sometimes, with depression, you can start to feel like *you're* responsible for the bad things that are happening. It can even be hard to figure out what's real and what's not. But listen to me, Sylvia. You are not responsible for anything that happened to anyone during that tornado."

"I knew it was coming, Dr. Forssmann, and I didn't do anything about it because I was selfish. And now all those people who died, their blood is on my hands."

"It's not your fault," Maria said. "There's something I can give you to make these thoughts that you're having go away. There's medicine that will help with the . . ." She hesitated long enough to remind herself not to say delusions. "The bad thoughts you've been having."

"Medicine can't fix this." Sylvia shut her eyes, walking her fingers from her temples to her forehead, kneading the skin along the way. "I know you can't see that, but I have to tell you what happened that day." Maria nodded for her to continue, but Sylvia wasn't waiting for her approval.

"There was a young couple hiding in the closet together during the storm. Shelby Whitten and John Ambers. They were twenty-five years old, they'd just gotten engaged, and they were riding out the storm together buried in some pillows and blankets. The tornado tore apart their house, and by the time it was over, John had been thrown into the field next door and Shelby had been buried under the rubble. Rescue crews found John right away, unconscious, with some broken bones, but at least he was still breathing. Shelby was dug out a few hours later and pronounced dead on the scene."

"Sylvia, I think—"

"Please, Dr. Forssmann." She held her hand up between them. "Please let me finish. I let Shelby die because, two years from now, I'll meet John and we'll fall in love and get married and live happily ever after. That's the way it would have happened if I didn't know about the tornado. The way it happened the first time, when I *didn't* know. But this time I knew, and I didn't do anything to warn those people because *I* wanted to be the one with him, not Shelby. And this time I just won't be able to bear it. The screams from his nightmares about that night. I won't be able to look him in the eye when he talks about all that suffering, and I'll never be able to forgive myself for that selfish decision that cost so many lives."

Sylvia's expression was a mixture of sorrow and resolve, as her eyes rose up to meet Maria's.

"Don't you see now? It's important to always do the right thing, even if you have to suffer the consequences. I made the wrong choice. God had a plan for me, but I chose selfishly, so now I'm here to make up for it. I'm here because something else happened in my life that I was powerless to stop all those years ago, and I won't let it happen again."

Sylvia's story swirled through Maria's head as she traced over the names John and Shelby on the notepad in her lap, wondering if those people ever existed and contemplating her next move. There was no talking away this illness, no therapy that could reverse the course of her psychosis. Sylvia would need medication.

"What is it that you plan to stop?" Maria asked.

"Something bad. I'm here to save you, Dr. Forssmann. I'm here to protect you and your baby."

The air went stale as Maria forced it into her lungs before she choked out her next words. "Protect us from what?"

"The first time I was here, our lives intersected in an unimaginable way, and you ended up being someone very important to me. Now I finally understand why. I know from that past how much you worry about your son, but if you listen to me, he's going to grow up to be a happy and healthy boy."

"I guess I worry as much as the next mom." Her voice was unwavering, but Maria's heart pounded against her chest as Sylvia's words, so confident and sure, reached a place inside of her that was so rarely exposed. No one knew about the fears she harbored for her son, not even her husband.

"Your pregnancy is not cursed," Sylvia continued. "Not anymore. But you have to listen to me. Stay away from Rachel. There's a laptop of hers in that storage unit you share with her that needs to get to the police, but don't go there until after your baby is born."

A flush of heat washed over Maria's body before it landed in her face, the sweat from her neck dripping down her back as she struggled to maintain her composure. Sylvia was delusional and rambling and psychotic, and Maria was reading too much into her words. But how did she know about the storage unit? And how did she know Maria was worried about her son?

The prescriptions she handed to Sylvia were barely legible, and Maria wasn't even sure she'd signed them, but she pushed them into Sylvia's hands as she rose from her chair.

"Thank you for your concern, Sylvia. I don't want you to worry about me, though. I want you to get these prescriptions filled so we can get you feeling better right away."

Sylvia placed her hand over Maria's arm, her composure a

marked contrast to Maria's uneasiness. If someone who didn't know better walked in at that moment, Maria would have been mistaken for the patient and Sylvia for the doctor. "Dr. Forssmann," she said, "if you don't listen to me, something bad is going to happen. You'll see."

"Just get those meds and start taking them." Maria pushed her way past Sylvia and yanked the door open before ushering her out. "And I'll see you back next month."

It was unfamiliar territory, being flustered by a patient. Most of her patients had at least a decent respect for personal boundaries and wouldn't dare make cryptic comments about her unborn child. Psychotic or not, it seemed grossly inappropriate. She watched from the doorway as Rachel tried to schedule a follow-up appointment, but Sylvia was talking over her, reciting some kind of poem. It wasn't until she heard "forgive us our sins and purify us" that she knew it had to be scripture from the Bible.

Sylvia was sick, probably even sick enough for the hospital, but Maria watched in culpable silence as her patient slipped through the front door and out of their lives forever.

CHAPTER THREE

HAD SHE KNOWN THAT SUICIDE WAS ever on Sylvia's radar, Maria would have done things much differently. The benefit of hindsight and a night of sleep gave her a clearer vision of how her actions, or inactions, had sent her patient to an early grave. She was tired. Her mind, once sharp and perceptive, was now dull and bogged down with menial and inconsequential tasks: car appointments, school field trips, soiled bedsheets. She couldn't focus on the important things and couldn't forgive herself for failing her patient.

Her hands trembled as she slid them off the counter and out of view of the receptionist who greeted her with a forced smile. She somehow stumbled through an awkward explanation of who she was and what she was doing at the police station, and the woman pointed her to a vacant waiting room where rows of blue plastic chairs sat in stark contrast to the whitewashed concrete walls. The room wasn't designed for comfort, but Maria didn't wait long.

"Dr. Forssmann?" A ruddy-faced, stout officer entered, his grip solid and his hands rough and calloused. "I'm Detective Andrews," he said. "Thanks for coming by." They snaked through the station to the detective's spacious and well-adorned office, where an empty wingback chair awaited her. "Can I get you something to drink? Coffee?"

"No, thank you." Maria patted her ripe, pregnant belly. If she was about to be exposed as a second-rate psychiatrist, she could at least make herself out to be a decent parent. "No caffeine for me," she said. "Maybe a cup of water?"

With a curt nod the detective left her to her angst, her mind churning through what-ifs and whys as her eyes scanned the overabundance of commendation awards on his walls. He was a military man at one time, and quite distinguished, with certificates and medals landscaping his walls and spilling over to his bookcase. It was her first time in a detective's office, and while she wasn't naive about suicides, she'd certainly never had to answer for the actions of her patients—or her treatment of them—until now.

The door creaked over the sound of the detective's labored breathing as he kicked it shut behind him, a mug in each hand. Maria inhaled the aroma of freshly brewed coffee, watching longingly as he placed the steaming mug in front of his own chair. A stained cup of lukewarm tap water found its way to her hands before the detective settled his stocky frame behind a faux mahogany desk. He was a large man, likely solid muscle in his youth, but as he eased onto his chair, an aged and neglected belly protruded over his pants and his shirt collar squeezed his neck like a tourniquet.

"Thanks for coming in on such short notice," he said. "I assume you know what this is about?"

Maria clutched her mug with clumsy hands, looking for an empty spot on the desk between them. "You have some questions for me about one of my patients," she said. "I mean, one of my former patients."

"Sylvia Woolf," he replied. "She passed away last night . . . But I'm guessing you already knew?"

Maria nodded.

"We're trying to find out a little more about her state of mind

the last time you saw her," he continued. "Maybe she said something that stuck with you? Something out of the ordinary?"

"Do you mean something that would have clued me in to the
fact that she was suicidal?" The tremor in her hands had spread to
her voice, and Maria knew better than to continue.

I just messed up.

Was that a good enough excuse? She teetered on the edge of
tears before she clutched the mug of stale, coffee-flavored water
from the desk and forced a sip. The hardened lines coursing through
the detective's face finally softened.

"I'm sorry," he said. "I hate to question you like this after everything you've been through with your secretary." He glanced at the
notes on the edge of his desk. "Ms. Tillman?"

"You know Rachel?"

"No, but I searched her records before I called you in and found
the information about her son."

Maria shifted in her chair, the mention of Rachel's name stab-
bing at her conscience. She had no reason to distrust her secretary,
but Sylvia's warning to steer clear of her hadn't been forgotten. *Stay
away from Rachel.* That tiny seed she'd planted, however outrageous
it sounded, was already starting to sprout.

"I didn't ask her to come in," the detective continued. "I
thought I'd talk to you first, see if we can get some of this straightened out so we can wrap up the investigation, and maybe she won't
have to come in at all."

Investigation. It didn't matter how she turned it, Maria couldn't
get the word to fit into her mind. It had sharp edges that jutted out
beyond the margins of her comprehension, and the more she repeated it, the more foreign it sounded. Why was there an investigation into Sylvia's suicide? Were they suspecting foul play? The
detective smiled as if her thoughts had been broadcast throughout the room.

"You're not a suspect," he said, but the crooked smile on his face offered little relief for her festering guilt. Sylvia's death was a crime of negligence, a failure of Maria to do what she had been entrusted to do, and whether her clinical judgment was being called into question or not, it was her complacence that gave Sylvia the chance to act.

"I guess I've just never seen such a thorough investigation into a suicide."

"We don't normally go to these lengths with an obvious suicide. And, to tell you the truth, it's not really her death we're investigating." He leaned forward and rested his burly forearms on the top of his desk. "It's the letter she left."

"What letter?"

"We found it on her kitchen counter, stamped and sealed, ready to go. She was planning to mail it to you before she died. I'm not sure why it never found its way to the mailbox."

"I can't imagine why she would write me a letter. What does it say?"

"I guess you could call it a suicide note. I can't discuss it, though." The detective's shoulders sagged, almost imperceptibly, as he contemplated his response. "It's considered evidence."

"Evidence of what?" she asked. "Maybe if you let me read it . . ."

"I can't." He pulled his arms from the desk before crossing them over his chest, weighing his options and clearly tempted to let her read it. She could see, from the way he watched her, that he wanted her to read the letter. "When you saw her in your office yesterday," he said, "did she seem like she was concerned about you? Like she was trying to warn you about something?"

I'm here to save you, Dr. Forssmann.

"She had some warnings," Maria said, as the detective pulled a notebook from his top drawer and flipped to an empty page, pen in hand, ready to record her memories. "But I'm sorry," she continued. "I can't discuss her appointment without a subpoena. Patient confidentiality laws."

"I understand, and we'll get one if we think we need it, but maybe you could just give me some details about Sylvia's behavior *outside* of the doctor–patient setting." He leaned over his open notebook, the empty blue lines eager to be filled. "Did you see her interact with other patients in the waiting room? Or with your secretary, Rachel? Anything you can tell me would be helpful."

It was a memory she was reluctant to revisit, the cryptic warnings and odd behaviors that were such obvious symptoms of Sylvia's illness but also were the very things that forced Maria to usher her out the door. "She quoted some Bible verse to Rachel before she left."

"Do you know what verse it was?"

Maria shook her head, embarrassed that her shameful lack of biblical knowledge was about to be exposed, wishing she'd paid more attention all those years ago.

"Do you remember what you thought it meant? Anything would be helpful."

"It was something about God forgiving you for your sins. Or asking for God's forgiveness. Something like that. I just don't remember."

"If we confess our sins, he is faithful and just and will forgive us our sins and purify us from all unrighteousness."

"That sounds like it," she said.

"It's from the first book of John."

His voice was apologetic, almost empathetic, like he understood the humiliation of being the only kid in Sunday school class to forget his Bible verses, but Maria was impressed by his knowledge, if not a bit jealous. By ten years old, and taking her father's lead, she was a Sunday school dropout, and whatever paltry knowledge she took from those classes didn't survive past year fifteen. "You sound like a biblical scholar, Detective Andrews."

His laughter filled the air, spiraling around them as the tension began to unravel. "My wife would have a field day with that one. She's been trying for over twenty-five years to get me to church." He leaned over his desk as the laughter died down and lowered his voice. "The only reason I know that is because it was in the letter. And please, call me Walt."

A kinship wound its way around them as she got a glimpse into the detective's private life; the adversities of their professions were more similar than she could have imagined. They both saw people at their worst, sometimes damaged beyond salvation, and their stories were woven into their cores, making them who and what they were as much as the diplomas and awards that hung from their walls.

"I'm sorry about this, Dr. Forssmann. I know it's unpleasant."

"I understand," she said. "And you can call me Maria."

His smile was tinged with an unexpected sadness as he nodded his head and straightened the notebook on his desk. There was something itching at the surface of his thoughts, something he knew better than to say. He jotted something down in his notebook, the blue lines disappearing under the black strokes of his pen, before he pulled his eyes up to meet hers.

"I have a personal question for you, Maria, if you don't mind. Do you and Rachel share a storage unit somewhere?"

It was such a trivial bit of information, and had Sylvia not mentioned it one day earlier, on the very day she killed herself, Maria might have brushed off the question. But it had gnawed at her deep into the night and right through her dreams the previous evening, long after she'd crawled into bed alone, wishing her husband good night over the phone from their bed to his hotel room.

"She put that in the letter, didn't she?" Maria said. "I still can't figure out how she knew it, though."

"So, she was right?"

"Not exactly. My husband and I have a unit that we gave Rachel a key to a while back. Her boyfriend at the time had racked up some credit card debt in her name, and he took off shortly after the baby was born. We felt bad for her because she couldn't afford the apartment she was in and had to downsize to a studio, so we let her put some of her furniture in there."

"Has she been there recently?"

"I have no idea. I never go there, and she has her own key. Is there something in particular you're looking for?"

She already knew the answer, of course: the laptop. It must have made its way into the letter, along with other things the detective wouldn't be divulging. Did he know that she'd been instructed to get the laptop to him, or that she'd been warned to stay away from Rachel, or that the fears she'd been having for her unborn son were seemingly validated by Sylvia? She was hoping she might get her hands on that laptop, if it even existed, and she had a feeling that if the detective got to it first, she'd lose her chance.

"There's nothing in particular that we're looking for," the detective continued, "but I wouldn't mind taking a look through the unit if you're okay with that."

"I guess," Maria said. "But I don't have a key on me."

"Do you think you could get it to me by Monday?"

"Sure," she muttered, certain there would be no time to go snooping through the storage unit before the end of the weekend. There was never any time.

"That'd be great. I'll be out of town this weekend, but I'll go through it early next week if you can get the key here by then. The lady at the front desk can get you a consent to search form on your way out. If you could just sign that for me now, that'd make it easier."

Despite the flippancy of his request, it seemed like something she should discuss with a lawyer, or at least her husband, but the hour was growing late, and one glance at her swollen ankles was enough to convince her she didn't have the energy to argue logistics.

"Just one more thing," he said, "and then I promise I'll let you go."

Maria nodded for him to continue.

"Did the police ever question Rachel, or anyone, about her son's death?"

"Of course not," she said, remembering that the coroner who'd performed Jonathan's autopsy had called it a classic case of sudden infant death syndrome. There had never been any mention of foul play. "Why would they investigate that?"

"Sometimes the police will do a preliminary investigation into accidental and natural-cause deaths. I didn't see one when I checked the case file, but I just thought I'd ask."

"I guess I can't be sure, but I think Rachel would have told me if she was investigated." Maria couldn't think straight. *Had* Rachel been investigated? She couldn't even remember what she'd had for breakfast that morning, let alone what Rachel had told her six months earlier about her son's death. Maybe she'd just assumed there was no investigation because, in addition to being her secretary, Rachel was also her friend. She could never believe her capable of hurting her own child.

"What about the baby's father?" the detective continued. "Was he around? Or did Rachel have a boyfriend around the time her son died?"

"Nick," Maria said. He'd been just one in a long line of on-and-off relationships that defined Rachel's adult life, a tradition that ended shortly after her son's death. "Nick Turner was the baby's father. He was in and out of Rachel's life, but he went back to New Orleans, where he was from, before Jonathan died. You don't think he had something to do with it, do you?"

"No," he replied. "We're not investigating anyone for anything at this point. I'm just trying to be thorough." He paused as he studied Maria's face, the same itch surfacing in his thoughts and tempting him to scratch it. "I'm sorry I can't let you read the letter, but I want you to know that Sylvia thought very highly of you. She didn't blame you for any of this."

"Thank you," she said. "Do I ever get to read it?"

"Of course." The detective rose from his chair and made his way around the desk. "It's yours. We'll close the investigation in a couple of weeks, once we get the autopsy report and finish up with the details, and then I'll give you a call, so you can pick it up."

He was by her side with a hand extended before she could attempt to hoist herself from the chair. There was a gentleness to his strength that she'd missed when they first met. "Looks like it could be any day now," he said, glancing down at her belly. "Is it a boy or a girl?"

"It's a boy." She rubbed the bulge of baby beneath her maternity dress. "We already have two girls, so I think we'll have our hands full."

The pained smile that broke across his face didn't escape her. "Do you have a name picked out yet?"

"Not that I'm telling anyone."

"Oh, come on," he said, winking as he helped her from the chair. "I won't leak it."

Maria had known her son's name since the first flutter of his existence, like the universe had named him long before he was given to her, but she hadn't even shared it with her husband yet, certain he would veto her choice. Only the journal in her nightstand drawer knew that secret.

"I'm sorry. My lips are sealed on this one."

Walt steadied his frame against the fake mahogany desk, another battle taking shape in his mind.

"It's Blaise," he finally said. "Isn't it?"

CHAPTER FOUR

B *LAISE.*

How could the detective have known? How could Sylvia have known? Had she been in Maria's house, snooping through her drawers? It was the only logical explanation, but it was a terrifying explanation, and one she couldn't even bring herself to share with the detective for her own selfish reasons: she didn't want her husband to find out. She didn't want to be reminded that her job could potentially be putting her own children in danger, a belief her husband had carried for years. Couldn't any job do that?

Maria needed to get to the storage unit before the end of the weekend if she was going to get a head start on the detective and find out what Sylvia had meant with the warnings about her unborn son. Maybe the answers to her questions were on the laptop, or maybe Sylvia had been to the storage unit and left her another clue, or maybe Maria was putting too much credence in the psychotic ramblings of a sick woman whose ghost she needed to stop chasing.

Too many scenarios swirled through her mind as a brisk chill churned through the night air, brushing over her skin like the breath of winter. Spring had never felt so cold. Maria shuddered before she curled up on the backyard lounge chair, the seams of her sweater screaming as she pulled it over her belly. With her daughters tucked safely into bed, dancing through dreams of princesses and ponies, she sipped her caffeine-free Coke from a scotch glass and waited for her husband to return from his conference.

Blaise was fighting for his freedom, kicking more fervently now than just hours ago, and with each kick Maria was saddled with guilt. Was he trying to punish her? Did he know she once considered letting him go?

It was a Thursday morning when she'd learned about her pregnancy. She'd viewed those double blue lines from every angle and in every light. Not even running water could wash away that blue. Then she'd gone back to the drugstore and bought two more pregnancy tests, just to be sure. When it was six dark blue lines staring back at her and no time to run back to the store, she wrapped the sticks in toilet paper, secured them in their boxes, and bagged the boxes with double knots before dropping them into the garbage bin by the street. Weeks slipped by before she finally confessed to her husband, utterly mistaken in her certainty that he would not be on board with having another baby. He was thrilled.

You've been lucky in love.

Those had been her mother's words. Maria last heard them two years earlier, just days before her mother lost a hard-fought battle to breast cancer. She'd been right. Maria *had* been lucky in love, lucky to find her husband halfway across the country, far away from her home in the middle of Alabama. Medical school in Ohio would have been a lonely venture if not for the boy from Toledo.

But that was a long time ago, and while Maria loved her husband without fail, their relationship and their roles looked far different today than they had all those years ago. Every day they crossed paths in a monotonous routine of life, with stolen kisses between breakfasts on the go. Finances were handled while laundry was folded, kids were discussed while dishes were washed, and futures were contemplated while children were bathed. They had become masters of efficiency and multitasking out of necessity, but she wondered if perhaps they were missing the point. She would never admit it to him, but she was heartbroken by his response when she asked him how they were going to manage the chaos of their lives when baby number three arrived. Words she never could have imagined him saying so nonchalantly left his mouth.

You don't have to go back to work.

That was his solution. As if her work was meaningless. As if she hadn't given the most significant years of her life for this career. As if she alone would be the one to balance these burdens. Will didn't see it that way, of course. He thought he was doing her a favor. But Maria could only see it as a sacrifice she was being asked to make. She wouldn't engage him in that conversation, though, because she could never admit to what she had really considered sacrificing: the beating of her own son's heart. How was it possible that she'd ever considered letting him go? It was one of the few secrets she didn't dare put in the journal beside her bed, one that she would have shared only with her mother, had she still been alive. What wouldn't she give to see her mother again, to curl up into a ball on her lap and let all of the stress and worry and anxiety of her life wash to the ground in a shower of tears?

Maybe her patients were right. Maybe there was catharsis through tears. It wasn't that she didn't have her own yearnings to weep; she did. They had been shadowing her for weeks, becoming too familiar, popping up at all hours and surprising her with their insistence and bravado. There was just never time to indulge them. Some of her patients admitted to crying in their cars because it was the only place they could find the time and privacy, but Maria couldn't remember the last time she was alone in her car, except on the short hop between school and work, and she certainly couldn't show up to either of those places with red-rimmed and swollen eyes.

The plastic table beside her buzzed as her cell phone vibrated across it. She blinked back the tears that were threatening to surface and then picked it up. It was a text from her husband:

b home 10 min

She replied:

OK-out back

Her eyelids drifted shut and her skin shuddered beneath another crisp breeze, as the tension that had been coursing through her body started to ease. Despite the stress of their lives, Will's presence was as comfortable to Maria as her own skin, and as the garage door started to groan, her pulse quickened. She didn't open her eyes until his lips brushed the top of her forehead.

"Hey, you," he said, caressing her cheek with the palm of his hand, the cobalt blue of his eyes penetrating the dim light. A warm smile broke across his face under the shaggy brown hair that was matted to his head from a long couple of hours of sleeping on the plane. He was the same handsome man she'd married fifteen years earlier, with the same charming smile, but time had started to carve out the first hint of crow's-feet around his eyes.

"I'm so glad you're home," Maria said.

"I'm so glad to *be* home." Will's smile broadened before he scooped up her empty scotch glass. "It's cold out here. Let's go inside and I'll fix you another drink."

"Jack and Coke," she said. "Hold the Jack."

"I bet you could use it tonight. I'm sorry I haven't been here for you." Will led her to the kitchen, placed her cup on the counter, and pulled the caffeine-free Coke from the refrigerator.

"It's not your fault." She hoisted herself onto a bar stool at the counter, wondering when their lives had reached this blistering pace. Had it always been this way, or had it, unbeknownst to her, been picking up steam along the way until it reached this breakneck speed? "Duty calls," she said. "I'm just glad you're here now."

The spaghetti she'd made for dinner and eaten with her daughters two hours earlier still sat in a lidded pot on the stove, looking more like a congealed science project than supper. Will dumped the entirety of it onto a plate and stuck the hardened blob into the microwave, a punch of nausea striking Maria as the aroma of melting marinara sauce hit her nostrils. The thought of rehashing Sylvia's death and her meeting with Detective Andrews only made it worse.

She'd been through this before, the loss of a patient, but this one felt different. This one was more personal. As Will downed the reheated spaghetti, Maria started in on Sylvia's ill-fated final appointment with an awkward mishmash of words and phrases and pauses that took them down the rabbit hole of her psychosis. She told him all about the time travel delusions and the letter that was waiting for her at the police station and the consent to search form she had signed for the detective to enter their storage unit.

What she didn't reveal were Sylvia's warnings about Rachel or her instructions to get the laptop to police or her knowledge of the secrets in Maria's journal, about their unborn son. There was danger linked to those things. They were personal, specifically connected to Maria, and at least one of them involved Sylvia sneaking into their home. She wasn't ready to discuss the inherent danger of her job with her husband, who was so eager for her to quit it.

"Can you imagine having to make a decision like that?" Will said, poised on the edge of his seat by the time she'd finished speaking, ready to dive back in. "On the one hand, it's your husband and your kids and your entire life. And then on the other it's the lives of all these other people. You're going to suffer either way. It's like the ultimate test from God."

"From God?" Maria stammered. "This wasn't real, Will. She was psychotic."

She spoke with a confidence she no longer possessed. She had to believe that Sylvia was psychotic and had broken into their house, because if that wasn't true then Maria was dealing with something that defied logic, something impossible.

"Did you search online for the people she mentioned from the tornado?" Will asked.

"Why would I do that? I can't spend my life trying to disprove the delusions of my psychotic patients. What makes her any different?" It was supposed to be a rhetorical question, but the answer was glaringly obvious between them, even if Maria refused to admit it: Sylvia's delusions had names. "Are you suggesting I misdiagnosed her?"

"Of course not. I'm sorry if it came off that way. You know how I am, I just have a soft spot for people who are . . . I don't know. What would you call them? Spiritual?"

How many years had it been since they'd had one of these conversations? How many lifetimes ago did they stay up all night drinking wine and debating the presence of God? How many times had she listened to her husband recount dreams of his dead sister, who he swore visited him in his sleep? And now, after all those years and all her headstrong certainty that God and spirits and the supernatural were for people who weren't strong enough to shoulder their own burdens and grief, there was a crack in Maria's armor. But she would fix it. Before her husband could drag her down that path, she would mend the opening and put a stop to his words.

"She wasn't spiritual, Will. She was sick. And I was her doctor. She came to me for help and I didn't give it to her, so she killed herself."

She swallowed down the tears that were threatening to surface, not sure if they were stemming from anger or guilt or frustration, too full of pride to let them flow. She could tell from the clenching of her husband's jaw that he had more to say, that he would have been content to go on all night about the meanings of dreams and the people who visit us while we sleep. Maria was overdue for her own sleep, and she didn't have the energy to indulge him. Once upon a time, she'd enjoyed those all-night discussions, during their courtship and the early years of their marriage, when she'd wanted him to think she was deep and philosophical. But a couple of kids later, when she didn't have the energy to fake it anymore, the discussions came to a screeching halt.

"I'm sorry, Maria." He scooted his stool closer to her and ran his hand across her back. "I know as well as anyone how hard it is to not second-guess yourself when you lose a patient, but you know I'm not blaming you, right?" When she didn't respond, he turned his attention back to the spaghetti. "Let's just forget about it. Tell me more about your meeting with the detective. You said you had to sign something so he could search our storage unit?"

"I don't know if I should have signed it or not," she said, relieved at how willingly her husband had dropped the conversation, knowing what it meant to him. "I haven't given him the key yet, in case you think I shouldn't."

"No, give it to him." He twirled the last heap of spaghetti around his fork, shoved it into his mouth, and then froze with half a noodle still dangling from his lips. "We have nothing to hide in there. Right?"

"Of course not. But doesn't it make you a little nervous that he wants to search our unit?"

"It's obviously about Rachel." He pushed the empty plate away and paused before going down a road they were both hesitant to traverse. "Do you think it has something to do with Jonathan's death?"

Maria shrugged. "I don't know," she said. "The detective asked me if Rachel and Nick were ever questioned about Jonathan's death, but I told him I didn't think so."

"That's weird," Will replied. "I guess we'll find out what it's all about when they give you the letter."

"Aren't you curious, though?" Maria gulped down a swallow of her watered-down drink and turned to face her husband. "What if there's something important in there that we need to know about?"

"Like what?"

"I don't know," she replied, wishing she had the courage to ask her husband to walk her through her anxieties:

I'm worried that something bad is going to happen to our son.

I'm certain my patient broke into our house before she killed herself.

I'm convinced there's something I need to see on Rachel's laptop in our storage unit.

The words never left her mouth. In the end, she couldn't force herself to confess, because even to herself she sounded neurotic, and if Will was ever looking for proof that she needed a break from her job, here was the evidence.

"Maybe we should go see for ourselves," she said.

"No, Maria." His finger shot up between them like a scolding parent. "Do *not* go snooping through that unit."

"Of course not," she mumbled, swirling the half-melted ice and the remnants of her Coke in small circles and wondering how she was going to get herself to the storage unit before the end of the weekend.

"I mean it, Maria. For once in your life, just listen to me. It could be a crime scene, for all we know."

"I'm pretty sure if it was a crime scene, they wouldn't need a search warrant."

"Please don't do this, Maria."

"Do what?"

"Get one of those crazy ideas in your head that you try to drag me into."

"Okay," she said, unable to meet his gaze. "I won't go there."

"I want to hear you say 'I promise.'"

"I promise," she laughed. "Now settle down."

"You're a mess." Despite his best efforts, the corner of Will's mouth curved up, and the crooked smile that had first endeared him to her all those years ago drew her in again. The wooden stool creaked as she heaved herself from it before draping her arms over the furrows of her husband's shoulders and pressing her lips into the curve of his neck. His body was lean and muscular, like a distance runner's, and she was suddenly conscious of all the ways her own body had changed over the years.

"You're so cute when you're serious," she said.

"I'm not cute." He slid his hands over her belly before wrapping them around her back, and Maria could feel his breath brush across her cheek before he pressed his lips into hers. "But I am serious," he said. "Go upstairs and get ready for bed and I'll be up in a minute."

As the dishes clanged in the kitchen, Maria heaved herself up the stairs, pausing for a contraction on the landing between floors, breathless and sweating. By the time she made it to the top and into her bathroom, a vortex of images was churning through her thoughts and spiraling into a knot that contained a dead patient, a cryptic suicide note, and now the lie that she'd lobbed to her husband not five minutes earlier.

"Are you okay?" Will's reflection in the mirror startled her as she watched him approach from the doorway.

"I'm fine," she whispered.

"Why are you crying?" He stepped closer, his image watching hers as he closed the distance between them. She hadn't realized the tears were flowing until he was standing beside her, his hands running down the sides of her arms as he watched her reflection in the mirror. "What's wrong?"

"Nothing," she replied, wiping the tears away, wondering if she would ever have a moment of privacy in her life again. "I'm just a little stressed right now. It's nothing. I just need a minute."

He kissed the back of her head and watched her in silence as she tried to explain away the tears and the anxiety and the stress, wondering why she had to provide an excuse for a perfectly reasonable response to her situation. He was hesitant to leave her, but when he finally slipped out the door, her tears went with him. She was too tired to cry. It took too much energy, and she didn't have any to spare.

She pulled her maternity dress over her head and dropped it onto the floor at her feet, examining her belly from every angle in the mirror and cringing at the damage control looming on the horizon. It was just one more thing to deal with. What would she look like after three babies? At least her son would arrive before her fortieth birthday, though just by a few weeks. She pictured her fifty-year-old self at a book club with other women her age, commenting that all her children had been born while she was in her thirties; somehow, that seemed important to her.

Will was already asleep by the time she climbed into bed. With her back turned toward him to shield the glow, she eased the laptop open and punched at the keyboard with the tip of her index finger. "John Ambers and Shelby Whitten" flashed back at her from the search box on the screen, the names of the lives that Sylvia was certain she had destroyed before her death. It was a mistake to search for them. It wouldn't prove anything if they were real, just that Sylvia had somehow incorporated them into her delusion, but even before her finger came down on the button, Maria knew she couldn't resist.

FIANCÉE FOUND DEAD UNDER RUBBLE.

CHAPTER FIVE

jenny

Calebasse, Louisiana

HER HANDS TRACED THE CONTOURS OF her hips and slid over the taut muscles of her stomach. Nineteen years had passed since her last and only pregnancy. She stretched out on her son's abandoned bed and took in the memories of his childhood. They hung on the walls in the form of posters and medals from his varsity baseball career and the dust-covered picture frames that captured the eternal smiles and laughter of high school friends who swore they would always return. Jenny remembered those same broken promises with her childhood friends.

"Jenny?"

Her husband's voice bellowed from the kitchen, but she didn't respond. The door creaked when he pushed it open.

"What are you doing?" He glanced at his watch. "One more cup of coffee before we head to New Orleans?"

"Sure," she mumbled, watching her husband from the bed and taking in his image as if it were the first time, amazed at all the ways he'd changed over the course of their marriage. His beard was more gray than brown, his skin was thick and tanned from countless hours in the sun, and his face was etched with the creases of time. Despite the years of abuse to his body, he was somehow more rugged and handsome in his forties than in his youth.

"What's up, Jen?"

"Don't you miss him?" She straightened the wrinkles from the covers as she slid to the edge of the bed.

"Of course I miss him," he replied, with a guarded step forward, stopping a few feet short of her. "But he's just at college. He'll be by in a couple weeks to visit."

She imagined her husband not stopping a few feet short but sliding onto the bed beside her and draping an arm around her shoulder. She couldn't remember the last time he had done that, but he wasn't the only one to blame.

"I know you miss him," Hank said, his tone softening. "It's got to be pretty lonely around here with both of us gone now. Maybe I'll look into that onshore welding job."

The conversation was as timeworn and weary as their marriage, but she nodded her approval, knowing it would never come to fruition. Their lives had been dictated by Hank's work schedule, two weeks on the oil rig and two weeks off, and she had her suspicions that more than two weeks together would be the end of them.

"Or maybe we could get a dog to keep you company," he said, with another quick glance at his watch.

"I don't want a dog," she said, following him down the hallway and into the kitchen. "I was actually thinking that maybe I'm ready to do something different with my life."

Hank sighed and sank into his chair, just like she knew he would. This was one of his least favorite conversations, and one that rarely got off the ground. He was, without fail, disinclined to engage in it. He didn't want Jenny to work outside the house and would do anything to preserve the rhythm and flow of the two-week breaks he had between oil rig stretches. She'd given an honest effort a couple of times over the past six months to breathe life into it, to let him know how she felt she was destined for something greater than the trivial life she'd been living since Dean left for college, that maybe it was her turn to do something selfish for once, to find out what she might have been if motherhood hadn't stolen her youth. But Hank had been unwilling to humor her in the slightest. He was scared he was going to lose her. On some level, she understood this about her husband, but it was never something they put into words.

Hank swallowed a large gulp of coffee before he pulled the cup from his mouth, his expression lost in the steam billowing between them.

"What did you have in mind?"

"I don't know," she mumbled with a shrug. "I guess I just feel like I'm in a little bit of a rut. I seem to have a lot of time on my hands lately."

"You should check out the high school," he said. "Remember when Dean was a student there and they were always nagging parents to volunteer?"

"I already do that on Monday and Wednesday afternoons." She hadn't considered a task so inconsequential, or that her husband's expectations for her could be so trivial. Her ideas were on a much grander scale. "And I go to cooking classes on Tuesdays, yoga on Thursdays, and volunteer at the hospital two Fridays a month. I'm not talking about more volunteer work," she said. "I think I might want to go back to college."

If she hadn't heard her own words churning through the air, she wouldn't have believed she'd voiced them. She'd been trying to get to this point for months, embarrassed by what she considered her *overconfidence*, as if she belonged in a class of people who graduated from college. She'd been a couple of years into an undergraduate program at the University of New Orleans when she ended up pregnant, but that had been a lifetime ago, and any thoughts of returning had been stashed away in the back of her mind, gathering dust and cobwebs, last item on a long to-do list. Hank didn't nod or smile or even appear to be breathing, until Jenny repeated her words. "I want to go back to college."

"You mean like one of those online courses they offer now?"

"No," she said. "I mean I want to go back to college and finish my degree. I only have a couple of years left. And I can commute from here."

The chair creaked when Hank eased his back into the wooden slats with his arms crossed over his chest. His biceps bulged in Popeye fashion from beneath his cotton shirt, and Jenny admonished herself for allowing her eyes to wander. When she pulled them up, they landed on the smirk that was creeping onto his face.

"Don't look at me like that."

"Like what?" he said, but the grin that had surfaced on his face was all she needed to see. She already knew his thoughts: that she was foolish and naive for believing she could dive back into that world and be a part of something significant and transformative, that she was not destined for greatness but for mediocrity.

"Like I'm not good enough."

"I never said that. I never said anything."

"You don't have to say anything. I can tell by the look on your face that you don't think I can do it."

"Is that right?"

He sighed as he pushed his chair back from the table, stepped over the linoleum tile floor they had talked about upgrading for over a decade, and dumped his half-full cup of coffee into the sink. As she listened to the water from the tap rain down and rinse away the remnants of his coffee, she wondered if her dreams were destined for the same fate.

She'd once believed that she could have been successful in business, finance maybe. She'd been good with numbers and had even thought about working for a nonprofit organization, to give back to the community. Her dreams were old now, though, and faded. She couldn't even remember what color suit she'd be wearing as she rushed to catch the train, or if her hair would be cropped short or pulled back in a power bun, or how late into the night she'd work while she helped Dean with his homework at the kitchen table. The little details, the things that once brought her dreams to life, were all gone now.

"Do you have an opinion?" she said, following her words to her husband, who was still standing at the sink.

"You don't want my opinion, Jen. You just want me to agree with you and support your decision."

"You're right. I'd like your opinion to be that you agree with me and support me, but I guess that's not the truth."

"You want the truth?" Hank said, and when the water stopped running and there was nothing left to rinse away, he turned to face her, the weight of his question bearing down on her. "I think it's a waste of time and money."

"How can you think doing something to better myself is a waste?"

"Having a college degree doesn't make you a better person. It's just a piece of paper you put in a frame and hang on the wall. It's not going to change who you are."

It could have been her mother standing there giving her the same lecture. The similarities of their words were striking, but the differences in their intentions were undeniable. Hank wasn't trying to stop her because of jealousy and apathy; he was a candid, commonsense type of guy, frugal to the point of cheap. If the ends didn't justify the means, then it was a waste of time and money.

Her mother had been his polar opposite, oblivious and unpredictable, jealous to the point of vindictive. Even as a child, when

Jenny's actions took the attention off her mother, there was a price to pay, and it usually involved dropping everything to nurse her drug-addled mother back from an overdose. The only time Jenny had refused to play that game, the night before a big exam during her second year of college, her mother had upped the stakes and ended up in the morgue.

The guilt she owned was more about her *lack* of guilt over the death of her mother than about the death itself, but at the funeral she'd played the part she was expected to play. She cried when cued, made up memories when prompted, and took on the role of the grieving daughter with such gusto she could have won an Oscar. The handful of mourners at the grave site scattered when the funeral was over, and Jenny had taken the opportunity to cut ties with the family that had fostered addiction and apathy and everything dirty that her mother had tried to pass on to her.

She didn't know it at the time, but she was four weeks pregnant when her mother passed away, and if she'd believed in hexes and curses, she would have sworn that her mother had planted that baby in her womb just to destroy her dreams.

"This is important to me," she mumbled. "I wish you could see that."

"I do see that," Hank sighed. "And I'm not trying to stand in your way. If it's really that important to you, I'll do whatever I can to support you, but it seems like a whole lot of work just to get a piece of paper that says you did it."

"It's not just a piece of paper," Jenny said, but she stopped herself there. It was futile to argue. What a college degree meant to her, Hank could never understand. He came from a middle-class family that carried work ethic and principles in its genes. They took care of each other and provided food, shelter, and encouragement to their offspring. They took in other peoples' children and raised them as their own. He could never understand her need to distance herself from the cesspool she had clawed her way out of, and how a college degree could permanently sever the chains that she could still feel wrapped around her ankles and dragging her back into it.

"Can we talk about this some other time, Jen?"

"Like when?"

"Like maybe when I have more than an hour to get to the dock."

Jenny didn't reply but yanked the screen door open and let it slam behind her on her way out. Hank was trailing close behind, somehow keeping pace as words poured from his mouth. "Give yourself a couple weeks to think it through," he said, "and when I get back, maybe we can get a puppy."

"I don't want a dog."

She stopped so abruptly that Hank almost barreled over her, and when she turned to face him, their bodies just inches apart, it was his eyes that ceased her rant. The beauty of his eyes was a mystery to her. Green was the official color listed on his driver's license, but they shifted through hues of aqua and blue as effortlessly as a chameleon. If anything about her husband could render her defenseless, it was his eyes. Amid his rugged exterior were the most inviting and soulful eyes she had ever seen, and if eyes really were a window to the soul, then Hank's were wide open. He was a good man, an honorable man, who had loved her son unconditionally and provided her with more than she deserved.

"Just forget it," she mumbled, before turning back around.

Hank was still on her heels, though, and paused just long enough to scoop up his duffel bag. He trailed behind his wife over the gravel, raced ahead of her, and had the passenger door open before she even reached the truck. He was a gentleman to the point of excess.

With her head turned away from him, Jenny gazed out the

passenger-side window and watched her home fly by. Spanish moss hung from the colossal oaks that dotted the fields between bayous, great herons and egrets meandered through the marshes, and an osprey soared from its nest among the tallest trees.

After all these years, Calebasse was still foreign to her. Someone else's home. She'd never forget how Hank had clutched her hand and proudly introduced her to his family, nineteen years earlier. She had been seven months pregnant with another man's baby, scared and insecure.

"Why don't we stop in to see your cousin Nick when I get back to New Orleans in a couple weeks?" Hank said. "Is he still breeding German shepherds? I wouldn't mind having one around the property, now that Dean's not here with you."

"For the last time, Hank, I don't want a dog. And the last person I want to see is Nick."

Nick was the only person from her family she still had contact with, but she limited her visits with him as much as possible. He was an emotional drain on anyone who spent more than five minutes with him, and he was just shrewd enough to outwit and manipulate even his closest friends and family. The last time they spoke was at his son's funeral, six months earlier, when she'd left an open invitation for him to call or stop by any time, which she considered more than congenial.

"Come on, Jen." Hank leaned a weathered and muscular arm against the window. "I don't want you to be sad about this. If you don't want a dog, we can always try for another baby. You know I'm always up for the challenge." He was trying to be funny, so Jenny laughed for his sake, but she didn't find much humor in his words.

"I'm too old for a baby," she muttered, watching an egret skim over the bayou as their car glided over a bridge. She wondered what her husband would do if he knew the secret she'd been harboring all those years. Hank had always wanted a house full of kids, but motherhood hadn't come easily to Jenny, so she'd made sure Dean was an only child. She loved her son unconditionally, but there was no denying that her husband was the more nurturing parent, and while Hank was certainly not the kind of man to play favorites, especially between children, she wasn't willing to test his devotion with a biological child of his own in the house.

They festered in a lengthy silence before Hank's hand found her leg, and she wondered, as she stared at it, if it felt as awkward to him as it did to her. Her natural reaction should have been to lay her hand over his, but the more she stared at the dried calluses of her husband's massive hands, the less familiar they were to her. At one time in their marriage, Hank's hands had been a safe harbor. The world could crumble around her, and sometimes it did, but those hands would always be there to pick her back up and keep her safe. Now it was like a stranger's hand sitting upon her leg, and she couldn't force herself to give one little bit to her husband.

How easy it would have been, and how valuable to their marriage, if she could have just reached out and taken his hand. But that vulnerability was more than she could bear, so with her arms crossed before her, Jenny watched the city's horizon emerge through the windshield. The marshes and oak trees had turned into alleys and housing projects, but Jenny watched with the same fascination, remembering a time before Hank, a time when the voodoo priestess on Bourbon Street had warned her about the bayou.

CHAPTER SIX

maria

I'M SORRY, MARIA. I THOUGHT IT *would end differently."*

Sylvia's words bounced off the walls of Maria's office as they sat face-to-face in the same chairs they'd occupied just days earlier, on the last day of Sylvia's life. The impossibility of their encounter didn't elude her, but a calming sensation washed over her as she took in the tranquility of Sylvia's face.

"I'm sorry," she said, peering into Sylvia's eyes, so alive with a depth she'd overlooked until that moment. "I should have done something to protect you. To stop you from wanting to hurt yourself."

"It wouldn't have made any difference." Sylvia's smile held the warmth of a summer sun shining through a westward window, giving Maria a glimpse of the woman she must have been before psychosis stole her life. "The ending wouldn't have changed."

Words were lost on her as she took in the shifting shapes of Sylvia's face, as if the woman before her and the woman she would one day become were melded into one, with the lines of her face coursing through years of sorrow and joy.

"You're just like they described you," she said, pulling Maria from her trance.

"What do you mean?"

"Your patients. They loved you."

"How do you know my patients?"

"I don't," Sylvia said. "I just heard their stories." She slid forward to the edge of the chair, graceful and silent, her gaze on Maria's face untiring. "I've known you for ages, Maria. Your memory was laced into my life so many years ago, shaping my character and inspiring my faith, and I wanted so badly to make it right for you."

"Make what right?"

"One purpose," she said. "You get one chance."

"What do you mean?"

"Every day people make choices without knowing the outcome. Can you imagine, though, if you knew the outcome before you made the choice? Wouldn't you bear the responsibility of it, even if it didn't happen by your hand? It's important to always do the right thing, Maria, even if you have to suffer the consequences."

"Why are you telling me this?"

"Come on," she said, rising from her chair. "I'll show you."

The wind picked up and night invaded the sky as they made their way from Maria's office into a dusky shadow. The park across the street, once lined with flowers and paths, now held a field sprouting with tombstones and weeds. A flurry of birds taking flight caught Maria's eye, and in the midst of the commotion stood a little girl, her cobalt blue eyes piercing the darkness.

It was her husband's sister, the little girl who never made it past eight.

"Beth?" Maria's feet stepped cautiously toward her. "Is that you, Beth?"

A giggle rang through the air as the little girl darted farther into the cemetery, and without hesitation Maria gave chase. Behind bushes and between headstones they ran, like a game of hide-and-seek, until the patter of feet ceased and the wind stilled.

"Beth?" Maria's eyes searched the perimeter of the cemetery as her words resonated in the emptiness.

"She's over there." A skeletal hand emerged from Sylvia's burlap dress, pointing Maria toward the grave at her back. Through the gloom of night, the headstone was clearly visible.

ELIZABETH ROSE DANIELS

A cavernous hole stretched from the headstone, and as Maria approached, Beth's discolored and distorted face came into focus. The bruises on her neck glowed through the darkness, and her lifeless stare bored through Maria's eyes.

"Oh, God!" She spun back toward Sylvia. "You have to help me save her!"

The marble-like eyes that stared back from Sylvia's sunken face were unseeing, though, as her body crumpled to the ground and disappeared.

"No! No! No! This is not real!" With her face buried in her hands, Maria fought to drive the images out of her mind, but as her knees sank into the soft ground and her hands fell from her face, the dirt surrounding Beth began to cave in.

"Oh, God, no!"

She stumbled into the grave, digging and clawing at the earth piling up around Beth, as blood seeped down her hands. It dripped from her fingertips, soaking into the dirt, and then Maria realized it was pouring from the gashes running down the insides of her own wrists.

"No!"

The stillness of her bedroom was shattered by the screams that followed her from sleep and the gripping pain that gnawed at her belly. Her heart pounded against her chest like a percussion mallet beating a rhythm into a bass drum, commanding and unyielding.

"No," she whimpered, pushing sweat-soaked strands of matted hair from her face and examining the soft, supple skin of her wrists. There were no wounds, just the icy memory of a nightmare that lingered like a ghost. Her arms searched the bed for her husband, but the sheets were cold.

"Will?" Her voice was frail and pitiful, and her mind couldn't vanquish the images of Sylvia and Beth that were branded into it.

Sunlight filtered through the cracks in the blinds as morning forced its way into the room, and by the time Maria hauled herself from the bed, the chills from her sweat-drenched nightgown had settled in. Her body knew her intentions before her mind, and as she reached for Will's wallet on the bureau across from their bed, her skin was rife with goose bumps. Her hands fumbled with the cards and photos stuffed into the tiny compartments until she found the one she sought.

The eight-year-old little girl with the cobalt blue eyes smiled back at her from the twenty-three-year-old picture, but Maria could only see the haunted eyes that had found her in the night, and the blue tinge of Beth's lifeless body.

"What are you doing?" Will's silhouette hovered in the doorway, a coffee mug resting in his hand, and for a moment she couldn't be sure he was real.

"I don't know." The shivers surging through her body rendered her hands useless as she tried to shove the photo of Beth back into its slot. "I'm sorry," she said. "I just wanted to see the picture of your sister."

The steam from the coffee billowed between them as he set the mug on the bureau, easing the wallet from her trembling hands and pushing the lingering strands of hair from her forehead.

"My God," he said. "You're drenched. Come sit down." The strength of his grip saved her from collapsing as he ushered her back to the bed, his hands palpating the roundness of her belly. "Are you in labor?"

Maria managed to shake her head before the tears broke

through, unintelligible words spilling from her mouth as she struggled to convey her dream.

"Come here." He slipped his arm around her shoulder and pulled her to his side. "What happened? I don't think I've ever seen you so upset."

"It was horrible . . ." Her words were scattered with sobs. "Beth was . . . and the ground was caving in . . . and Sylvia . . . and my wrists . . ."

"Wait. Start over," he said. "You had a nightmare about Beth?"

"What was her last name? It wasn't Forssmann, was it?"

She kept seeing the image of the headstone behind the hole where Beth's body was sinking into the ground. *Elizabeth Rose Daniels.* She'd always assumed Will and his sister shared the last name Forssmann, but it would make sense that they didn't; they didn't have the same father.

"Her last name was Daniels," he said. "I thought you knew that."

Did she? It seemed like something she would know. She'd visited the grave site with her husband a handful of times before they left Ohio, but the little girl shared a headstone with her mother and there was no sign of the name Daniels on it, no mention of the man they all wanted to forget.

"Did Beth come to visit you last night?" Will reached for a box of tissues as Maria wiped her nose with the sleeve of her shirt.

"It wasn't a visit," she said, brushing away his words. "It wasn't real."

She could still smell the fresh dirt on her hands and see the blood trickling from her fingertips. The pain in her wrists was almost palpable as she checked again to be sure there were no wounds. She'd never felt anything so real, except life itself, but there was little Will could do to convince her it was anything other than a nightmare. There had to be a reasonable explanation for it. Didn't there?

"It was just a dream," she said. "I think I'm just a little overwhelmed. There's so much going on right now, and maybe my mind was just trying to sort it all out in my sleep."

"You know you can talk to me, right?" Will brushed his lips over the skin of her knuckles. His hands were soft, almost delicate, as if they'd been designed to guide intricate wires and catheters through tiny blood vessels in the heart, and as Maria pictured Detective Andrews's hard and calloused hands, she was struck by how well suited both men were to their particular professions. "You're not alone, Maria. If you don't want to take time off work, you don't have to, but at least let me help you." Will pulled himself from the bed, crossed the room to the dresser, and pulled out some dry clothes for her. "I think you should stay in bed today. Get some rest. I'll take care of the girls."

Maria didn't answer him, but he was right. She needed a break. Her body was fatigued and swollen, craving rest like a hibernating bear, but she'd never been good at accepting help, even from her own husband. She was too stubborn to let someone else take the reins, and she certainly wasn't willing to head back into sleep. She was too afraid that Sylvia and Beth would be waiting for her.

"I think I'll take a shower first," she said. "And then maybe I'll get some rest."

The water cascaded over her head like a summer rain, but a deep chill had settled into her core, peppering her skin with goose bumps. She couldn't seem to get the temperature hot enough, and by the time the shower was over, her skin was red and splotched. She'd barely gotten a brush through her hair when squeals of laughter echoed through the hallway, following her daughter as she barreled into the room.

"What are you doing up so early, Emmy?"

"I didn't pee, Mommy!"

"Great job, baby." Maria hugged her three-year-old as tightly as her belly would allow and followed her daughter's giggles as they drifted through the air like a flight of butterflies. "I'm so proud of you."

"We don't have food," Emily said, freeing herself from her mother's embrace. "Daddy said we need grossies."

"It's *groceries*." Charlotte's words found them before her five-year-old peeked her head around the corner of the bedroom door. The cobalt blue eyes she got from her father, the same ones that had been haunting Maria all morning, sparkled like sapphires in the light. She looked at her little sister. "It's not *grossies*."

"Hello, beautiful girl." Maria pressed her lips to the top of Charlotte's head and inhaled the scent of bubblegum shampoo. "What are you up to this morning?"

"Daddy's making us go with him to get *groceries*." She stared at her little sister as she emphasized the word. "When we get back, Mommy, can you take me to ride my bike? Please?"

"I wish I could, sweetie. But I don't think I'm going to be up for it today." Maria rubbed her belly as if that would explain it.

"But you promised, Mommy! It's not fair!"

"Let me see how I'm feeling later on."

She smoothed her daughter's hair back out of her face as knots gathered down the length of it. She'd been meaning to take both of her daughters for a haircut before she got this deep into her pregnancy, but time hadn't been on her side. She didn't think Will would be able to get a brush through it, or even try, but she didn't have the energy to do it herself, and she had other things on her mind.

The key to the storage unit was where she expected it to be, beneath the journal in her nightstand drawer, the journal that was supposed to be keeping her secrets safe. She wondered if it really had been breached, if Sylvia really had been slinking through her house, rummaging through her drawers, and invading her privacy, or if there had been another way. Was it possible that Sylvia was telling the truth? It was a thought she would never have entertained even three days earlier, but things were different now. It was almost as if Sylvia was trying to tell her something, trying to reach her through her dreams and warn her about something. Whatever it was, Maria had a feeling the answer was in the storage unit.

She slipped the key into the pocket of her dress just moments before her husband walked in, but she was certain he could see the hardened outline of it burning a hole through the fabric like a glowing red ember. She was sure he could sense the deception in her voice when she told him she would be resting in bed while they ventured out for groceries, but if Will suspected anything, he didn't let on. He kissed her on the forehead and wrangled their daughters into the car before he drove off and left Maria to do what she'd promised she wouldn't.

She felt for the key in her pocket one last time before she slipped out the back door and into the garage. She'd have to hurry if she was going to beat them back from the grocery store, but as she slid into the driver's seat of her car a contraction gave her pause.

The skin on her belly was tight and the muscles below it rigid. It was time to head to the hospital, time to meet her son, but she had one more stop to make, one last little thing before she could go.

jenny

THE BOAT CARRYING HER HUSBAND WAS a speck in the distance by the time Jenny peeled her eyes from it. She blew Hank one last kiss for luck, like she always did, before she climbed back into his twenty-year-old Ford Ranger and steered it back to their home in Calebasse.

Tucked away on a high ridge overlooking the bayou stood a solitary house that Jenny had called home for nearly two decades. It had been built by Hank's grandfather and passed down through his family, but it was in need of some aesthetic repair. The red brick was faded to a deep pink, the shingles dotting the roof were mismatched, and the porch was no longer level, but at least it was still standing, which was more than the neighbors could claim. Their homes had all been washed away by Hurricane Katrina, and what was left behind had eventually been devoured by nature. Just a few concrete slabs were still visible through the overgrowth, and a few wooden pillars that stood defiantly tall. It was a constant and chilling reminder of their vulnerability.

The house was the last thing Jenny noticed, though, as she guided Hank's truck through the oak-lined canopy of their gravel driveway. The black sedan parked beside the shed, and the two men with their visible gun holsters, watching her from the edge of the front porch, stole her attention.

The cold metal of Hank's nine-millimeter Glock under the driver's seat should have been a calming reassurance, but Jenny wasn't even sure she could remember how to use it. She was a proficient shot when her target was a piece of paper nailed to a tree—Hank had made sure of it before he brought her out to the country and left her on her own for two weeks at a time—but she'd never been tested under pressure, and her heart was racing at the thought of having to use it.

Her intentions, when she reached beneath the seat to get a grip on the gun, must have been obvious, because both men had their badges on display by the time the truck rolled to a stop, and one of them had his holster undone. She held her hands up to show them she was unarmed, hoping the tremor wasn't visible through the windshield.

Never show fear.

She could hear the words in Hank's voice and see the stony expression he'd worn on his face when he'd been trying to toughen her up all those years ago, but she couldn't seem to convince her body to cooperate. She was scared. She was all alone in the middle of nowhere, at the mercy of two armed men who she hoped were in fact police officers, and she was supposed to be brave. But she wasn't. She was a city girl in a country girl's life, and no amount of target practice could change that.

The officers descended the stairs as she slid out of the truck and shut the door, her thoughts shifting to her son, praying he was still safe at college.

"Mrs. Fontaine?" The older officer spoke first. He was at least a couple of decades older than his partner, who looked uncomfortably out of place and far too young to be entrusted with a police badge or a gun. "Sorry to show up unannounced," he said, his

Cajun accent blending perfectly into the bayou around them. "I'm Detective Marcel and this is Detective Parker." He gestured to the man behind him, who was still fidgeting with the strap of his holster, before turning back toward Jenny with a conspiratorial wink. "You'll have to forgive my partner. He's not from around here, and a woman with a gun makes him a little nervous."

Jenny didn't return his smile or offer him a response. Guns made her a little nervous, too. In anyone's hands.

"What can I do for you gentlemen?" she said, leaning against the truck door and forcing herself to look them both in the eye when she spoke.

"We were hoping you might have some information about a friend of yours," the older officer replied, halting his footsteps at the bottom of the stairs and resting his elbow on the post of the weathered and paint-chipped rail Hank had been meaning to touch up for the past two years. "We spent the morning chatting with your cousin. Nicholas Turner?"

Of course it was about Nick. If a police officer showed up at her door, it had to be about him. Her cousin had a rap sheet a mile long, and when she was young and dumb, Jenny had imprudently played the role of alibi provider on more than one occasion. Police officers would show up at her door with questions about where Nick had been the night a convenience store had been robbed or a car had been lifted from a lot. *He was with me, having a few beers and watching TV.* She thought she was unconquerable back then, but after life threw her a few curveballs, she realized she'd just been reckless and irresponsible. She hadn't covered for him in years, not since moving to Calebasse.

"Whatever Nick's done this time, I wasn't a part of it," she said. "I haven't seen him in ages. Or spoken to him."

"We didn't come here to talk about Nick. We're trying to find an old girlfriend of his. Rachel Tillman?"

The guilt was sudden and unforgiving. Just the mention of Rachel's name did that to her. They'd become friends when she and Nick started dating a few years earlier, but when Nick stopped bringing her around, shortly before their son died, she and Rachel got out of the habit of calling each other. Jenny hadn't spoken to her since the funeral, six months earlier. She'd been meaning to call her, but days turned into weeks and weeks turned into months, and while she kept promising herself that tomorrow would be the day, tomorrow never came.

As far as she knew, Nick and Rachel hadn't spoken to each other since the funeral, either. Nick certainly hadn't been in contention for father of the year when Rachel found the boy dead in his crib one morning—SIDS according to the coroner's report—but he was pretty shaken up by the whole ordeal, and Jenny felt a trace of guilt for not having called him, either.

"I haven't talked to either one of them since their son's funeral," she said. "I guess it's been about six months."

"You'll let us know if she contacts you?" With his arm outstretched and a card tucked between his fingers, the older officer took a few steps forward, waiting for Jenny to close the distance between them. She met him halfway and took the card.

"Is she okay?"

"Far as we know," he replied. "But she's considered armed and dangerous, so be careful if she shows up."

"Armed and dangerous? I don't think we're talking about the same Rachel."

"I'm pretty sure we are. From Bienville, Mississippi? Used to date your cousin, Nick Turner? Lost her son last year?"

"Why would you think she's armed and dangerous? Did she do something?"

"She shot someone," he said. "And then ran."

"Shot someone? Are you sure it was her?"

She couldn't make sense of his words. Rachel was one of the most passive people she'd ever met, a stark contrast to the man who'd gotten her pregnant and left her to fend for herself. The one time they'd tried to take her out for target practice, she wouldn't even take the gun from Hank's hand to shoot at a tree. There was no way she would point a gun at a person. "I really can't imagine Rachel doing something like that. I don't think she's even fired a gun before."

"Well, she has now." He pulled out a crumpled pack of cigarettes and fished through it with a nicotine-stained finger, easing out the last one before tucking it into the corner of his mouth and crushing the empty pack. "She shot a pregnant lady," he said. "Her boss."

"What? Is she okay?"

"It's not lookin' good." He cupped his hand around the Bic to shelter it from the wind before lighting the cigarette, then took a heavy drag and blew out a plume of smoke. "But I guess we'll see."

Jenny was trying to read the card in her hand, but too many questions were running through her mind to concentrate. Where? When? Why? How? No matter how she turned it, she couldn't come up with a scenario involving Rachel, her boss, and a gun. They had to be mistaken.

"Thanks for your time, Mrs. Fontaine." She'd almost forgotten the men were standing beside her until they started for their car. The older officer with the nicotine-stained fingers turned back and winked at her, pointing at the card in her hand with his cigarette. "Make sure you call me if she contacts you."

"I will," Jenny mumbled.

It was a reactive response. She didn't know what she'd do if Rachel showed up, though she doubted she'd ever find out.

When the dust finally settled behind the black sedan after it made its way down the gravel lane, she hurried into the house to get the television turned on. Rachel's flawless complexion and auburn curls filled the screen as her image flashed across the local evening news. Jenny reached for the remote, but the segment was over by the time she got it turned up. The internet connection in Calebasse was always vengeful in its unwillingness to load, and her laptop offered little more than a spinning hourglass icon. From the few words that made it to the screen, though, she could almost believe what the officers had told her:

Doctor fighting for life after shooting . . .
Secretary wanted for questioning . . .
Police not releasing details . . .

She sank down into Hank's old leather recliner, the same one she'd been hounding him to park on the curb for the past three years, and pulled out her cell phone. Prudence and curiosity were battling each other in her mind, one nudging her to call her husband, and the other to call her cousin.

In the end, neither answered, and she was left to endure the night with the danger of an unbridled imagination. Who would Rachel turn to now? Who did she have on her side? Jenny wasn't so naive as to think that she couldn't have ended up like Rachel—always falling for the wrong guy, unable to care for a son she couldn't keep alive, never able to make ends meet. But for Jenny, it always came down to one question: Who would she be if not for Hank?

PART II

maria

THE AIR WASN'T RIGHT. IT WAS the smell. It wasn't unpleasant; in fact, it was vaguely familiar and quite comforting. But it was not right. And the room was too dark. Maria could almost feel her pupils dilating, searching for light, but inky blackness was all that trickled in.

"Will?"

Her whispered word bounced off a wall that was far too close, a wall that shouldn't have been there, and echoed back to her ears. It wasn't until she reached for her husband, though, whose presence was replaced by scratchy, rough-threaded sheets, that Maria was certain she was not in her home.

The nightstand beside her was piled high with a haphazard array of papers that spilled to the floor when her hands fumbled for the lamp, and when the room was illuminated with the yellow glow of soft light, Maria was breathless. She slipped out from beneath the pink comforter she hadn't seen in more than twenty years, the crumpling of papers under her feet shattering the silence, as visions of her childhood flooded through her eyes.

She was dreaming. She was home in Alabama, under her parents' roof, and as much as she wanted to surrender to the moment and absorb the beauty surrounding her, she was scared. Her pulse quickened as the smell and feel of dirt and blood invaded her memory, and her eyes scanned the room for signs of Sylvia and Beth, fearful that they would return with their enigmatic warnings. She was met instead with a corkboard full of memories that hung from the wall.

Pictures, ribbons, and magazine clippings three rows thick flooded her mind with long-forgotten images, and as she crept closer, her eyes trained on one particular photo that was tacked to the middle of the board, she was overwhelmed with sorrow. It was her mother and her, their arms wrapped around each other, tennis rackets dangling from their hands, and laughter floating through the air around them. They were oblivious to how it would all end. She gripped the photo between her fingers before pulling out the strategically placed thumbtack, and she watched the other papers drift to the floor and land carelessly around her feet.

Behind her, below the only window in the room, sat a familiar desk, brown and aged, with her name still carved into one of its legs. The wood beneath her fingers was smooth as she ran her hand across its surface, and though she could picture the contents of each drawer, she dared not open them. Instead, her eyes landed on a white teddy bear perched atop the desk, holding a satin heart with the words *I Love You* stitched across it. It was the one Marc had given her for Valentine's Day her senior year of high school, the one she threw out with a cache of love letters and photos when her heart was first broken all those years ago. She could still taste the bitterness of it.

On the far wall of the room, beyond the overstuffed corkboard and the sheets of paper littering the floor, stood three doors. She knew what once lay beyond them, but she was wary of venturing through them now. What world would they lead her to tonight? Would it be the one with Sylvia's skeletal fingers pointing her toward death? Or would this be the kind of dream her husband spoke of, where friends and family gathered together with memories of better days?

The handle to door one was like ice beneath her fingers, but it opened with ease and bought her entrance to a place she had long forgotten. A red hair dryer, a pink crimping iron, and makeup in every shade of blue floated across the bathroom counter, and when her eyes drifted up to the toothpaste-riddled mirror, they landed on a girl who shouldn't have been there.

Her skin was like porcelain and her eyes were wide and searching. Her hair, radiant and black, gleamed under the warm glow of the artificial lights, and Maria couldn't resist the feel of her skin. From her face to her body, Maria examined every curve and bend like a lover's first touch. It wasn't until she reached the tautness of the muscle-lined stomach, muscles that had never been stretched by a growing baby, that she was thrust back into reality.

Blaise.

Every fear she held for her unborn son magnified as her hands searched her belly for signs of him. The photo, warm and moist from the sweat of her palm, drifted to the counter as she reached for the handle of the sink. The water was colder than she anticipated, shivers gripping her body as it struck her face and trickled down her neck, soaking the front of her shirt. The girl in the mirror stood resolute, staring back at Maria as water dripped from her flawless skin, confusion etched onto her face. They both drew deep breaths into their lungs as Maria turned away from her. It was just a dream. Blaise would be there when she woke up.

She forced herself through door number two, apprehension warning her to return to her son but anticipation prodding her to see who might be waiting beyond her room. It opened to a familiar hallway where wall-mounted portraits from a lifetime ago tracked her movements with pervasive eyes. To her left, moonlight glinted off the surface of the kitchen counter just beyond the den, and to her right, the door to her parents' bedroom beckoned her.

She was powerless against it, the magnetism that pulled her to her mother, and when she pushed the door open, the dim light from the hallway spilled over the bed, illuminating two faceless shapes beneath a mound of covers. Her temples pounded in time with her pulse as stealthy steps carried her across the floor, and as she kneeled beside the bed, her mother's breath brushed across her face. It was a cruel reminder of what she'd lost.

"Mom."

The word floated between them, Maria at the mercy of her emotions as the soft features of her mother's face shifted with every breath.

"Maria?" Her mother bolted to attention, her shock knocking Maria to the floor. "Is that you?"

"Yes," she whispered. "It's me."

The light that continued to filter in from the hallway spotlighted her mother's confusion as her attention shifted from Maria to the nightstand. "What are you doing?" She squinted at the tiny numbers on the alarm clock. "It's four thirty in the morning. You need to go back to bed."

Maria sat in silence, barely breathing, and crouched beside her mother's bed, waiting for more. Waiting for the moment the woman before her would recognize the gift they'd been given, the moment clarity would reach her and they would embrace and laugh and cry—the moment she'd longed for since her mother's death.

"Come on," her mother finally said, gathering her robe from the chair beside her bed and stepping past Maria. "Let's not wake Dad up."

In a dazed silence, Maria followed her back through the hallway of roaming eyes and to the room where it all began, where drifts of crumpled papers and photos littered the floor.

"What happened in here?" Her mother shook out the pink comforter that had been discarded on the floor, and Maria watched as it billowed in the air and settled in a cloudy heap atop the bed. She stacked the books in a precarious pile on the nightstand before gathering the papers and photos into a pile on the floor. "Look at this mess," she said. "What have you been doing in here?"

"I just . . ." Maria scanned the room before glancing down and noticing the photo she was still clutching in her hand. "There was so much stuff in here that I'd forgotten about," she said, holding it up between them. "I found this picture on that corkboard over there. Isn't it great? I wish I could take it back with me."

Her mother took the photo from her hand and with barely a glance tossed it onto the nightstand, as if the memory was meaningless to her. "Take it back with you where?"

"Home," Maria mumbled.

"You *are* home." She pulled the covers back to the freshly made bed and motioned for Maria to climb in. "What's going on with you, sweetie? I've never seen you like this."

Maria eased onto the edge of the bed, studying the lines and angles of her mother's face, determined to burn them into her memory. Had she ever been this young? She could remember only the face her mother wore after years of cancer had ravaged her body. She could still see the frail arms that had clutched her children until the agonizing and bitter end, and as she took her mother's hand she noticed that the wrinkles that had once adorned them were conspicuously absent.

"You haven't even asked about Charlotte and Emily," Maria said. "Don't you want to hear about them?"

"Maybe you can tell me about them tomorrow."

"Tomorrow?"

"It's four o'clock in the morning, Maria. We both need to get some sleep."

"But we won't be here tomorrow," Maria said, desperate that her mother not waste this precious gift they'd been given. "Why haven't you asked me about them?"

"Asked you about who?"

"Your grandchildren. Why haven't you asked about your grandchildren?"

"My grandchildren?" The skin of her mother's hand was so warm when she pressed it against Maria's forehead and ran it down her cheek, that Maria could almost believe there was real blood pumping through her veins. "Your nightgown is drenched," her mother said. "You must have a fever."

"It's not sweat." Maria patted her hand over the dampness. "I just splashed some water on my face before I woke you up."

"Why would you do that?"

"I had a bad dream the other night, and I thought this was going to be the same thing, but now . . ." Maria's words drifted away as Sylvia reached back into her mind, pulling her back to the graveyard where Beth's body was drowning in the earth.

"Is that what this is about?" her mother said, tucking the blankets around Maria's slender frame. "Did you have a bad dream?"

"I don't know," Maria whispered. She'd never imagined this moment. She'd never wondered what her mother would look like if she met her in a dream, or how she would act, or if she would even recognize her. She'd never envisioned herself on a bed, in a room that was a part of their history, having a conversation as mundane and ordinary as this. She'd once been daring enough to imagine them meeting in heaven, though. And when they met in that heaven, her mother would wear a warm smile and yearn to hear all about her grandchildren. She was never like the woman who sat beside her today.

"You'll feel better in the morning," her mother said. "Get some sleep now."

She pressed her lips to Maria's forehead and, like a ghost, rose from the bed, drifted across the floor, and had almost slipped from the room before Maria bolted upright.

"Mom, wait!"

Her mother slid the door shut and retraced her footsteps back to Maria's bed before she sank down beside her again and smoothed her hair back. "What is going on, sweetie?"

"Please don't go," Maria begged. "Don't you want to spend more time together? To talk about everything that's happened since you left?"

"I haven't gone anywhere." Her mother fluffed the pillow one last time and with a firm insistence assured Maria that they'd spend the following day together, and the weekend, and every moment thereafter. "I promise," she said, tucking the covers even more tightly around Maria's body, as if she could secure her to the bed. "I'll be here when you wake up."

The clock read 4:52 A.M. when Maria forced her eyes shut, but the residue of adrenaline that trickled through her veins was potent, and sleep was elusive. It wasn't what she expected it to be, this rendezvous with her mother, but Maria couldn't wait to share her experience with Will, to apologize for the years of doubt. His face was all she could see as she slipped away into sleep, searching for him on the other side of her dream.

CHAPTER NINE

"WILL, YOUR ALARM CLOCK."

Even with her eyes clenched shut and her head buried beneath the pillow, the incessant, nagging beep that pierced the air still managed to leach its way into Maria's ears.

"Will!"

Her arm struck the nightstand when she reached to shake him, and when she peeled her head from the mattress, the Sony cube alarm clock from her dream glowed back at her.

7:01 A.M.

Her fingers fumbled with the controls, pressing buttons and turning dials until there was silence, and when her eyes were finally able to focus, she was forced into the realization that she had never made it home.

The textbooks were still balanced on the nightstand where her mother had piled them, the teddy bear still watched her suspiciously from the desk, and the photos that had drifted so carelessly from the corkboard to the floor still rested where they had fallen. The one of her mother and her, with the thumbtack holes and rolled-up edges, lay by her side.

The bathroom hadn't changed overnight, either, and the girl, looking much more forlorn in the light of day, watched Maria from the same hazy mirror, with the same radiant black hair and the same moon-shaped doe eyes. She wore her confusion without shame, and Maria was almost tempted to apologize to her, though she couldn't imagine why.

The hallway that had brought her to her mother the previous night, the one she had thought might lead to a thicketed graveyard with ghastly corpses, was nothing more in the light of day than an ordinary corridor with outdated wallpaper, and the portraits that she swore had been tracking her movements seemed to take less interest in her. They were just the dusty, still images of her family that had hung on that wall for years: grandparents, aunts, uncles, cousins.

Her footsteps were delicate and deliberate as she padded over the plush carpet, feeling like an intruder in a house that had once been her home, as she snuck toward the kitchen to watch her mother from the shadows. How could a dream be so bland and tedious? Everything in that house, including her mother, was like a page out of the life of an ordinary American family. It wasn't until the footsteps coming from the bedroom found her that things started to get interesting.

"Good morning, Maria." Her father's words crashed through the stillness around them, but she barely recognized the man who spoke them. The gray wisps of hair that had managed to cling to his scalp since her mother's death were now thick and black, and the kyphosis that had been stealing his height by the day was noticeably absent. He stood as strong and proud as a pharaoh's staff, and Maria was speechless at the sight of him.

"Maria?" Her mother was hovering behind them, wearing the same youthful and benevolent smile she'd worn the previous night. "How are you feeling this morning?"

Maria didn't bother answering. It seemed an unfair question, and she couldn't peel her eyes from her father.

"You can't be here, Dad." Her voice was hoarse and cracked, and her words were barely decipherable, but she expected more of a response than the silent stares and bewildered expressions on both of her parents' faces. She cleared her throat before she tried again. "You can't be here. This can't be possible."

"What do you mean? Of course I'm here."

"Everyone else is dead," she said. "Everyone who's visited me in my dreams has been dead. Sylvia, Beth, Mom."

It was the gasp that came from behind her, from her mother's mouth, that finally forced Maria to see the obvious. Her mother didn't know she was dead. She didn't know that her only daughter was grown and married, with children of her own, that her husband's booming voice and black hair had both faded, or that her body was buried next to her parents, just a few miles away.

"That's enough, Maria."

Her father stepped between them, as if he could stop Maria's words from assaulting her mother, as if his presence alone would limit the damage that cancer had done to her.

"But she doesn't know what's going on. She doesn't even remember Charlotte and Emily, or even Will. He was like a son to you, Mom. How could you forget them?"

"Stop it," her father said. "I don't know who any of those people are, either. Just stop this nonsense."

"'Those people'?" A tight band worked its way across her forehead, compressing like a boa constrictor as it inched its way around her skull. "They're not just some people. They're my family. My daughters and my husband. You were there when they were born. And don't you remember my wedding day, Mom? You gave me that pearl necklace that Grandma left you when she died?"

"Grandma's not dead." Her mother's words lacked their usual confidence, but she carried on as if she meant to convince Maria of the impossible: that they were all alive and healthy, that Grandma was coming to visit over the summer, that she wasn't buried down the street. "Why don't you go lie down?" she said. "You've been studying so hard for that AP test, I think you've just worn yourself out."

The look that flashed between her parents was one she recognized well. It was the same one she and Will used when they didn't want to speak in front of the children. The same one all parents used, she supposed. It was a look that signified the gravity of a situation.

"I don't need to lie down," she said, her words falling on deaf ears as her parents carried on with a conversation that was worlds away.

We can't send her to school like this.

She'll miss her AP test if she doesn't go.

She'll just have to reschedule it.

It was a conversation about choices and consequences that would seem dire to any high-achieving teenager, but as she listened to it play out before her, nothing had ever felt so meaningless. She wanted it to end. This dream that she believed was the most magical of gifts the previous night was turning into a nightmare of sorts, and she just wanted to wake up. As her parents droned on, Maria picked up the newspaper from the counter and scanned the front page. She didn't recognize the headline, "Operation Praying Mantis: Success," but there was no mistaking the date in the top right corner: April 19, 1988. She was seventeen years old.

"Please," Maria said, her voice bringing her parents' debate to a halt, dissolving between them, the air thickened by the sudden silence around them. "Please listen to me. This isn't what you think it is. This isn't real life."

The stillness was absolute, like a photo behind a glass frame. No breaths. No twitches. No words. She waited for the image to crack, for a thin line to spread through them before they shattered to pieces. She flinched when her mother reached out for her hand.

"I think you should get some rest," she said. "Maybe you can go back to school tomorrow if you're feeling better."

"There is no tomorrow." Maria stumbled back into the stool at the counter, her hand resting over the gentle curve of her stomach. "I'll wake up before then. I have to. My son will be born any day now."

A subtle gasp escaped her father's lips, followed by a whisper that could have come from either of them. "Are you pregnant?"

"No . . . I mean . . . I'm not pregnant now. But in real life I'm nine months pregnant and I already have two daughters and a husband and . . ."

As the blood drained from her mother's face, Maria's eyes drifted back to her father. Disappointment. Embarrassment. Regret. Everything she would expect from the father of a pregnant seventeen-year-old was etched across his face, but before she could explain herself to him, her mother was dragging her back down the hallway. Maria's eyes followed the textured wallpaper with the giant blue flowers they'd once picked out together, her fingertips grazing over its scratchy fibers and sending a signal to her brain through the tiny nerve endings that she was, perhaps, not dreaming.

Her mother shut the door behind them as Maria slid onto the edge of the bed she'd woken up in that morning, the one with the pink comforter. "Are you pregnant?"

"I don't know," Maria replied. "I mean, I never got pregnant in high school. Will's the only person who ever got me pregnant, and obviously I haven't met him yet since you have no idea who he is."

"Stop it, Maria." Her mother stood against the far wall by the door, as if entering any farther might negate the possibility that this was all just a misunderstanding. "What is going on with you?"

"I don't know," Maria whispered. "But none of this is real."

"I'm taking you to see Dr. Warner today. I'll call his office and let them know it's an emergency." Her mother reached for the handle of the door but turned back before she pulled it open. "And don't talk like this in front of Dad. I'll tell him you were just confused from a nightmare you had last night. It would kill him if he found out you were pregnant."

Maria stared at the door long after her mother disappeared, her limited options flickering before her like a burned-out marquee sign fighting to stay alive. She dug her nails into her arm as deeply as they would go, waiting for the pain to pull her from sleep, before she finally released her grip and watched the indentations that were left behind fade into four red splotches. When she slapped herself across her face, the throbbing in the palm of her hand almost matched the sting across her cheek, but there she sat, staring into a wall of pictures that had been lost to time many years back.

Maybe her doctor would know what to do. Or maybe he would just think she'd lost her mind. The latter seemed more likely. She reached for the pink phone on the nightstand, the one she'd gotten all those years ago to match the pink comforter, and dialed Will's cell phone number. The call wouldn't go through, so she tried her own number, even though she knew it was useless. She had to get back to Bienville. If she could get to her house, back to the bed where she'd fallen asleep, maybe she could somehow force herself awake.

Her closet shelf was scattered with neon shirts and acid-washed jeans, but the pair she grabbed were tapered so tightly at the ankles it was a battle to get them on, and she'd barely gotten a sweatshirt pulled over her head by the time her mother was back at her door.

"Is that what you're wearing?" Maria followed her mother's eyes as they both took in the grease-smeared sweatshirt she'd pulled from the floor of her closet and the dingy white socks dotted with holes around the toes. "Are you at least going to brush your hair?"

She ran her fingers through the tangles in her hair as her

thoughts pulled her back to her home in Bienville and one of the last memories she had before waking up in this strange world. Had Will gotten a brush through Charlotte's hair? Had he tried? She needed to get back, because her daughters were both due for a haircut and Will didn't know the number or the address of the salon they used.

"I'm not ready yet," she said, looking up at her mother. "I need to take a shower."

"Twenty minutes," her mother replied. "Then we have to get going."

Twenty minutes didn't seem long enough, once the clock started ticking, and since there was no time for hesitation, Maria got the water running in the shower and the radio turned up before she started in on her plan. The hallway was empty when she slipped from her room, no voices hailing from either direction. Before she eased the door shut behind her, she pushed in the button lock on the inside handle. She slipped through the den and crouched behind the kitchen counter, scurrying across the linoleum floor on her hands and knees, not resting until she reached the laundry room.

Her father's car was already gone, but her mother's blue Toyota sat just twenty feet away. The keys dangled on the hook above her head. Maria couldn't force herself to move. Sweat beaded on her forehead and trickled down the front of her shirt, and when she leaned back into the cool metal of the dryer, she felt the sudden urge to vomit. It was all so foreign to her. She'd never snuck out of a house before, and her pulse was thundering so loudly in her ears that she couldn't think straight. She hadn't even thought to grab herself a pair of shoes from her room and had to slip on her father's old grass-stained Adidas, the ones he wore to mow the lawn. They were ridiculously big, but Maria pulled them on and tightened the laces as she recited the same words over and over in her head.

This can't be real. This can't be real. This can't be real.

Her head was spinning with nonsensical thoughts as she sat crouched in the corner of the laundry room, her legs unwilling to carry her out the door, and she couldn't seem to force enough air into her lungs as she tried to imagine various scenarios.

What would she do if her mother found her there preparing to run? What would she do if Will wasn't there when she got back to Bienville? What would she do if she never woke up?

The cold metal of the dryer against her skin was like a grounding wire, a safety check, harnessing all the energy and chaos that was vibrating through her body and forcing her to remain present. Will would be there. Everything would be fine, if she could just get herself to Bienville. When the knock on her bedroom door echoed down the hallway sooner than she expected, she knew she was out of time.

"Maria? Are you just about ready?"

Before she could reflect on what she'd done, Maria had the engine of the blue Toyota running. Then she was backing over the bushes that had once meticulously lined their driveway and was careering out of her childhood home in the middle of Alabama.

CHAPTER TEN

MARIA CHECKED THE REARVIEW MIRROR ONLY once on her way out of town, and as the miles ticked by, she paid no heed to the sixty-five-mile-per-hour speed limit signs, flying past them at eighty miles an hour. Traffic seemed to crawl along beside her as she sped past Pontiac station wagons and Oldsmobile sedans as if they'd swallowed up all the SUVs that frequented those roads. She tried not to think about her mother's frantic words to her father, or the call they'd make to the principal's office, or the questions the police would ask them about the outfit their daughter was wearing when she left home that morning. Or if any of that would happen. It didn't matter. She was going home.

Hours passed in a blur as Maria spun the radio dial through station after station of songs she hadn't heard in years, catching herself humming along to George Michael as she steered her car off the interstate at the Bienville exit.

The scenery was scarcely what she expected. What would one day be a four-lane highway, with traffic lights and housing developments, was a two-lane country road without another car in sight. Acres of farmland stretched around her, speckled with cows and horses; miles of sky expanded in every direction; and thickets of wild spruce, magnolia, and cypress trees dotted the horizon. It was beautiful, breathtaking really, but it wasn't home.

As she rolled into the center of town, the signs posted on the side of the road assured her that she *was* home, but the sights re-sembled little of the speck-on-the-map town that she and her hus-band had picked to raise their family. As if by instinct, her car rolled up to the entrance of what would one day be her neighbor-hood and cruised slowly past the dilapidated trailers lining the red dirt road. It ended in a copse of trees too thick to traverse. The hum of the car engine rumbled through the silence as Ma-ria climbed through the brush, fighting through the foliage. The road that would eventually lead to her house had yet to be paved, and even if she could force her way through the vines and thistles, there was no way she'd be able to reach the spot where her home would one day stand.

Where was her house? Where was the bed in which she'd fallen asleep? She must have fallen asleep, but her memory was so unreliable these days that she couldn't even remember going to bed. She couldn't get past the moment when she'd buckled herself up in the car and was about to head to the storage unit. Did she make it there?

Her tires kicked up dust from the parched ground as she raced past the trailers on her way out, panic flooding into her chest like water into drowning lungs. She had to find her children.

A cobblestone path with perfectly manicured juniper bushes led to a red door that had been painted and repainted too many times to count. It was chipped and peeling, ready for another coat, and when Maria pulled it wide it opened to silence. The sound of her footsteps bounced from the floor to the walls and back to her ears as she rushed through the corridor, and by the time she reached the windowless door of room 204, a thousand reasons not to open it ran through her mind.

"Excuse me," she said in the moment of silence that followed her entrance, the moment before stifled laughter spread through the crowd like a virulent infection. The faces looking back at her could have been stolen from her junior high yearbook, with their teased-up bangs, frosted lips, and shaded blue eyelids. "I'm looking for my daughter," Maria continued. "Charlotte Forssmann. She's in Mrs. Nelson's kindergarten class."

The woman poised at the front of the class with chalk in hand was not a woman accustomed to interruptions. Her words, as rigid as her spine, were curt and concise, and with the snap of her fingers, silence descended upon the classroom. "You're in the wrong building," she said. "This is the junior high school."

"But this used to be the pre-K and kindergarten building. Or, I guess, it will be in the future." Words tumbled out of Maria's mouth faster than she could control them. "I'm sorry. I didn't mean to interrupt your class."

As her thoughts scattered into a jumbled heap around her, the teacher wound her way through the desks and was halfway to the door before Maria's gut told her to flee. Her legs felt like stones, though, and she couldn't force herself to move. She knew the truth, that her daughter wasn't there, but hope wouldn't yield to logic.

"Chapter three," the teacher said, with barely a glance back at the students. "And not a word until I get back."

"I'm sorry about the interruption," Maria mumbled, following the woman's gaze to the clownish tennis shoes on her feet that had been stained green from the countless rounds her father had made of their lawn behind the old push mower. Intuition kept nudging her to run, but as an arm slipped around her shoulders, she stepped obediently through the empty corridors of a building she had frequented with such regularity over the past two years she could navigate it with her eyes shut. The woman at the front desk of the main office greeted them with a smile that disappeared the moment she spotted Maria's escort.

"Mrs. Gaston," she said, her posture straightening as if she'd been called to attention. "What can I do for you?"

"This young lady found her way into my classroom today. Can you please help her reach her parents?"

"That's not necessary," Maria stammered. She was struggling against a snare, a trap that should have been an easy escape, but the more she fought the tighter it squeezed.

"Would you prefer we call the police?"

"For what?"

"It's called truancy. When you leave school without permission, it's called truancy, and it is illegal." The teacher nodded her head toward the woman behind the desk. "Amy here is going to call Bienville High School to see if any of their students are unaccounted for, and then maybe we can figure out who you are. I hear there's a problem over there with some of the students skipping class and smoking marijuana."

Maria clung to her silence as the sound of Will's laughter bombarded her from all corners of the room. He was one of the few people who would appreciate the irony of it all. Maria was almost forty years old and had never once smoked pot, never skipped out on a class, never snuck out for a cigarette with friends. How had these become her crimes?

"My name's Maria Forssmann," she said, in a long exhale that presaged defeat. "And I don't go to high school here. I know I must look like a seventeen-year-old girl and that I couldn't possibly have a five-year-old daughter, but I assure you this is not what you think it is."

"You don't look older than fifteen to me."

Amy placed the receiver back into its cradle with quiet hands, as if the noise might send Mrs. Gaston into a frenzy. "No one's missing from the high school," she said. "And they didn't recognize her name as one of their students."

"Please," Maria said, inching toward the door. "This is just a misunderstanding. And I really don't see the need to get my parents involved. If you'll just let me get in my car and go, I promise I won't bother you again."

Mrs. Gaston pulled herself from the edge of the desk, her narrow body blocking Maria's path to the exit. It was a deliberate gesture, and though Maria outweighed the woman by at least ten pounds, there was no getting by her without a struggle. "I don't have time for this," the teacher said. "I have a classroom full of eighth graders waiting for me, so the sooner you give me your parents' phone number, the sooner you can go."

"I'm sorry," Maria replied. "I can't."

Call the police.

The words echoed in her mind even after Maria shoved her way past the teacher and watched her fall to the floor in front of the desk. She sprinted through the halls while footsteps, whether real or imagined, pounded behind her. There was no time for rest or reason, and when her father's shoes flew from her feet she skidded down the corridors in her socks, sprinting through a maze of hallways until she reached a door on the far side of a dead end. The handle crashed into the wall when she swung it open.

"Emily Forssmann," she gasped between pants. "I'm looking for Emily Forssmann."

There was nothing but silence staring back at her. No snickers from students or reprimands from teachers, just an empty room in a forgotten corridor of a school with stacks of abandoned and broken chairs littering the floor. Her children weren't there, and though she'd known that before she'd opened the door, the absence was more devastating than Maria could have imagined. Even the band of teachers that rounded the corner and barreled toward her like a seething lynch mob couldn't force her mind back into action. Her fight, her will to go on, sank to the floor beside her, and they sat like perfect bedfellows with nothing left to do but surrender.

CHAPTER ELEVEN

"MARIA!"

The militant voice that called her to attention came from the largest of her escorts back to the main office. He was a gym teacher, by the looks of him, with a whistle slung around his neck and the whitest sneakers Maria had ever seen. She curled her toes to hide the dingy, white socks on her feet, wondering what had happened to her father's grass-stained tennis shoes. The Bienville police were on their way. "You answer me when I ask you a question."

"I'm sorry," Maria said, plucking her thoughts from the fog that blanketed her mind. Escape was futile. Strategies to wake herself up had occupied every second of the day, and all she'd managed to do was get picked up by the police. Maybe there was no waking up from this.

Maria shook the thought away as the door opened and Mrs. Gaston emerged with two uniformed officers. They seemed disappointed when their eyes landed on Maria. She couldn't have been what they'd envisioned when they'd gotten a call about an unruly, drug-addled teen wreaking havoc at the junior high school.

The officer in charge was a tall man, the kind of tall that would make a boy hunch in his youth, but if that was ever his affliction, he had outgrown it. He carried himself well.

"That office in the corner there," he said. "Can we use it for some privacy?"

When the secretary unlocked the door, Maria shuffled in and took a seat in a stiff-backed, weathered chair that sat on the wrong side of an ornately carved wooden desk. It was the principal's office, but the man who filled that role was gone for the day. Maria wondered how many kids that chair had seen, how many prayers and promises it had heard. It was her first trip to the principal's office.

"Maria, is it?" The tall officer slid onto the high-backed leather chair that sat behind the desk and nodded at her. The chair fit him like a glove. "I'm Officer Reynolds and this is my partner, Officer Hamby." He motioned to the man standing behind her, guarding the door.

"It's nice to meet you," she mumbled, and tucked a stray hair behind her ear, before she ran her tongue over her unbrushed teeth and crossed her arms over the grease-stained sweatshirt she'd forgotten she was wearing. It hadn't crossed her mind to worry about appearances that morning when she fled from her mother, or to think about what she might do if her plan didn't work, but as she tried to see herself through the officer's eyes, she wished she'd spent more time on her hygiene.

"Mrs. Gaston gave us her account of what happened today," he continued, "and before she presses charges for assault, she'd like to talk to your parents."

"Assault?"

"You knocked down a sixty-year-old woman." The officer grinned at his partner, who coughed through a poorly disguised laugh. "What did you think was going to happen? And we'll need to get a drug test, which I'm guessing will be positive?"

"I'm not on drugs," Maria whispered, though she doubted either man heard her words. She was a seventeen-year-old runaway, dressed like a bum, with an outrageous story that would be enough to convince any sane person that she was either delusional or on drugs.

It was Sylvia's story. It was the same one she'd listened to on the last day of her patient's life, the story she refused to believe. But maybe Sylvia was right. Maybe people really did come back from the future.

"We're also going to need your parents' phone number."

The officer leaned forward and rested his lanky arms on the lavishly carved desk in a gesture so like Detective Andrews's that Maria could almost see him sitting before her, with the calluses on his massive hands and the constricting collar around his beefy neck.

"Walt Andrews," she said, glancing from one officer to the other. "Is there a detective at your station named Walt Andrews?"

They watched her in silence for a moment, the officer at the door shifting his weight from one foot to the other, before they both shook their heads no. Of course Walt wouldn't be there. He was busy preparing for a war in the Middle East. He had medals to earn and children to raise, and he wouldn't be finding his way to Bienville for at least another decade, maybe two.

"We're going to need that phone number," Officer Reynolds said, rapping his knuckles on the top of the wooden desk and breaking the stillness that had settled between them.

"Please," Maria replied. "I'm fine. I promise. I really just want to go home."

Home. Even as she said the word, she knew there was no home for her there. Her home was twenty years in the future, and any Bienville address she gave to that officer wouldn't even show up on a map. There was no other home for her but the one in Alabama, where her parents were undoubtedly awaiting their daughter's return.

"I can't let you go until you give me that number," he said. "Or

I can get it when I run the plates on the blue Toyota out front. I'm guessing that was your parking job in the tow-away zone?"

At Maria's silence, he slid a piece of notebook paper and a pen across the desk. She hesitated before she picked up the pen, trying to find the words to a story that would take her to her husband and children and make this all a distant memory. If only she knew how to make that story take shape. She scribbled down the names of her parents and their phone number instead and slid it back across the table to the officer.

"Tom and Anne Bethe?" The paper crinkled in the officer's hands. "Did I pronounce that correctly? Be-thee?"

"Bay-ta," Maria said. "It's pronounced like B-E-T-A."

"I see. And you are . . ." He glanced at the notes he'd gathered from his interview with Mrs. Gaston. "Maria Forssmann? Is that correct?"

It was a moment that stretched into endlessness, the absolute stillness that goes along with being caught in a lie. But it wasn't a lie for Maria. It was her being stripped of her identity. It was the loss of her home, the loss of her husband and two daughters, the loss of a son she never got to meet.

"No," she whispered. "Not yet."

She watched in silence as Officer Reynolds dialed her parents' phone number, wishing she'd paid more attention to Sylvia's warnings. *Don't go to the storage unit. Stay away from Rachel.* Had she gone to the storage unit? She'd been on her way, but did she ever get there? Had she stayed away from Rachel?

"May I speak with Mr. or Mrs. Bethe, please . . .

"Mrs. Bethe, this is Officer Reynolds from the Bienville, Mississippi, police department. I have your daughter Maria here with me . . .

"Yes, ma'am, she's fine . . .

"I'm sure you were very worried, but she's fine . . .

"She drove herself . . .

"Well, we're not sure yet, but she's in a bit of trouble . . . She had an encounter with one of the teachers at the junior high school here, and there might be some assault charges filed . . .

"Yes, ma'am . . .

"I understand, but I'm sure it's your daughter. Dark hair, brown eyes, blue Toyota with Alabama plates. She gave us your name and phone number . . .

"No, ma'am. I didn't realize she'd driven all the way from the middle of Alabama. She hasn't been very forthcoming with us . . .

"No, she didn't mention an AP test . . .

"Well, to be honest, we're a bit worried about drug use. She gave us a false name and has been talking about her daughters, who she seems to think should be here . . .

"I see . . .

"Yes, ma'am. That does sound concerning . . .

"It might not be a bad idea to have her checked out at the ER when we're done here, but the teacher she knocked down would like to talk to you before she decides if she's going to press charges . . .

"Yes, ma'am. I'll put her on the line, and then we'll go from there . . .

"You're welcome . . .

"Okay, I'll tell her."

A red light flashed from the base of the phone when Officer Reynolds pressed the Hold button, his attention focused on the officer standing behind Maria. "Could you tell Mrs. Gaston that Maria's mother is on line one for her?" He waited for the door to click shut, for them to be alone, before he continued. "Maria Bethe," he said. "High school senior. Straight As. Class president. Never been to detention. No drug use. No police record. Scheduled to take an AP calculus test in Pine Creek, Alabama, and somehow ends up in Bienville, Mississippi."

She let his words wash over her. While it was true she had once been that girl, too many years had passed for Maria to remember her, and there was nothing she could say to make sense of the situation for either of them.

"Your mom told me to tell you that she loves you," he added, before he leaned back in the chair and sighed. "Do you want to tell me what's going on?"

"I don't know," she said. "I wish I had a better answer for you, but I really don't know. I guess I'm just in the wrong place at the wrong time."

The officer rose from the high-backed leather chair, his height even more impressive than she'd remembered, and with two strides was by her side. Whatever words he had for her were drowned out by the voice that broke through the intercom.

"Officer Reynolds," it cracked through the speaker. "Mrs. Gaston would like to come in and talk to Maria."

"Send her in," he replied, his eyes following Maria as she rose from the chair before Mrs. Gaston pushed the door open.

"You don't know how fortunate you are to have such kind and caring parents." The teacher's words landed solidly on Maria's shoulders, and she sliced her hand through the air when Maria opened her mouth to respond. "I don't want to hear a word from you," she said. "If it wasn't for your mother, I would be charging you with assault. Try to remember that, next time you decide to run off on some wild escapade."

Maria listened to the woman's fading footsteps as she retreated from the room. They echoed with satisfaction.

"Come on," the officer said, pressing his hand into her back and guiding her toward the door. "I'll let your parents know they can pick you up from the station."

Less than four hours later, Maria sat unmoving beside her mother as they coasted up Interstate 65, her father trailing behind in the blue Toyota. Every movement she made threatened to be an invitation to conversation, so Maria sat motionless in the passenger's seat and let her mother's words drift away unreciprocated.

You could have gotten yourself killed out there.

Dad and I were worried sick.

Don't ever pull a stunt like this again.

She was running out of ideas, out of places to go, and as her hands drifted back to her belly, searching for the son whose life had yet to become his own, she could almost feel him slipping away.

Did Sylvia make it home? The woman who'd visited her in her dreams had been a different version of the woman who'd killed herself two days earlier. Maria could almost feel the blood running down her arms from the gashes in her throbbing wrists as Sylvia watched her from the periphery of that nightmare. She'd already killed herself by the time she showed up in Maria's dreams. Maybe she was trying to show Maria the way home.

jenny

"COME IN!" JENNY HOLLERED OVER HER shoulder to her son, who was knocking on the screen door off the kitchen. Dean was home for the weekend and he and his father had spent the morning fishing in the bayou off their pier. Jenny was busy pulling all the Tupperware containers from the cabinet beside the refrigerator. Some she hadn't seen in years, and she still couldn't find the lid to the one she'd already filled with the homemade marinara sauce she planned on freezing. He knocked again. "For heaven's sake, Dean. Why are you knocking?"

When she spun around, the face that greeted her was not her son's. The icy blue eyes that stared back at her from the other side of the screen door belonged to a woman who'd been evading police for almost three weeks. Her auburn curls had been shorn and dyed black, and she'd lost at least twenty pounds, but there was no disguising those eyes.

"Oh my God!" The words came out in a gasp before Jenny covered her mouth with both hands and tried to stop herself from fainting on the kitchen floor. They watched each other through the mesh screen as the silence stretched between them, taut like a bow.

"I'm sorry to come here," Rachel said. Her voice was scratchy and hoarse, absent of the melody it once carried, and Jenny had to lean in to hear her. "I didn't know where else to go."

"You can't be here." Jenny swung the door open and grabbed Rachel's wrist, pulling her into the kitchen, unable to ignore the odor that followed them inside. "You have to leave," she continued, thinking better of bringing her into their house. She dragged Rachel back out the door and behind the toolshed. "The police have already been here looking for you, and your face is all over the news. They're looking everywhere for you."

"I don't have anywhere to go."

"Did you do it? Did you shoot that pregnant woman?"

The nail marks that were embedded in Rachel's skin when Jenny finally released her grip took a moment to fade. Rachel rubbed at them before moving on to the mosquito bites that pock-marked both of her arms.

"It was an accident," she said, her words barely a whisper and the dark hollows of her eyes giving her a ghastly appearance that was made more shocking by the unforgiving light of the sun. The terror that danced through them was more disturbing than any Jenny had ever seen. "Is she still alive?" Rachel said. "Please tell me she's still alive."

"For now." Jenny glanced back toward the bayou to make sure her husband and son were still fishing. "But it doesn't look good. And how the hell do you accidentally shoot a pregnant woman? What were you even doing with a gun?"

"It's a long story."

Rachel leaned back against the side of the shed and slid herself down to the ground, her sleeveless shirt catching on a nail and tearing. She didn't seem to notice, or perhaps she just didn't care. It had once been blue—Jenny could see the original color popping out from the inner hem of the collar—but it was a dingy grayish black now, along with the pants that had likely been khaki the day she shot her boss. The clothes she wore weren't heavy enough for the chilly spring they were having, and she was visibly shaking, but any pity Jenny felt for her was quickly whisked away. There was nothing she could do for her.

"You have to go, Rachel. I'm sorry. The police have already been here, and I have my family to think about."

When Rachel looked up at her, Jenny could almost see the girl she'd once thought of as a sister. She'd never had a sister and had never really understood how to be friends with another woman until Rachel came along. But that was a long time ago, and whether those feelings had died with Jonathan or when Nick finally left her for good, Jenny couldn't say. Like most of her relationships, though, it never really had a chance.

"Please," Rachel said, still looking up at her. "Could I just spend one night here in the shed? If anyone finds me, I promise I'll say we haven't talked. That you didn't know I was here."

Jenny squatted down beside her, wishing she could offer her something more, wanting to be a better friend, but not willing to risk herself for it. "Why don't you just turn yourself in?" she said. "If it was an accident, why are you running?"

"Because they won't see it that way."

The words had barely left Rachel's mouth when Hank's booming voice found them from the bayou. Jenny glanced back to see her husband and son giving each other high fives, celebrating a big catch, no doubt.

"I have to go," Jenny said. "If Hank sees you here, he'll call the police." Her words and warnings had little effect on Rachel, though. She was a woman who was out of options. From her head to her toes, she was soiled and battered and bruised, and as Jenny watched her with her knees bent up to her chest and her head bowed between them, she couldn't help but pity her. "One night," she said. "If you want to stay in the shed for one night, it's fine. But I haven't seen you, and if anyone finds you, I had no idea you were here."

"Thank you, Jenny." Rachel reached out for her, grasping at her arm with dirt-caked hands and staring up at her with tear-filled eyes. How could this be the woman Jenny had once admired, and even envied? The woman who picked herself up after the father of her son left her on her own? The woman who pulled herself together after her son was torn from her? The woman who had done it all on her own? "I won't let anyone see me," she said. "I promise."

"Just make sure you're gone by the morning." Jenny felt ashamed as she walked away. The words she'd left with Rachel had sounded cruel and merciless coming from her mouth, and as she pictured her friend cowering in the corner like a neglected dog, shivering and hungry, she was ashamed for having voiced them. It would have cost nothing to offer her a kind word or some encouragement or a moment of companionship.

Hank and Dean were still propped on the edge of the pier when she sneaked back into the house. They had fishing poles dangling from their hands and their heads were nodding in time with the bobbers that floated atop the murky bayou water. They looked like a couple of boys who'd just popped out of a Norman Rockwell painting, and as she watched the sun shift its position behind them, she wondered how much time she had left.

She knew she should have been telling Hank or calling the police at that very moment, but she couldn't force herself to do it. It was Rachel, and she was cold and hungry and scared, and she had nowhere else to go. Before Jenny could talk herself out of it, she pulled the bread and bologna from the refrigerator, as well as a bottle of Coke, and slapped a couple of sandwiches together. She snatched the quilt off the guest bedroom bed and hauled all of it out the kitchen door, careful to not let it slam behind her, then darted behind the toolshed. Rachel was curled up and shivering in the back corner and didn't stir when she opened the door. She was in bad shape, and probably in need of a doctor, but Jenny could only risk so much.

"I brought you some stuff," Jenny whispered, waking her up to witness the same terror coursing through her eyes. "It's not much, but the blanket should keep you warm tonight. And you look like you haven't eaten in weeks, so I made a couple of sandwiches for you."

Rachel tore into one of the sandwiches with an animal hunger that reminded Jenny of the hyenas she'd seen on a National Geographic special a few months earlier. She couldn't believe this was the same woman who had once eaten pizza with a fork and knife. Both sandwiches were gone, along with half the bottle of Coke, before she finally acknowledged Jenny's presence.

"Thank you," she said, wiping her mouth with the back of her hand. "I haven't eaten in days." She chugged the rest of the Coke and wrapped the quilt around herself.

"You don't look so good, Rachel. Why don't you let me take you in to the police station? At least there you'll get food and clothes and a doctor. You're not going to survive out here alone." Before Jenny could even finish her sentence, she felt certain she knew Rachel's intentions. Survival wasn't part of the plan. "Where's the gun?" Jenny asked. "You're not going to kill yourself out here, are you? Where is it?"

"I'm not going to kill myself," Rachel replied, pulling the quilt back around herself. "I got rid of it. It got too heavy and I couldn't carry it in my pocket anymore without my pants falling down." She gestured with her head toward the pier behind them where Jenny hoped her husband and son were still fishing. "I threw it in the bayou."

"Here?" The leaf blower banged against the wall when Jenny sprang to her feet, frantic to get it stilled before anyone heard them. "You left a murder weapon in my backyard?"

"It's not in your backyard," Rachel said. "It's in the bayou. And it's not a murder weapon. I didn't kill anyone."

It took some restraint to not snatch the quilt and send Rachel on her way, or to tell Hank, or to call the police. Jenny didn't know much about the law, but she knew she was committing some kind of crime by letting Rachel stay. What could she do, though? When she looked down, Rachel was slouched over on the concrete floor, her breathing deep and labored, and the brokenness of her too unbearable to witness.

One night.

Jenny would give her one night, but if Rachel wasn't gone in the morning, she'd have to turn her in.

"What happened in here?" The screen door slammed behind them as Dean followed his father into the kitchen and took a seat next to him at the table. Tupperware containers littered the floor, and slices of bread were spread across the counter like playing cards after a night of high-stakes poker. "Looks like a tornado came through."

"Just making some lunch," Jenny said, knocking over the condiments on the counter as she tried to quiet the tremor in her hands. "No fish today?"

"Nothing worth keeping," Hank replied. "You okay, Jen? You look a little shaken up."

"No, I . . ." Jenny wiped her forehead with the back of her hand and forced a laugh as she surveyed the mess around them. "I was trying to find a Tupperware lid and a roach crawled across my hand. Scared me half to death." She shook her head and laughed again before she smeared some mustard across a piece of bread. "I still haven't found him," she said, holding up the butter knife in front of them, "but I will."

They watched the news until dusk seeped into the house and the outside world was cast into darkness. Vigils were being held throughout Mississippi for the pregnant woman Rachel had shot, and while she was still lingering on in a coma, doctors didn't think she could hold on much longer. Rachel's face was popping up with alarming regularity on the local and regional news stations as the manhunt expanded to the surrounding states. The story was even starting to stake its claim in the hearts of the rest of the nation, with a blip here and there on national news stations.

Jenny couldn't stop thinking about Rachel, shivering in the shed, trying to stay warm beneath the checkered quilt, hungry for one more sandwich. Or the gun sitting at the bottom of the bayou. She'd been half listening to Hank and Dean go on all night about Rachel, both certain she was already dead, that she'd taken her own life instead of facing up to what she'd done. When she had finally heard enough, Jenny got up and took the remote from the armrest of Hank's recliner and turned off the news.

"Stop it," she said. "Both of you. It was just an accident."

"If it was an accident, then why is she running?" Dean was trying to open the news on his cell phone, but Jenny knew he wouldn't have any luck with the WiFi. "I haven't read anything about it being an accident. Was that on the news?"

"No," Jenny stammered. "But you know Rachel. She couldn't have shot someone in cold blood."

"Apparently we don't know Rachel as well as we thought we did," Dean continued. "Now they want to question her about her baby's death, too. There's some kind of letter the police have, but they're not releasing it yet."

"There is no way Rachel had anything to do with Jonathan's death," Maria replied. "She was crazy about that baby. And you know how much stress she was under after Nick left her, trying to raise that baby on her own."

"That didn't give her the right to kill him. There are plenty of single moms out there who manage to get through tough times without killing their children."

"She didn't kill her child," Jenny snapped back. "I know Rachel well enough to know that she couldn't have hurt that baby. And it's not as easy as you think, being abandoned by a man and having to raise a child on your own. You have no idea what that's like."

"And you do?" Dean's words were jagged and sharp, seamlessly ripping through Jenny's defenses. "You've never worked a day in your life," he said. "And you've certainly never had to worry about being abandoned by a man."

It was the hurt more than the anger that pulled her from the couch, and as she stood over her son, Jenny could only see his biological father in him. The man who'd abandoned them both before he even laid eyes on his son. The man who destroyed her dreams and left her to live a life that had always been one giant question mark: What could have been?

It would have been easy to spill the secrets of Dean's life onto the floor in front of him, to make him mop up his words, but she could feel Hank imploring her to stay silent, forcing her to swallow her pride.

"Don't ever talk to me like that again."

Her footsteps were soft and silent as she retreated to the bedroom, the shadows from the sun having disappeared from the walls. She sat in darkness, not wanting to be found, not wanting to hear anyone follow her down the hall or knock at the door, not wanting to deal with the secret in the shed. Hank slipped inside without a word and wrapped his arms around her before he pulled her into an embrace that broke through the layers of defenses she'd built up over so many years.

"Thank you," he whispered into her hair. "I know how hard that was."

She buried her face into his chest and let all the guilt and re-gret soak into the collar of his shirt with the tears that spilled from her eyes. Too many secrets were piling up—secrets kept from her husband, from her son, from the police. She could no longer con-tain them.

"I have something to tell you, Hank." She wasn't sure which one was going to spill out first, but she couldn't balance the weight of them, and they were about to topple.

"I have something to tell you first," he said, slipping a finger under her chin and tilting her face up toward him. "I don't know what's gotten into you today, but you would have done just fine on your own."

"You can't possibly know that."

"But I do." Hank swept his hand over her forehead and with clumsy fingers tucked a lock of hair behind her ear. "No matter what might have happened in your life, whether we ended up to-gether or not, you would have always been a great mom to Dean."

"But I'll never know for sure, will I?" Her thoughts churned to-gether in a jumbled mass of remorse and guilt as she sat transfixed, almost hypnotized by the green in her husband's eyes. Without Hank, she could have been the one shivering in the shed. "Because you saved me."

"I didn't save you, Jen," he whispered. "You saved me."

His words brushed against her forehead as he breathed them out, and Jenny didn't protest when his lips traveled down her cheek to her neck, or when his hunger for her blotted out any need she had to share her burdens. She felt her own hunger when he laid her back onto the bed, and so, for the first time in years, she gave her-self to him completely.

maria

THE SHEERS ON THE WINDOW FLUTTERED beneath the breeze of the fan as the first of the sun's rays peeked through them. The minutes ticked by on the clock beside her, with no regard to her predicament. What little fitful sleep Maria had found the previous night was occupied by Sylvia. Every time she closed her eyes, she saw the blood from her dreams pouring down her wrists and dripping from her fingers, and it was getting harder to force it from her mind. She didn't think she had it in her.

Her mother was waiting for her on the couch when Maria finally dragged herself from the bedroom. She'd been browsing through the coupon pages of the newspaper. "Good morning, Maria," she said. "How are you feeling?"

"I'm fine," Maria replied, clearing a spot for herself on the couch. "Just not quite myself."

They sat side by side, mother and daughter, too intimately close for eye contact as they stumbled through an uncomfortable session of You Can Tell Me Anything.

If kids are being mean to you at school, you can tell me.

If you're struggling with your classes, you can tell me.

If boys are trying to pressure you into doing things you're not ready for, you can tell me.

"It's nothing, Mom. There's nothing going on that you need to worry about."

It was an easy lie. Easier, perhaps, than it should have been. Who was there to help her, if not her mother? Her husband and her children and her life were somewhere out there, waiting for her, and all she had to guide her back were disjointed dreams and memories and the words of a dead patient.

I'm here to save you, Dr. Forssmann. I'm here to protect you and your baby.

". . . his lunch break today."

"What?" Maria asked.

"Dr. Warner. He said he'd see you on his lunch break today. And he wants to get some kind of scan of your head and do some blood work, too."

"Sure," Maria mumbled, but the two Sylvias in her mind—the sallow-faced girl who sat in her office vowing to protect her and the skeletal creature who pointed her to the grave—were struggling for her attention. Were they sending the same message?

"Are you okay, Maria?"

"I'm fine," she said, and as her mother rambled on, blissfully unaware that a dead woman's haunting voice was echoing through her daughter's mind, Maria could hear only Sylvia's words.

The first time I was here . . . you ended up being someone very important to me. Now I finally understand why.

". . . come out there with me? The tulips are already sprouting, and I think the lilies will start in the next week or two."

"I think I'll just hang out here," Maria said. She'd forgotten how important her mother's garden had once been, and the hours they'd spent out there in the kind of silence that taught them more about each other than a thousand conversations ever could. If only time had been on her side. There were no words to explain where she was going or why she had to leave. She dropped her head onto her mother's shoulder and wrapped her arms around her neck. It was a strange and uncomfortable embrace, not the kind either woman would have chosen for a last good-bye, and Maria dared not imagine what she would be leaving behind. Would her parents remember this? Would they mourn the loss of their daughter? Would they even go on living in this world after she left?

"I know this is going to sound crazy," Maria said, "but promise me you'll keep up with your mammograms. Don't skip any years."

"Mammograms? What are you talking about, Maria?"

"Just promise. Please."

Her mother reached over and pulled her in for a proper hug, the aroma of her Giorgio perfume flooding Maria's senses and forcing her back to a time when this really was her home, when the woman beside her could offer her sanctuary. "I promise I'll take care of myself," her mother said. "But let's focus on you today. Let's get you feeling better."

"I'm so sorry, Mom. I hope you know that I never meant to do this to you and Dad."

"You haven't done anything to us, sweetie. Don't worry yourself about it. Dr. Warner will know what's going on and you'll be back to yourself in no time."

Her mother eased away with a gentle grace, reminding Maria that her father would be home shortly to accompany them to the doctor's office and that she should rest before it was time to go.

And then she left.

She slipped out the back door with her gardening shoes and her wide-brimmed straw hat like their lives were not extraordinary, like her daughter was not about to disappear forever. Her mother's absence was more intrusive than her presence, and as Maria's fingers skimmed over the grainy, crisscrossed fabric of the couch, she could almost believe that this life was all she had. Through the window, she watched as the freshly sprouted weeds in the garden were plucked, one by one, and when her mother's steps finally led her to the tulips, Maria eased herself from the couch and slipped into the kitchen.

The car keys had all been hidden, but the knife block was waiting for her on the far end of the counter, the glistening steel blades lined up like perfect soldiers. Maria ran the chiseled edge of the butcher's knife over the tip of her finger, allowing the waves of angst to ripple through her body, before she returned it to its sheath.

It was the paring knife beside it that she needed—not nearly as grand and menacing, but razor sharp and wieldy. The cold metal pressed against the thin flesh of her inner wrist when she slid it up her sleeve, trying to conceal it from the watchful eyes of her grandmother, whose portrait hung on the wall. Maria slinked by her, and the rest of the family, down the narrowing corridor of the hallway and into the sanctuary of her bedroom.

The steel glistened from the side of the tub while the water rose higher and higher, sending an uncontrollable shudder through Maria's body. It was a deed that would take more willpower than she possessed, of that she was sure, and as she sank into the tepid water, sweat trickled down her chest and into the thin creases of her belly. Will and her daughters were waiting for her when she shut her eyes, splashing through the surf and beckoning her to them under a warm and radiant sun.

"I'm coming," she whispered, but her hands shook uncontrollably and the blue veins mapping across her inner wrists retreated like they were anticipating her actions. The knife handle was slick in her hand, and the cold steel against her skin nauseating, and despite the steam from the water, goose bumps dotted her arms. Her eyes stung from the sweat that seeped into them.

This was what Sylvia had been trying to tell her, she was certain of it. *Slit your wrists and you can go home.* But as the weight of the blade sank into the hollow of skin on her inner arm, Maria could feel her resolve waning. Maybe she was wrong. Maybe the images from her dream were just fantasy, and the gashes across her wrists that had throbbed even after she awoke were just lingering memories from a desperate subconscious trying to rid itself of guilt. Maybe Sylvia hadn't killed herself to go home and Maria really had just failed her as a doctor.

"Please make this stop." Her gaze floated up toward the ceiling, but her words crashed back down around her, drowning in the tub full of water. "I just want to go home. Please, just let me go home."

God brought me back for a special purpose.

Sylvia's words hammered into her thoughts, louder and louder, until she couldn't make sense of anything. How could she be a seventeen-year-old girl sitting in a bathtub about to end her life in a deed so selfish and grotesque?

"I'm going home." She repeated the words over and over, needing to believe them so her body could do what her mind wouldn't allow her to do.

I'm here to protect you.

"I'm going home."

Her body sank deeper into the water as a careless hand drifted over her barren belly and her mind grasped for the fluid image of her family. She reached for the knife one last time as an eerie silence blanketed the bathroom. The *ping* of water droplets dripping into the tub echoed through her ears, and the sporadic whispers of her own breath amplified in her head.

"I'm going home."

One purpose. You get one chance.

"Stop it, Sylvia!"

The tip of the blade eased into the delicate skin of her wrist, and with a tenacity she had never known, Maria pushed until the steel disappeared beneath her skin. The pain was exquisite, and as tendons and vessels were torn from her arm she watched in horrid fascination, as if she were no longer a part of her body.

Swirls of pink danced through the water around her before vanishing under her body, and when she pulled the knife from her arm, crimson blood poured from her wound. The only sound was the roaring of her pulse inside her head, beating in time with the flow of blood from her arm, and after the world around her dimmed, it disappeared through a narrowing black tunnel. When the pulsating beat in her head ceased, the silence was complete, and for a moment there was nothing. Not even pain. Just blackness.

"Maria . . ." The voice was barely audible. "Maria."

"Will?" She struggled to force the word from her mouth, but he was too far away to hear her.

"Maria!"

"Dad?" The sound of her name grew louder as her confusion deepened. The words, one moment her father's and the next moment Will's, intensified, until the man who spoke them was right by her side.

"Maria, hang on! Please, baby, hang on!"

"Will, it worked."

Her voice was so weak she couldn't hear her own words, but she was home and Will was by her side. Her smile faded under the watchful eye of her husband as she allowed herself to drift into blackness.

CHAPTER FOURTEEN

LIGHTS FLASHED THROUGH MARIA'S EYES AS conscious-ness seeped in. The wheels of a stretcher whisked her through a hospital corridor as a face hovered above her and a stifled voice tried to force its way into her ears.

". . . in there, Maria. Please, baby, just hang on."

When the face came into focus, it was Will's, but Maria's voice was weak and muffled and her words couldn't reach him. A hand from nowhere pressed an oxygen mask against her face. The mask fogged up with each breath, and the pain that tore through her abdomen, the hard contractions of labor, was unlike any Maria had ever known. Her vision waxed and waned like the tide, and when her husband came into focus again, his hands and face were stained with spatters of blood that could only be hers.

"Please don't let him die."

The words were just a whisper on her lips, but they echoed through her mind as she watched a terror she had never witnessed bleed through her husband's eyes.

"Please, Maria. Please, baby, just hang on!" The darkness closed in again, and Will's face faded away.

"Please," she whispered into the blackness. "Please don't let him die."

When the lights returned, unrecognizable faces floated in and out of view as white coats bustled around in a frenzy. Voices yelled in the distance.

"I think she's awake!"

"Get her sedated and intubated now!"

Maria fought with the oxygen mask still strapped to her face, and through shallow gasps of breath, pleaded with the woman standing over her.

"Please don't let my baby die."

As the voices shuffled to the background she felt herself drifting back to the darkness.

"Is she pregnant?"

"Someone get an HcG on that blood, stat!"

The scene was dimmed, and a calmness had settled in. There were no faces floating above her. Only silence, except for the hum of machines. Her throat burned, and when she tried to swallow, it felt like shards of glass were tearing through her esophagus.

"Maria?"

An unfamiliar voice attached to an unfamiliar face loomed over her. She was a bone-thin woman, likely in her fifties, but the wiry gray of her hair and the coarse wrinkles surrounding her eyes and mouth from decades of smoking made her look closer to seventy. She brought a Styrofoam cup of ice water to Maria's lips with a straw. "Your throat's gonna be real scratchy for a few days. Why don't you see if you can get some of this water down?"

"What happened?" Maria's words were just a whisper, but the pain was phenomenal.

"You had a tube in your throat that was breathing for you. We took it out yesterday, but sometimes it can take a few days before the swelling goes down."

The woman placed the cup on a table next to the bed, and Maria managed to glimpse the RN behind a name she couldn't quite make out on the name tag.

Her memory was hazy, but she knew that she was home, and she knew that her husband was there because she had seen him. It wasn't until she reached for the cup of ice water on the table beside her that she realized her wrists were bound to the bed by leather restraints.

"Why are my arms tied down?"

"It happens sometimes in the ICU," the nurse said. "You were givin' us a hard time trying to pull that breathing tube out and get at your IV. Once you're feeling more settled down, we'll get them undone."

"You can undo them now," Maria whispered. "I'm fine."

"It's not up to me, honey."

The room was empty but for some flowers and cards in the corner and a couple of empty plastic chairs by the bed. Recessed and dimmed lights provided a muted glow over it all, casting an artificial calm across the room. Maria's nurse kept herself busy recording vital signs.

"How long have I been here?" Maria asked.

"You came in about a week ago."

"Where is everyone?"

"I'll get your family in just a bit. Visiting hours are over, but they stay camped out in the waiting room. I can sneak 'em in for a couple minutes."

When she closed her eyes, she could almost feel the velvet of Emily's cheeks against her own and the grip of Charlotte's arms around her neck as her daughter's breath tickled her ear. She could smell Will's cologne as he leaned in to place a gentle kiss on her forehead and whisper that he loved her.

"Maria."

Her name rang through the air in a voice that didn't belong to any of them. It came from a woman who was supposed to be dead.

"What is she doing here?"

Maria's throat tore as she recoiled in terror, the restraints holding strong when she yanked against them, desperate to distance herself from her approaching mother.

"Maria, please," her mother said, as she reached for a hand that Maria was powerless to withdraw.

"Where's Will? Where's my husband? Where are my children?" Her eyes flashed to the hospital blankets tucked firmly around her flat, babyless belly. "Where is he?" she screamed. "What happened to my baby?"

A baritone voice boomed over the commotion of the room as a team of medical staff swarmed in and shuffled her mother to the background. "Give her five milligrams of Haldol IV and get psych back up here."

Maria thrashed and writhed against the leather restraints, and only when a familiar searing pain ripped through her arm did she remember what she had done. Her nurse approached, a syringe of Haldol at the ready, and reached for the IV bag hanging by Maria's bed. "We're just gonna give you a little something to help you relax," she said, her throaty voice and the twang of her backwoods accent heightened. Maria caught the name printed on her name tag: Joanie, RN.

"Joanie, please don't. I'll calm down. I promise. Please don't give me Haldol."

The nurse cast a hesitant glance toward the doctor who had ordered it, but he nodded his head and the medicine was pumped into Maria's veins.

"I'm sorry, sweetie, but this is gonna help you rest, and you'll feel better when you wake up." She smoothed Maria's hair back and pulled the matted strands from her face as Maria's body stilled.

"Why are you doing this to me?"

Her words were thick and heavy as the Haldol hit its target and she faded back into the darkness.

jenny

S TEAM SWIRLED UP FROM THE BLACKNESS, the scent of hazelnut coffee lingering in the air as Jenny set the mug in front of Hank at the kitchen table. He smiled up at her, his eyes still drowsy from sleep and the shadows beneath them accented by the natural light shining through the window. She added a spoonful of sugar and a splash of cream to her coffee before she glanced out the kitchen window toward the shed. She was too busy plotting her way out there to notice that his attention had drifted past her to the screen door. It squeaked just moments before it closed, but Jenny still jumped when it banged shut.

"Sorry," Dean mumbled as he crossed the kitchen. "Didn't mean to scare you." He pulled a mug from the cabinet and filled it with coffee before he turned back to Jenny. "You're awfully jumpy this morning."

"No, I just . . ." Her heart was pounding so fiercely, she expected both her husband and son could hear it, and she had to catch her breath before she continued. "I thought you were still in bed. What were you doing out there?"

"I couldn't sleep," Dean replied as he took a sip of coffee and sat down beside his father. "I got up early and went for a walk."

"A walk?"

Jenny glanced back at the door, trying to quell the urge to question her son about what he may have stumbled upon out there, certain he would mention if he'd seen anything peculiar. She cringed when she thought about what she might find when she finally made her way out to the shed. Would Rachel be gone? Would there be a note? Would she be dead?

"Where'd you go?" she said.

Dean shrugged as he stood up and walked toward the hallway. "All over," he mumbled, the tension from their argument the previous night still thick in the air between them. "I'm going to pack up and head back to school early today. I've got some projects due next week that I need to work on."

Jenny watched as he disappeared down the hallway, barely able to restrain herself from following him and pulling him into a tight hug and telling him how much she loved him. He was wrong for speaking to her like that, but he was her son, and what wouldn't she do for a little more time with her son?

"So, what was it you were going to tell me last night," Hank said, "before we got interrupted?"

When he smiled, the creases in the corners of his eyes deepened, adding an unexpected charm to his features. Jenny had those creases too, but hers didn't add anything but years to her face. She'd forgotten she was about to spill her secrets to him the previous night. In the sobering light of morning, she couldn't imagine how she'd ever thought that was a good idea. All she could think about as she sipped her coffee and watched her husband over the rim of the cup was getting him out of the kitchen so she could get back to the shed.

"I can't remember now," she laughed. "Must not have been too important."

"I guess not," he replied, rinsing out his coffee cup and placing it in the sink. "You have any plans for us today? I was thinking about heading out to Stark Bayou with some of the guys from work."

"No plans." Jenny gulped down the gritty remnants of her coffee and smiled up at her husband. "I have some things to take care of around the house, so take your time. Have fun."

She didn't leave the kitchen until her husband and son were both out of the house. She paced the floor, brewed another pot of coffee, and checked the clock on the wall at least a dozen times, praying to God that Rachel wouldn't appear at the back door or poke her head out of the shed before they were gone. Despite the promise Rachel had made to be gone by morning, Jenny had her doubts. She waited until the dust settled behind Hank's truck before she ventured out the screen door, careful not to let it slam behind her.

A thick film coated the window on the side wall of the shed, and even when Jenny pressed her face up to it, she couldn't see in. It wasn't until she opened the door that she saw Rachel lying in the corner, in the exact spot she'd been in the previous night. Her head was slumped forward, and Jenny couldn't pull her eyes from the quilt, straining to see if it was rising and falling over Rachel's chest.

She stepped over the concrete floor, careful not to bump Rachel, and leaned against the wall across from the window. The pane was equally filthy on the inside, and so little light penetrated it that the room had an almost underground feel, like a tomb.

"You're supposed to be gone," Jenny whispered, crouching down beside her. She was surprised to find Rachel fully awake, her eyes open and her fingers fumbling with a dirty piece of notebook paper that had been folded into a tiny square.

"I can't go back there," Rachel said, trying to fold the paper into an even smaller square.

"Well, you don't have to go back there," Jenny replied. "But you can't stay here. Hank is home for another week, and you know how he is. He'll turn you in if he finds you."

Rachel held the square of paper between them, gesturing for Jenny to take it. When she opened it, the words were faded, and the seams were almost torn from where it had been folded and re-folded, but Jenny could still read the words:

Dear Rachel,

You don't know me, except as one of Dr. Forssmann's patients, but I know you. In fact I remember everything about you from the last time I lived this life. How you tried to convince the jury that killing Dr. Forssmann was an accident and that you didn't deserve to rot in prison for the rest of your life. I remember that because I was on that jury. I was one of the people who convicted you of murder.

I won't let you do it again. I've already warned Dr. Forssmann to stay away from you, and I'm begging you, please leave her and her son alone. If you kill her, you are condemning her family to misery. Her father will die from the heartbreak and stress of the trial, her children will know their mother was killed by a woman they trusted, and her husband will cry himself to sleep each night before he visits her in his dreams. They don't deserve this. They deserve to live a long and happy life together—even if you couldn't have that with your son.

I also know about the letters you wrote to your ex-boyfriend. The ones about wanting to start over with a "clean slate" after your son died. I always thought the police should investigate those, but for some reason they didn't think you had anything to do with your son's death. Someone will be looking into them this time. I've made sure of it.

I'm leaving now. There's nothing left here for me and I can't

live with these memories or the knowledge of what I've done. I
have my own sins to atone for, just like you.

If we confess our sins, He is faithful and just and will forgive
us our sins and purify us from all unrighteousness. 1 John 1:9

—Sylvia Woolf

"What is this?" Jenny sank down onto the ground beside Rachel, her eyes never leaving the paper as she read and reread each
word at least three times. "Who sent this to you?"

"One of Dr. Forssmann's patients," Rachel replied. "She's dead
now. She killed herself after she sent me that letter."

"What the hell does it mean?"

"It means Maria's going to die," Rachel said, picking at the
hem of her tattered shirt, her face expressionless, as if she were no
longer in possession of emotions. "It means I'm going to spend my
life in prison if I go back."

"She was obviously crazy," Jenny said, pointing at the words on
the letter as she spoke. "How could she have sat on a jury for a trial
that hasn't even taken place? And Maria's not dead. This woman
was just trying to scare you. It doesn't mean this is what's going to
happen. This is just nonsense."

Rachel sat quietly as Jenny tried to convince her that the words
in the letter carried no consequences and that they were meaningless, but Rachel didn't seem to be hearing them. She mumbled under her breath as she continued to pick at the frayed edges of her
shirt before she moved on to the scabbed mosquito bites on her arms.
She jumped when Jenny touched her leg, her feral eyes scanning the
room before they settled back onto the unraveled hem.

"Rachel," Jenny said, waving the letter between them to get
her friend's attention. "This is nonsense. You don't have to worry
about this."

"I do, though," Rachel replied. "The woman who wrote that letter died before I shot Maria. She knew it was going to happen before I even did it."

"That's not possible." Jenny scanned the letter again, trying to piece together the significance of that information. "And Maria's not dead. And Jonathan . . . You didn't . . . ." She stopped short of asking. She couldn't bring herself to say the words, as if voicing them might bring them to life and make them true.

Rachel finally looked up at her. "Were you going to ask me if I killed my own son?"

"No," Jenny replied, although the question was on the tip of her tongue. It needed to be asked. If she was going to offer anything to Rachel, she needed to hear her say the words. She needed to believe that Rachel wasn't capable of killing her own child.

"I knew something wasn't right that morning." Rachel bent her knees up to her chest, and when she turned her head toward the muted light from the dirt-coated window, the blue of her eyes seemed to glow between them. "You just . . . you know those things when you're a mom. I couldn't say exactly what it was. Maybe it was the silence from the monitor. No cooing or babbling that morning. Maybe it was the stillness when I opened his bedroom door. No little fingers gripping at the bars of his crib. I knew before I even saw him. I thought to myself, maybe if I go back to sleep and wake up again, things will go back to normal. I didn't want to see him or touch him, because I knew I'd never be able to go back. But of course I went to him. He was so cold when I picked him up. I don't remember calling nine one one, but I must have. I didn't cry or say a word until they took him from me. I do remember that. And the screams. How loud they sounded, even to my own ears. How hard I tried to hold on to him. How they ripped him from my arms."

Jenny was the only one crying when Rachel stopped talking. She imagined that her friend had relived that moment every single day for the last six months, but she wished the story would just end. As selfish as it felt, Jenny didn't want to hear any more.

"So, no," Rachel continued. "I didn't kill my son. But I did write the letters to Nick."

"What letters?"

"They weren't even letters," Rachel replied. "They were just stupid rambling thoughts I typed out one night after I'd been drinking. I was sad and lonely and they didn't mean anything. I never even sent them. And I don't know how that patient knew about them, because I never told anyone they even existed."

Jenny listened in silence as Rachel detailed the pieces of one tragedy after another, each stemming from the one before it. Why did fate pick certain people for misfortune? Why was she spared? Why, when they both ended up pregnant and alone, had Jenny been offered salvation?

She couldn't send Rachel back there. There would be no one to stand up for her. A wealthy woman had been shot, a respected doctor with a family and friends and the full support of the country, and Rachel would show up with the smoking gun. She didn't stand a chance.

Jenny rose from the floor and dusted off her pants before she placed a board over the window to be sure no one could peek inside.

"It would be better if you didn't leave the shed while Hank is still in town," she said. "He'll be back on the rig in four days, and then we'll figure out what to do. In the meantime, I'll bring you some fresh clothes and blankets. And some more food."

Jenny was thankful for the thickness of the air in the darkened shed and how it served to veil the expressions on their faces. She couldn't stomach any more. She didn't think she'd be able to hold herself together if she had to watch her friend begging for mercy or crying from gratitude, especially when it so easily could have been her, so she closed the door behind herself as she stepped out into the blinding light and shuddered at what was to come.

CHAPTER SIXTEEN

maria

THERE WERE THREE PEOPLE IN THE room with her, three separate voices. Her mother and father were two of them, but she didn't recognize the third. Maria pretended to be sleeping while she listened to her parents tell the story of her life to voice number three. Her childhood sounded almost idyllic.

. . . such a happy kid.

. . . very social and outgoing.

. . . always popular.

She couldn't help but wonder if they were all recalling the same childhood. Maria's memories of youth involved watching from her window as the other kids in the neighborhood played kick the can. Every night she would pray that, just once, they would knock on her door and invite her to join in. They never did, at least not until she hit puberty.

"This just doesn't make any sense."

Her mother's frustration was pitiable, but as much as Maria wanted to decode the mystery for her, to show her the truth, she just couldn't do it.

"I'm so sorry, Mrs. Bethe. I can't imagine what you and your husband are going through."

Voice number three belonged to a woman. She was confident and concise, with a touch of compassion, as she effortlessly dictated the pace and direction of the conversation. She was no doubt the psychiatrist her doctor had been calling for earlier. "If you don't mind, I just have a few more questions."

"Go ahead," her father said. "It's fine."

"Does Maria have any family members, specifically blood relatives, who have ever suffered from depression or bizarre thoughts?"

"Not that we know of," her father replied. "The other doctor asked us the same thing a couple days ago, and we've been racking our brains trying to put the pieces together. Neither one of us has ever been treated for any kind of psychological problems. We've both had our ups and downs over the years, of course, but never anything we couldn't work through."

Ups and downs. If she'd been asked to describe her parents' marriage the first time she was seventeen years old, Maria would have likened them to June and Ward Cleaver. She couldn't have fathomed their marital problems until she became a wife, and it wasn't until her mother lay on death's doorstep, succumbing to cancer, that she learned a secret she had no business, or interest in, knowing.

Maria pushed the memory aside, wondering whether Sylvia had ever been able to convince anyone she'd come back from the future and hoping she wouldn't have to use that secret to convince her mother of the truth.

You get one chance.

What did Sylvia mean by that? One chance at suicide? One chance to get home? Had she already used up her only chance? There was an answer out there somewhere, a way home. She just had to find it. Who could help her, though? Sylvia would still be an infant, Rachel a toddler, and Detective Andrews a soldier heading off to war soon.

Bienville still seemed her best option. Her children hadn't been there, but she wasn't convinced she wouldn't find her husband if she went searching again. She could almost see him standing in the hospital corridor in his blue scrubs with a stethoscope draped around his neck. She couldn't remember the last time she'd gone to visit him there, and she was saddened by all the broken promises she'd made to herself, and to Will, to set aside an hour and have lunch with him.

The itch that had taken up residence beneath Maria's cast was daring her to ignore it again, inching its way from her hand to her fingers like the delicate legs of a spider. It was a useless endeavor, trying to will it away, and when she twisted her arm to alleviate it, a blazing pain shot through her wrist.

"Son of a bitch!"

The words catapulted from her mouth before she could contain them, landing in the circle of voices in the far corner of the room. Her father sprang from one of the plastic chairs like a gazelle ready to bolt, treading through waters so foreign that fight or flight must have seemed his only two viable options.

"Maria, please!"

"Please what, Dad?" She pulled her head off the pillow so she could see him. It was the only part of her body that had yet to be restrained, but it pounded with the effort. "I'm tied down to a goddamn hospital bed, my arm feels like it's being stuck with a hot poker, and I'm trapped in hell! So please *what*?" Her eyes darted between her parents before they homed in on her mother and the unmistakable quiver in her lip. "You have no idea what's going on around here, Mom. You don't even know . . ."

That you've been dead for the past two years.

She somehow stopped herself before she finished the sentence. She had enough sense to know that highlighting her psychosis in front of her new psychiatrist would not get her out of the hospital.

"Good morning, Maria." The woman peeking over the rail was stout, her girth nearly matching her height. "I'm Dr. Anderson," she said, "and I'll be your psychiatrist while you're in the hospital."

She paused as if expecting a response, but Maria rewarded her with silence before letting her head drop back onto the pillow. She was grateful when her parents were dismissed to the cafeteria, and they seemed equally grateful to be excused, almost tripping over themselves to get out the door. Her doctor settled her oversize frame onto the plastic seat of an undersize chair beside Maria's bed before she opened the notebook on her lap and readied her pen above it.

"Now," she said. "I know a little bit about the days leading up to your suicide attempt from talking to your parents, but I was hoping you could fill me in on some of the details."

Maria let the words seep in as she considered an explanation, an excuse for nearly severing her arm in two, knowing there was little she could say or do to keep the word *suicide* out of her chart.

"I guess everyone thinks I was trying to kill myself," she mumbled.

"Weren't you?"

The truth hung in the background of Maria's mind, a story so bizarre it was certain to rival any that Dr. Anderson had ever heard. But even if she could convince this doctor that suicide was not her intention, the diagnosis of psychosis would be waiting to take its place.

"I wasn't trying to kill myself," she said. "Not in the way that you think."

"What were you trying to do?"

Maria could almost feel the warmth of the water washing over her skin as she held the tip of the blade against her wrist, certain she was going home, certain her nightmare would end in that tub. *I was trying to get back to my family.*

Her memory was vague and sketchy, like a 1930s movie that had been poorly spliced together. She kept seeing the storage unit, the one place her husband had made her promise not to go. She must have been there. Why couldn't she have just listened to him? She could have stayed home in bed, resting and preparing for the birth of her son. She could have taken Charlotte to ride her bike and spent the afternoon with Emily. She knew she must have lied to him, because she remembered sneaking out of the house and standing on the concrete floor. Her memory was fuzzy and incomplete, but there was something there, just out of reach, a place her mind refused to go.

"Look, Maria." Dr. Anderson sighed into the silence as she closed the notebook on her lap. "I've been doing this for quite a while, and, unfortunately, I've seen my fair share of suicides. But in all this time I have never seen anyone do to their body what you did to that wrist." With the tip of her pen she pointed to Maria's casted arm, which throbbed from the unwanted attention. "It took two surgeries to put that wrist back together, and I can't even imagine the rehab you'll have to go through. So, whatever it was that led you to do that to yourself, it needs to be addressed."

"I guess I can understand how it looks," Maria said, seeing herself through the diagnostic eyes of Dr. Anderson. What could make her psychotic and suicidal if not schizophrenia or bipolar disorder or severe depression? There was only one thing she could think of that might get her out of the hospital without a more involved workup. "I didn't want my parents to find out," she continued, "but I took some pills the other night to keep me awake so I could study for my AP exam. I guess they made me a little confused."

"What kind of pills?"

"I don't know what they were," Maria continued, hoping her doctor had some experience with methamphetamines. "Someone from school gave them to me and said they'd keep me awake and help me concentrate."

Dr. Anderson flipped through the pages of Maria's chart, scanning through her lab results from the emergency room and shaking her head. "There was nothing in your system when you were admitted. They did a drug screen, and everything was negative."

Maria shrugged.

"What about the pregnancy?" Dr. Anderson asked. "You were really convinced you were pregnant when you came in through the ER."

"I was never pregnant." Maria tried to laugh it off, but the words seemed to catch in her throat, a difficult lie to swallow. "I don't know where that came from. It must have been those pills I took, because I barely even remember any of it."

"Well, some drugs can certainly do that." Dr. Anderson's pen landed with a thud on her notebook before she leaned back in the plastic chair and nodded her head. "I'd like to run another drug screen. A more specific one to make sure there's nothing left in your system. I need you to be honest with me, though, Maria. Was it just that one pill or were there others? And how long has this been going on?"

"It was just that one. But I took it for a few days before bed while I was studying. Just to help me do better on the exam."

Dr. Anderson picked up her pen and jotted something in her notebook before she continued. "You know I have to tell your parents about this, right?"

"I'm ready to tell them, but I don't want them to think I'm on drugs. It was just a onetime thing."

"I think they'll understand," she said. "Before I go, though, I have a few questions to make sure your memory is functioning. Would that be okay?"

Maria nodded for her to continue, relieved to have gotten over that hurdle. It was almost too easy. Once she was out of the hospital, she'd find a way home. She'd figure it out. There had to be some sort of loophole, some clue she was missing. She'd been rash, acting on impulse, but she'd be more careful now.

"Can you tell me your full name?"

"Maria Bethe."

"What year is it?"

"1988."

"What month is it?"

"April."

"What state are we in?"

"Alabama."

"What country are we in?"

"The United States."

"And who is the current president?"

Who is the current president?

The question echoed in her mind until the names of former presidents were spinning through her thoughts faster than she could hear them. Reagan, Bush, Clinton. Who was the president in 1988? She'd imagined it would be the little, day-to-day details of life that would trip her up, not the significant chunks of history that were printed in books and taught in school.

"Maria." Dr. Anderson tapped her pen on the notebook. "The president?"

"The first Bush," she said.

"The *what* Bush?"

"I mean . . . there's no first or second yet. It's just Bush. George Bush."

"There's no first or second yet?" The doctor closed the notebook on her lap and placed it on the table before she capped her pen and tucked it into the front pocket of her white coat. She didn't bother with a response. She rose from the chair and brushed the wrinkles from her skirt before she raised the bed rail and collected her note-book from the table. "What does that even mean?"

"It's Reagan, isn't it?"

"I'd like for you to get some rest, Maria. I'll be back to see you tomorrow and maybe then you'll be ready to tell me what's going on. I can't help you unless you're honest with me."

"No, please don't go. I promise I'm not lying to you. I'm just still a little fuzzy from all the medicines they've been giving me."

"You're not being honest with me, Maria. I've been doing this long enough to see that quite clearly. I don't know what you're hid-ing, but if it's drugs you're taking, then we need to get a handle on that. And if it's something else, and you're trying to downplay your symptoms, then I need to know so I can make sure we keep you safe. There's something going on that you're not telling me, and my job is to find out what it is."

Her instinct was to beg, but Maria kept her mouth shut, count-ing down from five so she could rein in her compulsion. It was a setback, but it didn't have to be a disaster.

"I'm sorry," Maria finally replied. "I'm not quite myself, with ev-erything that's happened. I'm just ready to get out of the hospital."

"Nobody wants to be in the hospital, Maria. Let me get that drug screen back and talk to your parents and then we'll discuss our options. For now, though, I'd like you to get some rest." She glanced at Maria's casted arm. "You still have a lot of healing to do."

CHAPTER SEVENTEEN

T HE RAIN PATTERED AGAINST THE WINDOW and the clouds cast a darkness over the room that no artificial light could penetrate. It fit her mood well. Her mother's hands fidgeted as she sat otherwise motionless in the plastic chair by the bed, and when Maria peeked over the rail, she could almost see the abandoned hope in her eyes.

"Good morning," her mother said. Her voice held the same defeat as her eyes.

Maria owed her an explanation, an apology at the very least, but the thought of it was too exhausting, so she watched in silence as her memories dragged her back to a similar scene from two years earlier. Their roles were reversed back then, as her mother rested in a hospital bed while Maria sat vigil by her side, stroking her hair and praying for a miracle. When it was clear there would be no miracle, she prayed for comfort, and when it was clear there would be no comfort, she prayed for death. She never told anyone that. She could never bring herself to admit that she had prayed for her mother's death, even if it was to end her suffering. Tears gathered in her eyes as she watched her suffer again.

"I'm so sorry, Mom."

"We'll get through this," her mother replied. "Whatever it takes. We'll do it."

Maria examined the plastic splint that had replaced the cast on her arm, relishing the newfound freedom of her limbs after the leather restraints and wondering how long she would play this role of daughter, teenager, and patient. She wanted so desperately to warn her mother again about the cancer that would be coming for her, but how could she do that without digging herself deeper into a hole? She'd have to leave her a note, a letter to inform her of all the catastrophes to come.

"Do you think maybe I'll get to go home today?" Maria asked, but her mother wouldn't meet her eyes, and shrugged in response. "I'm feeling much better."

The door swung open with a bang before her mother could respond, and Nurse Joanie ambled into the room with a wheelchair in tow and a crooked smile across her weathered face.

"Just like a teenager," she said. "Sleeping 'til noon. I'm glad you woke up before I left for the day. I wanted to say good-bye."

"I'm going home?" Maria breathed out an exaggerated sigh of relief and glanced from Joanie to her mother, who still refused to make eye contact with her.

"I'm sorry, honey." Joanie's throaty voice cracked before she coughed into her fist and shot a quick glance at Maria's mother. "I thought you already knew. You're being transferred to Three West." She secured the wheelchair next to the bed before she continued. "The psych unit."

"The psych unit?" Her voice caught on her words when she spoke, but it shouldn't have come as a surprise. It was so obvious it was almost laughable, but somehow Maria hadn't seen it coming. She'd fallen into a trap even Sylvia had enough sense to avoid. "I'm not suicidal," she said, pleading with Joanie, as if her nurse had any say in the matter. "I'm just ready to go home. Please call Dr. Anderson back here."

"I meant to tell you," her mother said. "I just—"

"Mom, listen," Maria interrupted. "You can stop this. Just tell them you're willing to take me home. That's all you have to do."

She could hear the desperation in her own voice, but she knew it was useless. She'd already cemented the deal with her psychiatrist the previous day, and her mother was barely keeping herself afloat while trying to save her drowning daughter. Maria was surprised by the unexpected comfort she found when she reached out and placed her splinted hand over her mother's arm. She missed the familiarity of her role as caregiver. Looking back, she felt she'd always been the caregiver—for her husband, her children, her mother—but it wasn't always that way. She wondered at what point in her life their roles had changed.

The hospital was a labyrinth of halls, but Maria recognized the steel doors with the tiny, prison-like windows at once. She flinched when those doors slammed shut behind her, feeling like an imprisoned warden. It was the first time she'd ever been on a psych unit without the keys in her pocket, and the view was quite different from the other side. It was a world she knew well, though, a world that had once offered hope and healing but now gave meaning to the phrase that swam through her head and refused to desert her.

Abandon all hope, ye who enter here.

Joanie and Maria's mother were escorted off the unit just moments after their arrival, before a nurse with no name tag wheeled Maria through a vacant corridor and stopped in front of a room with an unobstructed view of the nurses' station. The walls were a cold and steely gray, and the fluorescent glare from the oversize lights that hung from the ceiling did little to soften the atmosphere. A twin-size bed with faded and worn sheets sat against one wall and a wooden desk rested under the only window in the room, its heavy bars blotting out the sunlight.

"You can put these on," the nurse said, dropping a pair of hospital pajamas onto the bed and then hovering in the doorway.

Maria eased herself onto the bed, listening to the springs creak as her weight sank into them and wondering if Will had changed the sheets on their own bed at home. She tried to do it once a week but it rarely happened more than twice a month. There was just never time. How could she have let dirty sheets cause her so much stress? Even Emily's urine-soaked sheets seemed so trivial to her now.

"Could I have some privacy, please?" Maria motioned toward the pajamas beside her on the bed.

"No closed doors while you're on suicide watch," the nurse replied. "We'll go over the rules this afternoon. There's a group therapy session going on right now that your doctor would like you to attend."

Maria already knew the rules of suicide watch: no closed doors, no shoelaces, no utensils. She'd enforced them for years, but she never imagined she'd be on the wrong side of the rule book. The nurse watched her from the doorway as Maria dropped to the floor the open-backed gown she'd worn from the ICU and struggled to get the hospital pajamas over her head with her bulky and awkward splinted arm. She was too proud to ask for help.

"I can't imagine therapy would do me any good," she said, still fighting with the sleeves of the pajamas. "I'd rather stay here, if that's okay."

The choice wasn't hers, though, and as Maria was escorted down the corridor to the group therapy room, she could hear the muffled voices on the other side of the door growing louder and more distinct. When the door opened, and the flow of conversation ceased, Maria's eyes landed on the boy who'd been speaking. For a moment, just a breath or two at most, they watched each other, as if they'd known each other at some point in their lives, maybe crossed paths at a familiar coffee shop or sat in the same waiting room at a doctor's office. Maria could tell that he was trying to place her, too, but the moment was fleeting.

"It must have just been a side effect from that new medication," he said, pulling his gaze from Maria and turning his attention back to the group. "Because I feel better now, and I don't have those thoughts anymore."

"That's wonderful, Henry. Thank you for sharing with us." The leader of the group couldn't have been much older than twenty, with hair the color of ground ginger and curls that screamed Ogilvie Home Perm. She looked decidedly too young to be leading a group, but her words were beyond her years. "Sometimes the truth in our minds doesn't match the truth that those around us see, and our lives become more about perception than reality."

Chair legs scraped the floor as the circle widened to create a spot for Maria. A small group of children, as young as six or seven, huddled together on the far side of the room, but teenagers made up the bulk of the patients. Until that moment, Maria hadn't considered she'd be on a child psych unit.

She slid onto a chair among the teenagers as all eyes in the room tracked her movements, forging their own interpretations of the bulging bandages under her splinted arm. As interest waned, though, Henry's eyes didn't waver. The boy who'd been speaking when she entered watched her with rapt attention, words almost forming on his lips as a disquieting anticipation settled over them.

"Welcome to the group, Maria." The ginger-haired woman's voice crashed through the silence. "I'm Tonya, and this is our afternoon group session. There's no judgment here. You can ask questions, talk about your experiences, or just listen, if you prefer. A couple of weeks ago, Henry shared with us his belief that he'd already been through all of this." She nodded to the boy with the short-cropped hair, whose eyes hadn't left Maria. "Sort of like déjà vu, right, Henry?"

"That's right," he said, reluctantly peeling his gaze from Maria. "Just like déjà vu."

"Sometimes the medications we use can do things like that," Tonya continued. "Play with our minds and trick us into believing things that just aren't possible. But eventually, once they work their way into your system, everything will balance out and you'll think clearly again. Has anyone else noticed problems like that with their medications?"

"What do you mean, déjà vu?" Maria's words were floating through the air before she realized she was speaking, a meek voice piercing through the suddenly curious gazes around her. Her eyes were trained on Henry. "You mean like you've lived this life before and you've somehow come back?"

"I don't know about coming back or reliving my life," he said. "It was more like Tonya said. Déjà vu." His smile broadened as he gestured to the woman with the Ogilvie perm, but Maria knew that, despite his answer, her words had shaken him.

"But when you thought you'd done this before—"

Henry silenced her before she could continue. It was just a subtle shake of his head, but Maria let her words drift away unfinished and unreciprocated. He was right. Group therapy wasn't the place for this conversation. The other patients around them sat captivated, with perked ears and riveted attention, unaccustomed to voluntary participation, and it wasn't until the clap of Tonya's hands shattered the stillness that Maria realized the room had succumbed to silence.

"Well, we're just about out of time for today," she said. "Maybe we can continue this tomorrow?"

Maria sat motionless, unable to pull herself from her seat, as the other patients clambered around her. Shuffling chairs and screeching shoes echoed across the floor as the room emptied, until it was just her and the boy.

"Was it really just déjà vu?" she asked, when she was certain they were alone, but Henry didn't offer a response. His eyes never left her face, as if he, too, was struggling to remember where they'd met, struggling to put a name to her face. He scooted forward on his chair, narrowing the gap between them.

"Do we know each other?" he asked.

"I don't know," Maria replied. "But it happened to you too, didn't it?"

"I don't know what you're talking about." He shook his head and glanced back at the door before leaning in even closer and lowering his voice to a whisper. "But I'd suggest you don't mention things like that to anyone, if you ever want to get out of this place."

"Please," Maria begged. "Tell me what you meant by 'déjà vu.' Have you been here before?"

"I can't talk right now." Henry glanced at his empty wrist, like a man with a watch who had somewhere to be, and rose from his chair. "I'll find you in a little bit."

"Wait. Tell me what you meant." Maria trailed him to the door, her voice rising. Henry turned to face her, their bodies just inches apart. His square jaw and deep-set, piercing eyes held an intensity that could almost be described as intimidating, but at the same time there was safety within them. He was broad shouldered and confident even at this, likely one of his weakest moments. He was the man you wanted showing up when you were trapped inside a burning building.

"Not now," he said. "I'll find you, but you have to be patient. And trust me when I say this: it wouldn't hurt if you learned how to keep your mouth shut."

CHAPTER EIGHTEEN

W HEN DAY TURNED INTO NIGHT, MARIA started to
worry. She couldn't find the boy from group, and the more
she pestered the nursing staff about his whereabouts, the more
closely they watched her. She was starting to wonder if he had
been discharged, or maybe even imagined, but half an hour before
lights out he finally showed up in the dayroom and dropped onto
the couch beside her. She was so relieved to see him that she almost
wrapped her arms around him and violated one of the most important rules of the psych unit: no physical contact between patients.

Maria hadn't noticed it at first, but there was a charm to Henry
that couldn't be denied. The same sandy-brown hair that her husband wore in loose messy waves was shorn close to his skull, but
that was where their similarities ended. Henry was a boy with
the physique of a man and the eyes of a timeworn traveler. There
was something so achingly familiar about those eyes, but she just
couldn't place it.

"Where have you been?" Maria asked, startled by her own
brashness when the question left her mouth, as if she had the right
to question Henry about his whereabouts. She nodded toward the
clock on the wall. "I thought maybe you'd find me sooner. It's almost lights out."

"I had a meeting with my doctor and my family," Henry

replied. "I'm going on a day pass tomorrow to see how I do off the unit. Apparently, if I can hold it together, I'll be discharged in the next few days."

There were no day passes on the horizon for Maria. She'd been on the psych unit for less than twenty-four hours but had already managed to raise alerts with her doctor, the nursing staff, and the group therapist. Henry was right. She needed to learn how to keep her mouth shut.

When she turned to face him, she was suddenly aware of how close they were sitting, and that her pajamas were too baggy, her hair was too messy, and she hadn't brushed her teeth all day. It was like a veil being lifted to reveal insecurities and vulnerabilities she didn't even know were there. Who was this boy beside her who made her feel these things that she hadn't felt in years? When he leaned in close, she could smell the mix of coffee and faded mint toothpaste on his breath.

"You weren't here last time," Henry said, turning his body to block out their conversation from the other patients, who were settling into their evening routines of crocheting and reading and staring off into space. "I was here over twenty years ago, and everything was exactly the same. The same doctors, the same nurses, the same patients. Until you showed up. And when you started asking me those questions in group therapy today, I knew you'd come back too, but I just couldn't figure out why."

"You did come back," Maria said. "I knew it. What happened to us?"

"I don't know what happened to us, but we know each other, don't we?" He studied her face until the moment became uncomfortable, until Maria turned her head away and shrugged her shoulders beneath the sagging hospital pajamas.

"Who are you?" he asked.

Who are you?

Who was she? It was no longer an elementary question, and as Maria thought about the answers she could give, they all felt like lies, or at least half-truths. Who was she? Maria Bethe? Maria Forssmann?

"I'm Maria," she whispered back to him.

"But how do I know you?"

She dropped her gaze to the stark white fabric of the freshly rolled gauze around her splinted arm and let Henry struggle with his memories. She had her own memory lapses to resolve, her own missing chunks of time that were essential to her return home, so while she could believe they'd once crossed paths, the question of how they knew each other didn't seem as pivotal as why they were thrown together now. "I don't know," she said. "But it's hard to believe us meeting here is coincidence."

"But how did you end up here in the hospital, in the psych unit of all places, if you weren't here last time?"

"I didn't know what else to do," Maria said. "Everything was happening so fast and I . . ." The events that had landed them together played over in her head—the drive to Bienville, the suicide attempt, the disastrous meeting with her psychiatrist—and Maria didn't realize she'd stopped talking until Henry tried to finish her sentence.

"You just wanted it all to end?"

"No," she said, feeling the weight of his stare burning into the side of her reddening cheek. "I thought this was what I was supposed to do to go back."

"To go back where?"

"Home."

Henry leaned back in the couch with his arms crossed over his chest. He had the calloused and rough hands of a laborer, and though he couldn't have been more than eighteen, he seemed like a man more than twice his age. "You can't go home, Maria."

"Of course I can." The parched and barren red dirt road wound its way through her memory and rose up to meet her, reminding her of the failed journey home that had landed her in the hospital. "I have to get back. My family is waiting for me."

"What about your purpose?"

Purpose.

Hadn't Sylvia used that same word? *God brought me back for a special purpose.* It hadn't occurred to Maria that she'd been sent back for any particular reason. She'd been so focused on returning home, she hadn't considered there might be a purpose to her being there.

"What do you—"

"Lights out! Five minutes!"

Before Maria could get the question out, the night nurse was walking through the halls, announcing the end of another day. Patients were scurrying around, trying to get crossword puzzles done and letters written and teeth brushed before their worlds were shut down. Henry was drawing himself up from the couch when Maria grabbed his wrist.

"What do you mean by 'purpose'?" she asked.

Henry pulled his arm away, gently but firmly, and checked to make sure they weren't being watched by any of the nurses. "You can't do that," he said. "I'll find you before I'm discharged, but you need to be more careful, Maria. You're never going to get out of this hospital if you can't figure out how to play the part."

Maria was too shocked to respond. She was so accustomed to being in control that she didn't know how to handle being scolded. She watched Henry disappear down the hallway and into his room before the nurse's voice reverberated through the corridor again.

It chased her into the sanctuary of the cold and steely gray room that had become her new home, and as she thought about Sylvia's words and warnings, she knew she'd be hearing her dead patient's voice ringing through her head over the course of another long and sleepless night.

CHAPTER NINETEEN

D ON'T BE SCARED." DR. ANDERSON MOTIONED Maria into the visitation room. "Come on in and take a seat next to your parents."

It wasn't fear that Maria carried with her. It was caution. She hadn't planned on an eight A.M. meeting with her parents and her doctor, and she'd been up half the night trying to make sense of Henry's words from the conversation that had been so abruptly interrupted. She hadn't had a chance to ask him about his purpose, and while she knew what Sylvia's had been, she wasn't convinced that she'd been sent back with one of her own.

She slid onto the only chair available, the one between her parents, guardedly hopeful that another day pass was about to be handed out and discharge was in her near future. Henry would be off on his pass by the time she got back to the unit, but she was determined to catch him before he was discharged for good. He was her only lead, and she wasn't about to let him slip away.

"Thanks for joining us," Dr. Anderson said, welcoming her as if she'd accepted an invitation instead of being pulled from a half-eaten breakfast. Maria tried to ignore the enthusiasm radiating from her parents as they nodded their heads and parroted their approval of whatever was to come. "I was just telling your parents about an interesting new development in your case," she continued. "I spoke with a doctor from Iowa this morning, a specialist in schizophrenia who's been reviewing your chart, and he's very interested in being a part of your treatment team."

As Maria tried to find meaning in Dr. Anderson's words—*Iowa . . . specialist . . . schizophrenia*—they churned through her mind like a thick stew.

"I don't understand," she said. "What specialist?"

"I know it's a lot to take in," Dr. Anderson replied. "But he's a specialist in your particular type of schizophrenia."

Schizophrenia. It shouldn't have come as a surprise, but there was a permanency to the word she'd never fully appreciated until that moment. It felt like a brand, a scar that had been carved into her psyche and was as much a part of her now as the wound on her arm.

"I know this doesn't make any sense to you, Maria." Her mother's voice, which had seemed a divine gift just days earlier, grated in her ears like the faulty brakes of a rusted-out steam engine. "But Dr. Anderson was telling us that schizophrenia is when people—"

"I know what schizophrenia is." If she'd been able to fake civility, she would have let her mother finish. She would have pretended she was grateful to have her there, grateful to be given this chance at recovery, grateful to have such an invested physician. "I'm just surprised it's my diagnosis." She turned her attention to Dr. Anderson. "What about the pills I told you about?"

"There was no trace of anything in your system from your admission through the ER," Dr. Anderson replied. "In your blood or urine. I'd be happy to go through everything with you." She cleared her throat before opening the folder sitting on the table between them. It was Maria's medical chart, weathered and worn, frayed at the edges, and thick with doctors' notes, lab results, and imaging reports. It shouldn't have belonged to a seventeen-year-old girl.

"I'd rather not," Maria mumbled. Dr. Anderson nodded before shuffling through the loose papers in the chart and pulling out a small stack that had been fastened together with a paper clip.

"This is the résumé of the specialist I was telling you about." She slid the papers across the table to Maria's father, who thumbed through them with feigned interest before passing them on to his wife. "His name is Dr. Johnstone and he's an expert in the field of prospective hallucinations."

Maria's mother flipped through the papers, seemingly impressed with the doctor's expertise in a field of psychiatry Maria was certain she'd never heard of before that moment.

"*What* kind of hallucinations?" Maria reached for the papers that her mother was pretending to read, certain she'd misheard her doctor.

"Prospective," Dr. Anderson replied. "It's a very rare type of hallucination where people have memories of events in the future that haven't even taken place. It's fascinating, really. I don't know much about it, but Dr. Johnstone gives lectures all over the world, and I checked out a couple of his journal articles from the library."

The room swayed ever so slightly as Maria contemplated Dr. Anderson's words, a new scenario taking shape in her mind. What if she was wrong? What if it *was* all a hallucination, a delusion created by an illness of her mind? The implications were unthinkable. Her family, her profession, every detail of a life that spanned more than twenty years into the future . . . it would all vanish.

"Is it real?" she whispered.

Dr. Anderson hesitated, casting a cursory glance toward each of Maria's parents before responding. "Is *what* real?"

"Prospective hallucinations," Maria said. "Is that a real diagnosis?"

Dr. Anderson nodded.

"But I've never heard of it. Is it in the *DSM*?"

"Well, no. Not yet." Her doctor hadn't quite learned to expect the unexpected from Maria, and she stumbled through an ill-prepared response. "I mean . . . it's not actually a diagnosis, so it wouldn't be in the *DSM*. It's a *symptom* of a diagnosis."

"What's the *DSM*?" her parents said, almost in unison.

"It's the *Diagnostic and Statistical Manual of Mental Disorders*." Dr. Anderson retrieved a handheld copy from the front pocket of her white coat. "It's what we base all of our diagnostic criteria on in psychiatry. How we come up with specific diagnoses." She slipped the book back into her pocket before she continued. "But I'm not sure how Maria knows what it is."

Maria shrugged and mumbled a nonresponse under her breath. Would she know about the *DSM* if she were a seventeen-year-old girl with schizophrenia? She couldn't make sense of it in her mind. The timeline of her life was not only disjointed but also fluid and elusive, and she was having a difficult time grasping reality. "Who is this doctor?" she said. "And why is he so interested in *me*?"

"He's doing some research with imaging of the brain and psychiatric disorders," Dr. Anderson replied. "And there was something he saw on the MRI of your brain that led him to this diagnosis."

"But you can't diagnose schizophrenia with an MRI," Maria said. "You can't even do that . . ."

Twenty years from now would have been the next words out of her mouth, if she hadn't thought better of it. How could she know that if she wasn't a psychiatrist?

"Maria, please." Her mother patted the fingers of Maria's splinted hand, which rested on the circular table between them. "You don't even know what an MRI is."

"But why me?" Maria said, pulling her hand away from her mother's reach. "How did he even know I was here?"

Dr. Anderson paused, the briefest of hesitations, which Maria was certain went unnoticed by her parents. "I received a fax yesterday," she said, tucking the doctor's résumé back into the folder. "A letter asking for patients with your particular diagnosis to participate in a study that's being conducted at the University of Iowa. When I gave them a call, the doctor who's spearheading it said he was interested in you."

"Well that seems a little coincidental," Maria replied.

"I've completely vetted him, if you're worried about his legitimacy." Dr. Anderson shifted her attention to Maria's parents as she spoke. "I called the university where he works, talked to the dean of the department and several of his colleagues, and, like I said, even read a few of his journal articles."

Her parents didn't have to be sold on the idea, though. With their wrinkled clothes and washed-out complexions, defeat already stitched into the creases of their brows, they would have agreed to just about anything her doctor recommended. Maria wasn't quite so willing to concede defeat. She knew she'd already put her parents in a situation that would push them even closer to the edge they were about to fall over, but she was still considering another battle for her freedom. She was ready to argue that Dr. Anderson couldn't keep her locked up on the psych unit without their permission or a court order, to beg them mercilessly for their pity, and to pull the threads of their sanity, which were already beginning to unravel.

"He should be here in the next day or two," Dr. Anderson said, cutting off the momentum of Maria's thoughts and bringing her back to the reality of her life: she was a seventeen-year-old girl with a diagnosis of schizophrenia, she was locked up on a psychiatric ward, and she wasn't going anywhere until she cooperated.

CHAPTER TWENTY

jenny

S HE HATED THE BAYOU. EVEN AFTER all these years, it was
still foreign to her. It reeked of decay and its music crashed
through the air in a cacophony of unblended notes. She stood at
the edge of the pier and let her thoughts descend into the depths
of darkness below her feet, almost believing she could see the outline of the gun.

Hank was gone on an overnight fishing trip with some buddies, and Jenny had taken the opportunity to let Rachel into the
house to take a shower and a nap in the guest bedroom before
heading back out to the shed. Night was creeping in, and it was
too dangerous for Jenny to keep a fugitive in the house when she
couldn't have one eye on the driveway. They both agreed they'd
feel better not risking it.

What they couldn't agree on was their next step. Jenny thought
Rachel should be planning her defense strategy for when she eventually turned herself in. She even offered to reach out to some
high-profile defense attorneys who might take her case for free,
but Rachel wouldn't hear of it. She had no intention of returning
to Mississippi. Ever.

The silence of the empty house brought with it a comfort Jenny hadn't anticipated. With a glass full of wine in one hand and the freshly washed quilt in the other, she found her way to the guest bedroom to remake the bed and search through some of her old clothes to find something that might fit Rachel. Bins that housed more half-finished projects than most people had even started were stacked on top of the closet shelves. Boxes of photos and birthday cards and school projects spilled across the wire shelves, all in line to be assembled into albums and scrapbooks. Jenny pulled down a few of the clothes bins before her eyes zeroed in on the red plastic bin in the far corner of the top shelf. The one she hadn't touched in almost twenty years. The one she'd broken more than a few promises to herself to get rid of.

It was heavier than she remembered, or perhaps age had weakened her, and when she dropped it onto the bed, dust fibers billowed into the air. A tinge of guilt pricked at her conscience before she pried off the top, inhaling the smell of stale smoke and musk that permeated the air around her. It was the scent of *him* invading her senses and filling her with a memory so real that she was once again sitting by his side in a smoke-filled lounge where he'd just performed, counting out dollar bills and phone numbers that had been left in his tip jar, listening to him hash out his plans to get signed by that highly coveted record label.

The plastic lid fell to the floor as her eyes fixed on the man in the top photo, her breath catching in her throat. It could have been her son staring back at her from that bin, tall and thin, with roguish, dark eyes that matched his mischievous grin.

"David." She breathed out his name and blinked away the tears before she took the photo in her hands. She didn't remember the photo, but David's name was scrawled across the back in handwriting that had a marked resemblance to Hank's. She'd often thought about how similar her life could have been to Rachel's if Hank hadn't spared her that fate, and though she sometimes lacked appreciation, there was no denying what her husband had done for both her and her son. David, Dean's biological father and the man Jenny was set to spend her life with, disappeared ten months after they met, which happened to be the week she revealed her pregnancy to him. She'd been naive to think she could change David with that baby. It turned out that a family was too much to ask of a struggling musician who was in love with his wandering lifestyle. Within days of the announcement, what few belongings he had kept at her apartment disappeared, and then one day so did he. Three months later, when a handsome oil rig worker and his buddies sat in Jenny's section for lunch at the Oyster Reef Restaurant, her fate was sealed.

She placed the photo on the bed and dug deeper into a world that had been calling her back for years. A world where a young, beautiful girl smiled up at her in photo after photo. It was hard to believe that carefree girl was once her. Soft, brown eyes peered out from charcoal-lined eyelids, and pearly teeth gleamed between scarlet-painted lips. As she ran her fingers over the silken beauty of her youth, she wondered if David ever thought of her. What would she say to him if she could go back?

She thought about him from time to time, about what her life would have been like if she hadn't left New Orleans, but as she soaked up the memories of her youth, she realized it wasn't him she had missed. It was what he represented to her: independence, freedom, dreams. He'd always lived by his own set of rules, and even though he did it selfishly, he was out there following his dreams while she was here, living someone else's.

The wineglass was dry by the time the bin was empty, and Jenny took a moment to survey the mess she'd created on the bed around her. She felt like she'd just cheated on her husband, and a renewed sense of guilt washed over her as she cursed herself for holding on to that bin. Dean had always been the feeble excuse to hold on to David and her past; it was to be a keepsake for him, a window into the truth about his biological father. The only problem, though, was that Hank and Jenny had never gotten around to telling him he was adopted, and after a certain number of years and too many missed opportunities, the moment was never right. It made no sense to tell him the truth. He already had a father who adored him; why tell him about the one who'd abandoned him?

At the bottom of the bin, beneath the dust of Jenny's life, lay an old business card with a black raven on the front and the Bourbon Street address of a voodoo priestess scrawled across the back. She shuddered as she thought about that day all those years ago. She'd been warned. She hadn't stumbled into this life unaware of what was coming. The voodoo woman had given her plenty of notice when she'd stood Jenny up and faced her toward the door.

This is west. Choose this direction, and you will see all the gifts you have to offer the world.

Then she'd turned her to face the other direction, the one that would soon take her to Calebasse with her new husband and the baby she didn't yet carry.

But choose east, and you will see the woman in the bayou whose home was not meant for you.

She'd ignored the warnings, of course. What else could she do when she found herself five months pregnant with no family, no money, nothing? Hank had offered to rescue her, and after hearing about the woman in the bayou one too many times, the jokes got old and his tolerance reached its limit. Jenny promised to stop talking about her, but she never forgot.

She tossed the card back into the bin and started in on the mess around her on the floor, throwing in albums and loose pictures and letters in haphazard fashion. She'd almost filled the bin by the time she saw it, an old envelope that must have been tucked between the pages of a photo album.

It was an envelope she was certain she'd never seen before. There were others beside it, cards and letters that had been torn open with haste and excitement, but this one was different. This one wasn't addressed to the Jenny from New Orleans, the one with the black eyeliner and scarlet lipstick, but to the Jenny who was living in Calebasse, Louisiana, with her soon-to-be husband and son. It was postmarked just two weeks after Dean's birth and had been sliced open with a whetted letter opener, just like the one Hank used.

The paper was soft between her fingers, and when she pulled it from the envelope, she instantly recognized the beautiful penmanship as David's. Her eyes pored over the pages, devouring word after word, until there were none left to read, and then she started over. Words flooded her mind and consumed her as she read the letter again and again, each time slower than the previous, until she could take it no more. The paper slipped from her fingers and drifted to the floor at her feet, her tears dripping down beside it.

The wine ambushed her when she pulled herself from the bed, and when she fell into the nightstand, the empty wineglass fell to the floor beside her, dripping wine onto the carpet and bleeding into the words of David's letter, blotting them out forever.

What would Hank's excuse be?

She stumbled through the hallway to her bedroom, feeling her way along the wall with clumsy hands as the floor spun beneath her feet. Her head was swimming with merlot and her tongue was too thick for the slurred words she spat out at her absent husband.

"Whyjoo do that to me, Hank? How couldjoo?"

The room continued to spin, even when she fell onto the bed and covered her head with the pillow, as if she were floating above herself, waiting for it to end, waiting for the moment when it would all come crashing down.

maria

FIBERS OF DUST FLOATED THROUGH THE meek rays of sunshine that trickled past the prison-barred window of Maria's room. They danced around her like they were drifting down from heaven but had lost their way. The Alabama spring sky was an impossible shade of blue, mocking her from the side of freedom, where people worked and lived and loved with no regard for the torrent of grief that washed through her. Was her agony any worse than theirs?

Henry was on another day pass and the hours were terminally long. He'd returned to the unit just moments before bed the previous day, and she had yet to ask him about his purpose or his plans. The five minutes they found for each other were spent exchanging phone numbers and addresses in case they didn't get another chance to talk before he was discharged.

Maria could feel someone watching her as she stared out the window and counted the minutes ticking away on the clock. She could feel his eyes boring into the back of her head before she heard his raspy, nasal breath, and though she had no interest in company, she felt compelled to face him. No words were exchanged as they took in the sight of each other, his eyes lingering on her splinted arm as hers tried to reconcile the mismatched pieces of him. A mop of gray hair, well overdue for a trim, clung to the top of his head while a wiry pair of spectacles played an endless game of slip-and-slide off the bridge of his nose. His pants were cinched too high, his loafers were scuffed, and his shirt had most certainly never felt the heat of an iron. He looked like he could be one of her patients.

"Can I help you?" Maria said.

He smiled at her as cautious steps carried him into the room, and only when they stood eye to eye, just inches apart, did he speak.

"Maria." He breathed out her name as if she'd been lost to him for ages and finally returned. "I can't believe you're here."

"Were you expecting me?"

"I was, in fact. But still, what a nice surprise." His hand jutted out between them, but only with hesitation did Maria accept it. "I'm Eric," he said. "Eric Johnstone."

"*Doctor* Johnstone?" Maria replied. "From Iowa?"

"The one and only." With his hands held wide, he stepped toward the window, the sunlight casting the shadowed bars across his face. "You might find this hard to believe," he said, "but this is my first trip to Alabama. I was in Louisiana once, New Orleans, right during the heat of summer. I don't know how anybody survived down there before air-conditioning was invented." He turned back to her and shook his head. "Hotter than Hades."

Maria stood in awed silence as this man who'd stumbled into her life carried on about bayous and gators and the overabundance of seafood that was pulled from the Mississippi Sound, like he was an airboat tour guide.

"But why am I telling you all this?" he continued. "You're from the Gulf Coast of Mississippi, right?"

"I'm from Alabama," Maria muttered. "From right here."

"That's right." With a wink, he turned and stepped closer to the barred windows, his eyes peering down at the courtyard below. "Did you ever wonder what it would be like to be locked up on a psych unit before now?" He spun around to face her before he continued. "I mean, as a psychiatrist, did you ever think about stuff like that?"

It was the one secret she'd managed to withhold, the one piece of information she hadn't shared with anyone since returning. Her doctors knew all about the other delusions—her family, her unborn son, her home along the coast of Mississippi—but the fact that she had become what she spent her life trying to cure was the one secret she had guarded.

Dr. Johnstone was not who she expected him to be. She'd been prepared for a university professor with a clipboard and a checklist of symptoms, and maybe even an assistant. She'd planned on being a quick disappointment, a failed case study that would land him back in Iowa by nightfall, but this doctor was challenging her, casting out just enough bait to make her bite. When their eyes met, though, it was clear that he wasn't expecting a response.

"Why don't we head outside," he said. "A beautiful spring day like this shouldn't go to waste."

The courtyard was teeming with patients and visitors as she and Dr. Johnstone settled onto a concrete bench in a far corner, under the shade of a magnolia tree. Maria could see it a thousand times, the majestic bloom of the southern magnolia, and it would never grow old. There had been one in her yard when she was a child. It was probably still there.

A lone velvet petal drifted to the ground at her feet before her eyes searched the perimeter of the courtyard. It was an unconscious response, learned from just days of confinement. Where was the exit? The courtyard was full of them, gravel-lined paths and gates that hung open like gawking mouths, inviting her to amble through them to her freedom.

"Where will you go?" Dr. Johnstone's voice, along with his laughter, pulled her back to him as he watched her plan her escape. "When you break yourself out of here, what direction will you run? You already know your family's not out there, so where to next?"

"I don't know," Maria said, wondering how the man beside her seemed to stay one step ahead of her and follow her thoughts as if she was speaking them out loud. Did he already know her next move? Did he know that she was awaiting Henry's return to the psych unit so she could formulate a plan with him to get home? Did he know what "home" meant?

"I'm going to get myself a cup of coffee," he said, slapping his hands on the tops of his legs and startling Maria from her thoughts. "I'd be happy to bring one back for you, if you'd like."

Maria simply nodded and watched in silence as he rose from the bench and traipsed down the gravel path that led to the hospital, confident in the knowledge that his new patient would be waiting for him on the bench beneath the magnolia tree when he returned.

He was right. Thoughts of escape had faded from her mind, and as she awaited Dr. Johnstone's return, spring bombarded her from every corner of the courtyard: sunshine, blooms, and babies. People all around her laughed and lived as if cruelty wasn't lurking around the corner; they were oblivious to what could happen and what they might awaken to in the morning. A young couple ogled their toddling baby on their makeshift picnic blanket, a tray full of cafeteria food between them. Maybe it was better not knowing. Maybe the inevitable was easier to face without a countdown clock ticking away in the background.

Maria lifted her face toward the sky and closed her eyes as

a gust of wind spiraled through the tree above her head, sending a shower of petals over her body. When they settled at her feet, Dr. Johnstone was standing before her with a paper cup in each hand.

"'Listen to the wind, it talks. Listen to the silence, it speaks. Listen to your heart, it knows.'" He handed her one of the cups and eased onto the bench beside her. "That's an old Native American proverb that always pops into my head when I feel a big gust of wind. Do you know that some cultures believe the wind carries our spirits back from death to be reborn again?" He sipped his coffee and tilted his head back, sunlight sprinkling through the branches of the trees and trickling over his face. "Do you listen to the wind, Maria?"

His words forced her back to a place that was now so far out of reach, and a scene that wouldn't leave her mind: Will and her daughters laughing at the beach, in a dream that was worlds away. When had she ever just listened to the wind? And what wouldn't she give to go back and do it all over? Take her family from that dream and make it a reality?

"I'm sure we could all take more time to listen to the wind," she said, forcing a sip of the lukewarm coffee, which must have been sitting on the burner for hours. It seemed such a distant memory now, when her days were filled with worries about work schedules and day care drop-offs and her son being born before her fortieth birthday. She swallowed another gulp of the bitter coffee, unable to still the nausea in her gut. "You knew I was here before you sent that fax to my doctor, didn't you?"

"I did," he replied. "You're very perceptive. I was wondering if you were going to ask about that. How would a research scientist from Iowa know about a seventeen-year-old girl in Alabama? And why would he travel all the way down here just to see her?"

"Why, indeed?"

"Because you're not just any patient," he said with a wink. "And George is the one who told me you were here."

Maria's mind spun through the names and faces of every man she could remember named George, faster than a Rolodex. None of them made an impression. Was he a patient? A coworker? A friend?

The last drops of cold coffee left a bitter aftertaste in her mouth, but she gulped them down, stalling for time and trying to force the pieces of their conversation together.

"Who's George?" she finally asked.

Dr. Johnstone scooted to the edge of the bench, his excitement a palpable discomfort between them. "You don't remember George?"

"Should I?"

"He's been with you your whole life. In a way. He's been sick lately, otherwise he'd be here to visit." He shrugged away the thought before he continued. "Anyway, he's the one who knew you'd come back."

Come back.

Maria wanted to trust him. It would have been easier to throw caution to the wind and trust that the man beside her was on her side and not trying to trap her into a diagnosis. But she'd already fallen into a trap that wasn't even deliberately set by her first doctor, unable to name the current president, and she couldn't afford to drop her guard.

"From the future," he continued, winking at her again before scooting back on the bench and struggling to contain his restless energy. "But I was the one who figured out you were a psychiatrist. How else could a seventeen-year-old girl know what the *DSM* is? Or that schizophrenia can't be diagnosed with an MRI?" Maria picked at the edge of the paper cup as his words danced around her. "Okay, let me rephrase this and put your mind at ease. How does a seventeen-year-old girl without the *internet* know all those things?"

It wasn't a word she should have been hearing. It was a word that didn't belong to this time or place, and as her thoughts raced ahead of her, she couldn't remember if there was such a thing as the internet in 1988.

"You're trying to remember when the internet was invented, aren't you?" Dr. Johnstone laughed. "Technically, it's already been invented, but the term isn't in popular use yet. How about cell phones and text messaging?" The courtyard spun as the doctor's words swirled through the air, rustling the leaves of the magnolia tree above their heads. "And September 11, 2001? No American can forget that date. Does it ring a bell?"

Maria wanted to cry. The relief was sudden and overwhelming, like a dam breaking and spilling out all of the fear and anxiety that had been pent up inside of her. Finding Henry had been a blessing, but finding Dr. Johnstone could mean salvation.

"Were you there?" she asked. "Were you alive in the future, too?"

"I was."

"What happened to us? Why are we here?"

"The short answer is, I don't know." He leaned back and laughed, downing the rest of his coffee before crushing the cup in his hand and glancing at his watch. "And the long answer is too long for me to go through right now. But we'll get there."

"I thought this was some kind of test to see if I have those . . ." Her mind was still racing, and she couldn't remember what they were called. "Those hallucinations of the future."

"It's not a test, Maria. You're not hallucinating." His voice dropped to a whisper as he leaned toward her almost conspiratorially. "There's no such thing as prospective hallucinations. I made it up to find people like you."

"Then you'll help me?"

"I'll help you with anything I can," he replied. "I'm sure you have a lot of questions, and I've been around for a while, so hopefully I can answer them for you."

Henry was the first person who popped into her mind. Not her husband or children or her home in Mississippi. It surprised her, and saddened her in a way, but she was eager to share the excitement with him and to tell him all about the doctor who might be able to get them both home. Sylvia wasn't far from her thoughts, either, with her premonitions and warnings and purposes.

"Why are we here?" Maria asked. "Were we sent back for specific purposes?"

"Some people think that." Dr. Johnstone shifted on the bench, as if he could physically dodge the question, and if Maria hadn't been paying attention, she would have missed the subtle change in his restlessness.

"Do you?" she asked.

"I think you can find a purpose to anything if you look hard enough." He rose from the bench and tossed his crumpled-up coffee cup into the garbage, before he glanced at his watch again. "There's a lot we have to talk about, Maria. But I told Dr. Anderson I wouldn't disrupt your routine too much, so I have to get you back up to the unit before group therapy."

"Wait." Maria pulled herself from the bench, unable to settle her nerves or her racing pulse and not yet willing to abandon their conversation. "What about getting me home? Can you do that?"

Dr. Johnstone hesitated briefly as he studied Maria's face, as if her question had surprised him, as if she'd asked for something unexpected. It reminded her of Henry's response during their first meeting on the couch in the dayroom.

You can't go home, Maria.

"I'll be back first thing tomorrow morning," Dr. Johnstone continued, "and I'll explain everything to you."

Maria reached out and laid her hand over his arm, forcing his eyes to meet hers. "Please tell me you can send me home."

"We'll talk about it tomorrow, Maria." He placed his hands on her shoulders and held her gaze at arm's length, making her feel suddenly small again, like a child being comforted by her father. "I know how hard it is," he said. "Believe me, I do. But you're just going to have to trust me."

CHAPTER TWENTY-TWO

T RUST.

    People were popping in and out of her life and her dreams with such disturbing regularity that Maria couldn't keep track of them. How could she possibly *trust* Dr. Johnstone to return to her? There was nothing she could do about it, though. Whether she trusted him or not, she was at his mercy. He was the doctor and she was the patient.

Henry had been at group therapy when Maria was escorted in a few minutes late by her new doctor. He was excited to report that his visits with family had gone well and he would be getting discharged from the hospital the next day. Maria was waiting for him on their couch like he'd asked.

Meet me on our couch after group.

Our couch.

She wasn't sure why that made her smile, and she could feel her face flush when she noticed him watching her from the other side of the room. It was a habit that had haunted her in her youth, and one she had forgotten about until she felt the warmth climbing into her cheeks. There was something so intimate in the way his eyes landed upon her skin, as if he could see into her, leaving her feeling exposed and vulnerable.

"I have something really exciting to tell you," Maria said, as

Henry took his place beside her on the couch. "There's a doctor here who's come back from the future, just like us."

Henry surveyed the room around them before he responded, making a mental note of where the nurses were stationed, like he always did, and then he leaned back into the couch and sighed.

"Please tell me you didn't talk about this with one of the doctors," he said, rubbing at his temples with the tips of his fingers. "And please tell me that, if you did, you didn't include me in this conversation."

"Of course I didn't mention you," Maria replied. "And he's not one of the doctors from here. He's from Iowa, and he came all the way down here just to see me. He does this kind of work so he can find people like us."

As Maria stumbled through the events of the past couple of days—from the meeting with her parents and Dr. Anderson, to the conversation with Dr. Johnstone in the courtyard, to the information about the man named George who'd known she'd come back—Henry's skepticism seemed to only grow.

"I don't think it's a good idea to trust this man, Maria. You should be thinking about getting out of the hospital, not adding more doctors to your treatment team."

"Don't you at least want to talk to him and find out what's going on? He knew about things he couldn't have known if he hadn't come back from the future," Maria said. "He knew about September eleventh." Until she said the words out loud, it hadn't occurred to her that Henry might not know what she was talking about. Had he gotten that far into the future? Did he even come from the same future? "Do you know about September eleventh?"

"I made it a few years past 2001." Henry laughed, and when he winked, Maria could feel the blush creeping up her neck and into her cheeks. "I guess it wouldn't hurt to meet him, but I'm not talking to another psychiatrist until I'm out of the hospital. I'm not spending one more day in here than I have to."

"Fair enough," Maria replied. "But doesn't it seem pretty coincidental that we're all here in the same place at the same time?"

"I've been thinking about that." Henry leaned forward as he spoke, his focus on Maria's face so intense that she felt compelled to turn away from him. "I think I figured out how I know you. I think you must have been one of the people who was there with me between lives."

"What do you mean, 'between lives'?"

"When you left your last life," Henry said. "Don't you remember being with all your family and friends and learning about your purpose?"

Purpose.

There was that word again. Henry kept coming back to it, and as she tried to make sense of it, her thoughts kept mixing into the disharmony of the patients around them, until the muttering of voices and the scraping of chair legs and the cackling of laughter was like the deafening roar of a thousand beating wings drumming through her head. She couldn't remember coming back, or any moments between this world and the last. She shrugged as her eyes ran over the sculpted edge of Henry's jaw, but her mind was so unreliable and inaccessible that her head pounded from the effort of thinking.

"What purpose are you talking about?" she asked.

"The one I was brought back here to fulfill," Henry replied. "The reason I need to get out of the hospital."

God brought me back for a special purpose.

It didn't take Sylvia long to come crashing back through Maria's memory. Her dead patient was around every corner, taunting her with her ethereal presence. Was his purpose like Sylvia's? Would it change his life forever? And why was he willing to do it? Maria could think of nothing that would force her to quit her husband and children.

"I don't have a purpose," she said.

"Of course you do." Henry's fingers fidgeted with the stitching on the armrest of the couch, his nail scraping against the fabric, before he leaned back in toward Maria. "The dreams," he whispered. "The ones you had before you got here. They were telling you what to do."

"How do you know about my dreams?"

"Because we all have them before we come back. That's how we know what we were sent here to do."

She held up her arm between them again.

"Mine were telling me to do this," she said.

He laid his hand over her uninjured arm. It was such an innocent gesture, but the warmth of his skin filtered through the thin fabric of her shirt and there was a familiarity to his touch that made her long for more. A part of her knew that she should pull her arm away, that she shouldn't find comfort in the touch of another man, but a larger part of her wanted him to keep his hand there, to wrap his arms around her and tell her that he'd take care of her, that he'd make this all go away.

"Are you sure?" he said.

"I'm sure," she replied, but as Henry pulled his hand away, Beth and Sylvia crept back in. Two unwanted guests who refused to be ignored, slinking through her subconscious mind until they found an opening, forcing her to remember what she'd tried so hard to forget. Beth's lifeless body with the fresh bruises glowing through the darkness. The dirt falling onto her pale skin. The blood dripping from Maria's wrists. Sylvia insisting there was but one purpose, one thing she'd been sent back to do.

And then her husband's words.

May should be such a happy month, but I just can't bring myself to smile in May.

How could she have been so blind? May 9, 1988. Just weeks before high school graduation.

"May." The word came out of her mouth as barely a whisper, like a thought that hadn't been breathed into life yet. A single, unreciprocated word floating above them.

"Is it May yet?" she said, biting her words off at the ends, almost choking on them, while Henry struggled to dodge the unwanted attention surrounding them.

"What?" He glanced at his wrist, at the empty spot where a watch had once been, and then back to the crowd of faces. "I think so."

"She died in May of the year we graduated from high school." The bile creeping up her throat burned as she swallowed it down and struggled to quell the nausea. "I have to find my husband."

"Maria, look at me." Henry drew himself closer, the warmth of his hands and the depth of his eyes fighting to pull her back to him, struggling to keep her from falling into the void. "Calm down," he whispered. "The nurses are going to be here any minute if you don't settle down." His words were reaching her, but there was nothing he could say to save her. "What's going on? Who died in May?"

The vise around her head tightened as she searched his eyes for absolution, as if he could give that to her. As if he'd known all along that she'd just been too self-absorbed to recognize her purpose.

"I know why I'm here, Henry."

jenny

A STEADY HUM OF CRICKETS AND frogs filled the air as
Hank and Jenny sat on the back porch, the creak of the
swing harmonizing with the chorus. From their position, the shed
was in full view, but Rachel had kept her promise to remain invisible. The manhunt had turned into a nationwide affair, but the
police hadn't been back to question them further, and the woman
in the coma was still clinging to life. Jenny and Rachel had finally settled on a plan, but it was too risky to consider with Hank
at home. It was too risky to consider at all, but Jenny had already
promised she'd try.

A peaceful and comfortable silence bounced between her and
her husband on the swing, tempting Jenny to keep her mouth shut,
to leave the past in the past and pretend she'd never stumbled upon
the secret in the closet, which had been gnawing at her since she'd
found it. If she'd known how it would end, she would have shown
more restraint, but hindsight would prove to be a cruel companion.

"Do you ever wonder what our lives would have been like if
we'd never met?" she said, casting a glance toward the shed before pulling her eyes away, wondering if she would have fared the

same as the woman lying on the concrete floor behind the clouded window.

"What do you mean?"

"I mean, if we'd never gotten together. Do you think you'd still be an oil rig worker, or would you have moved on to something else?"

"I don't know," Hank replied. "I can't imagine us not being here, or not having Dean grow up in our home." It was a forced effort when he pulled his gaze from the bayou and reached out for her hand. "Or not having you by my side."

"But what if we had never met?" she said. "What do you think our lives would have been like?"

"I guess I would have been a lonely roughneck."

It was a conversation that had no meaning to him. If she'd asked him to describe how he felt the first moment he held Dean, he'd have been a flood of emotions, but there was nothing in Hank's life that was as meaningful as his son, not even her. They were a compatible couple, and at times she could believe that they were destined to be together, but it was doubtful whether their relationship would have survived without the glue of Dean to hold it together.

"I'm sure you would have met someone else," she said, "and had kids of your own."

"Of my own?"

It was an intentional jab, though she feigned ignorance and shrugged it away.

"What about you?" he said. "What do you think would have become of you and Dean if we'd never gotten together?"

His words were pointed and sharp, but she'd pushed him into it, this what-if conversation between husband and wife that never ended well. Hank was a man of immeasurable tolerance, but some lines in his life were not meant to be crossed, and his son was one of them.

"I don't know," she said. "I guess I would have been a single mom, or maybe . . ."

"Maybe what?"

After all the rehearsing, she still didn't know how to say it, how to tell her husband that he didn't deserve to be the father of her son and that, no matter how much he'd given, it wasn't enough. Now that he was sitting before her, it seemed gravely unfair to deny him what he'd earned, even if it was ill-gotten. "It's not important," she said. "I don't even know why I brought it up."

"Sometimes it's best to leave the past in the past." He pushed back with his legs and let the porch swing fall forward, the creaking of the rusted chain grating through Jenny's thoughts and the words of David's letter forcing their way back into her mind.

"But what if the past comes back?" she said. "Or if the past isn't really what you thought it was?"

"It probably never is," he replied. "I think most of us remember our pasts in very different lights. Even when we've gone through them together."

Jenny envied her husband's contentedness with life. It was almost physical, his confidence infusing the air around him like cologne. He never questioned his choices; he just made them and moved on. "I was going to say that if we never met, I probably would have tried to find David again. Just to make sure he didn't want to be a part of his son's life. Or mine." They never talked about David. It never seemed appropriate, given what Hank had done for her, but as she stared at the side of her husband's face, wondering what her life would have been like if the man next to her was David instead of him, she wished she hadn't waited so long. "I'm sorry," she said. "I just thought you should know that."

"No need to be sorry. It seems like a reasonable thing for a single mom to do."

"It doesn't upset you to hear that?"

"We all do what we have to do, Jen. If you think that would have been the best thing for you and Dean, knowing that he'd leave you in the end, then I guess that's what you'd do. I'm glad you never had to make that decision."

"No," she said. "I never had to make that decision, did I?"

The translucent green of Hank's eyes, once such clear proof of his honesty and integrity, faded into the muddled depths of a canopied, sun-starved forest, and Jenny couldn't fathom what was lying inside them.

"When did you read it?" he said.

"Does it matter?"

He shrugged as he gave the swing another push, then he leaned back and crossed his arms over his chest. "I guess not."

"Why didn't you tell me? How could you lie to me for all those years?"

"I never really lied to you. It was always right there for you to see."

"I wouldn't say hidden in an old box in the closet is 'right there.'"

"It's not really just some old box, though, is it?" he said. "I'd call it more of a tribute to your ex-boyfriend that you tried to keep hidden from me, right under my nose, for the last twenty years." He tilted his head to the side before he gave the swing another hefty push. "Kind of like your own little secret that you've been keeping from me."

Jenny's breath caught in her throat before she could speak. She had so many secrets stacked up, she wasn't sure which one he was referring to, but she was confident that if he knew about the one in the shed, the police would have already been there by now.

"You can't compare me keeping a box of memorabilia of my son's biological father to you not telling me that he came back for us," she finally replied. "It's not quite the same thing, Hank."

"He wasn't coming back for you. I did you and Dean a favor by not giving that letter to you. I probably should have just gotten rid of it, but I figured if I left it in that bin and you found it and went back to him, well, then it was meant to be."

"Unbelievable," she said, as Hank gazed out over the bayou, his expression nothing more than indifference, maybe even boredom. She couldn't imagine why she had thought he would care.

"You were in no position to make that decision. You had an infant son, no job, and this guy who you think you're in love with comes back to 'do the right thing.' He'd have been gone again before Dean was even crawling."

"It wasn't your decision to make, Hank. David was coming back for his son, and you took that away from him."

"I took nothing from him. Dean is *my* son, and he always has been. I gave that deadbeat exactly what he wanted: freedom from being tied down to a wife and a kid." Hank's voice crescendoed with each word, his body edging closer to Jenny's, until she could feel his words speckling her skin. "You think that loser was coming back to rescue you? He had a momentary lapse of judgment, a moment of weakness, where he thought he could do it. But where is he now, Jen? He never even came back for you. He sent that letter to the home of the man who took responsibility for *his* mistake, and never even bothered to find you again, just to make sure you got the message. And you think he really wanted you and Dean back?"

By the time his words reached the apex and began their decrescendo, he was standing above her with a finger buried in his chest. "I'm the one who rescued you, Jen. I'm the one who stood by your side and took in your son. So fantasize about David all you want. Pretend he's the self-sacrificing hero who unjustly lost his family. But you know just as well as I do, even if you won't admit it, that he's just some asshole who abandoned you and Dean."

He stood motionless above her, his finger still digging into his own chest, their eyes fixed on each other, both blind to the scenery around them and deaf to the sounds of the bayou. She'd never imagined she'd see this side of Hank. She'd never known it existed. And while she knew he was right—David wouldn't have lasted a season—she was furious that he had so frivolously tampered with her fate.

"Well," she said, unable to contain her venom, "since we're clearing the air, I've got my own secret to share with you." Hank's hand fell away from his chest as she slid off the swing to face him, and through the fading light of day she landed the final blow. "Do you want to know why we never had more kids, Hank? Do you want to know who made that decision? It was me. I thought it would be in *your* best interest for Dean to be your only child. You know, just like you thought Dean and me staying with you was in *our* best interest? Didn't you ever wonder why I was so careful to never miss my 'vitamins'?"

With her fingers still hooked into quotation marks, she slipped past him into the kitchen, relieved to have said it but ashamed at the same time, not sure which she felt more. The minute hand of the clock on the wall was tireless in its ticking, and when Hank finally entered, his eyes red and swollen, the green was again translucent.

"I'm sorry," he said. "For never giving you the option to go back to him."

"Hank, that's not what I—"

"No." He raised his hands between them, the same weathered and calloused hands that had held their newborn son more than eighteen years earlier and had never once come down in anger. The same gentle hands that knew every inch of her body. "I'm not saying this because I want your forgiveness. I can't ask you to forgive me, when I don't think I can ever forgive you for what you've done to me. I probably should have given you the option to decide, back then, but I'm glad I didn't. I can't imagine not having Dean in my life, and if I had to go back and do it all over again, I wouldn't change a thing."

She knew he had more to say, she could feel it, but when his hands fell to his sides, there was only silence. There was no good-bye, no hug or kiss on the cheek, no last trip to the boat dock with her husband.

Had she known it would be the last time she ever saw him, she would have done it all differently, but her final memory of Hank was of a broken man with slumped shoulders and bloodshot eyes, slinking out the back door of their home, into the dusk.

CHAPTER TWENTY-FOUR

maria

MARIA GASPED FOR AIR, HER LUNGS swallowing it down in gulps as the suffocating darkness faded away. Her oversize hospital pajamas were soaked with sweat and clinging to her skin when she pulled herself from the bed, and the doctor from Iowa was sitting in the chair by her side, battling with the glasses that were still slipping from his nose.

"Nightmares?" he said, dropping a copy of *Time* magazine onto the wooden desk. Maria's trembling hands were still clutching her belly, and the bandage on her arm was beginning to unravel. She eased back down onto the edge of her bed, where a silhouette of sweat was stamped onto her bedsheet, and let her hands fall away. Dr. Johnstone wore the same wrinkled clothes he'd worn the day prior, and his hair still jutted out from his head in an impossible mess.

Maria tried to speak, but her tongue was thick and parched like she'd endured a night of heavy drinking, and a throbbing ache wound its way around her forehead, edging dangerously close to her temple and threatening to plunge into her left eye. She let her eyelids drift shut and her head fall into her hands.

"Apparently, you got worked up last night about something," Dr. Johnstone said. "They said they had to sedate you."

Henry was gone. She could feel it. The sun was up, a new day had begun, and he would have been discharged by now. It had taken him to put the pieces together for her, but Maria finally understood what it meant to have a purpose.

"Do you know what the date is today?" she said, almost too afraid to hear the answer, certain she had already failed the little girl who was waiting to be saved.

"May fourth," he replied, and when Maria breathed a noticeable sigh of relief, he leaned his body against the desk and eyed her over the rim of his glasses which had slipped halfway down his nose. "Why? Is there somewhere you need to be?"

"Yes." She squinted up at him, the morning light from the window behind him unforgiving in the potency of its glare. "And very soon."

With his body propped against the desk, Dr. Johnstone watched her in quiet contemplation. There was something so visceral about him in that moment and in the way he seemed to be piecing together her history. It was the longest he'd kept his mouth shut since their introduction, and the air between them grew thick with anticipation before he broke the silence.

"I'm starving," he said. "Why don't we head down to the cafeteria for some breakfast and finish our conversation there?"

The cafeteria was nearly vacant when they arrived, just a scattering of patients and visitors mulling over half-eaten breakfasts. They paid Maria no mind as she settled into a far corner booth with her plain bagel and cup of coffee, or when Dr. Johnstone slid onto the chair beside her, his plate overflowing with bacon and eggs.

"Is that all you're eating?" He eyed her meager portions and dusted his eggs with salt and pepper. "The food here is really pretty good."

Maria tore off a piece of bagel and forced it into her mouth. "I'm not really a breakfast person."

He shrugged before diving into his pile of eggs, his appetite as voracious as his personality. As he wolfed down his breakfast, she tried to ignore the discomfiting gaze he set upon her.

"So, you think you figured out why you're here?" he said. "Your purpose?"

She nodded as he lifted his glass of orange juice to his mouth, which was still stuffed with eggs.

"Can I ask you how you figured it out?"

She hadn't thought to prepare an answer for a question like that, and as she considered all the lies she'd woven through her story over the past couple of weeks, she couldn't understand why this one felt so difficult. It seemed like something she *should* have been able to figure out on her own, even if she didn't. "I had some dreams before I came back," she said, biting into her bagel and shrugging off the question.

"Has anyone come to visit you since you've been in the hospital?"

He swallowed down half his juice with an audible gulp and set the glass on the table. Maria dropped her eyes to it, unable to disguise her surprise. Did he know about Henry? She wondered whether she'd ever see the boy from the psych unit again, and why she felt compelled to safeguard his privacy.

"Like who?" she asked.

"I don't know." He shrugged before he continued. "Anyone besides family?"

Maria shook her head.

"What about when you came back," he continued. "Do you remember anything about that?"

"Not really. I just woke up in the middle of the night one night and thought I was dreaming, and then when I realized it wasn't a dream, I thought I was supposed to kill myself to get back home."

"You don't remember any kind of transition? Like being in a hospital or seeing your family or anything like that?"

"Not when I first came back," she said, shaken by the memory of her husband's face hovering above her as she begged for her son's life to be spared. "But after my suicide attempt, I saw my husband covered in blood and pleading with me to hang on. I thought I had made it back home, but when I woke up in the ICU, I was still here."

"I'm sorry," he said. "Most of us have some difficult memories to deal with when we come back."

"What happened to us?"

"We're repeaters," he said. "Kind of like glitches in the system."

He shoved a bite of toast into his mouth and wiped his hands on his pants as he gathered the salt and pepper shakers from the surrounding tables and positioned them along the perimeter of his plate at varying distances.

"Let me explain. Let's say this plate is the sun, and the salt and pepper shakers are all planets. Now, each of these planets is spinning around its own axis to make days, right?" He spun the salt shaker closest to him in a clockwise circle as he watched Maria to make sure she was following along. "One rotation around a planet's axis is one day. But these planets aren't just spinning around their own axes; they're also circling the sun."

The salt shaker he dragged around the plate left a trail of salt in its wake, and when he released his grip on it, greasy fingerprints were stamped onto its sides.

"Our whole lives are measured in cycles: days and months and years. So all these planets are spinning and circling at different speeds and crossing paths with each other at different places throughout time and space."

The salt and pepper shakers circled the plate in a chaotic dance through Dr. Johnstone's solar system as Maria looked on.

"Well, it's the same thing with our lives. Imagine each person being a planet. One cycle is one lifetime, and we're spinning through these lives, interacting with people at various times and places throughout space. Does that make sense so far?"

"I guess," Maria replied.

"Good. Now this," he said, pointing at the scene before them, "is how things go when there are no glitches in the system. You complete a life cycle and then you're born into a new one, with no memories of the previous one. But every once in a while, an asteroid or comet or some other space debris comes along and crashes into a planet, knocking it off its axis and back in time."

He flipped the spoon in his hand end over end before crashing it into an unsuspecting pepper shaker and sending it tumbling off its trajectory into the plate of eggs. "That's what happened to us. We've been hit by something that's knocked us off track."

He'd worked himself into a frenzy by the time he was through, though that didn't seem a difficult task, and as Maria took in the mess on the table between them, her hope faltered. Her doctor seemed to be balancing precariously close to the edge of his own psychosis.

"You think we're planets?"

"Not the *actual* planets," he said. "I just think we're *like* the planets in the way we rotate through time. You know, like a metaphor. Using one thing to describe another?"

He sighed as he pushed the plate of eggs away and leaned back in his chair, his fingers fumbling with one of the salt shakers from the table. "I don't understand why no one ever gets my planet metaphor."

Salt spilled onto his pants as he flipped the shaker in his hands, oblivious to the mess he was making. "All right, then, try to think about it like reincarnation. We're born, we live, we die, and then our memories are wiped clean and we're reborn again. Now, where and when we're reborn isn't constant, so the people and places we encounter are always changing, but sometimes we catch glimpses into our past lives, when we meet someone we swear we know or find ourselves standing in a place we're sure we've been. It's so common there's even a name for it: déjà vu, which literally means 'already seen.' And then there's us." Dr. Johnstone spread his arms out wide. "The repeaters. For some reason, sometimes there's that glitch in the system, and instead of restarting at the beginning of a cycle when we die, with our memories wiped clean, we're thrown back into a time and place in the life we're already living."

When we die.

His words were jumbled and cluttered in her mind, their meaning ambiguous, as she tried to comprehend the only three she could remember: *when we die.* The storage unit flashed through her memory like a grainy slide show projected on the wall. The metal door with the painted numbers, the faint light of the hallway, the slick surface of the concrete floor. With a shake of her head, they scattered out of view.

"But I didn't die," she whispered, listening to the legs of the doctor's chair scrape across the tiled floor as he closed the gap between them.

"What do you mean?"

Will's blood-smeared face stared back at her with the same pleading eyes Beth had worn in a nightmare that was worlds away, forcing her into a place she refused to go. "I mean I didn't die," she said, and while she knew something terrible lay just beyond her memory's reach, she also knew that, somewhere in time, she was still with her family. She could feel it.

"I knew it." Dr. Johnstone slammed his hand on the tabletop with such force that it drew the attention of the few scattered diners throughout the cafeteria. "I knew it when I met you, Maria. This is so exciting."

"What does it mean?"

"It means you're still alive out there somewhere," he said. "It means we can get you back home."

It was a tempered excitement that coursed through her body, a yearning so deep she refused to acknowledge it for fear it would evaporate before her like a mirage. "You can really get me home?"

"I've done it before," he said. "I've only met one other repeater who didn't die before coming back, and, as far as I know, we got him home."

"How did you do it?"

"Hypnosis," he said. "The idea is that, if we can get you to a state where you're present in both realms, you can somehow choose which one to enter. The research I've done on this is quite fascinating. I think pretty soon I'll be able to prove that hypnosis is the key to unlocking areas of the brain and memories that are trapped in there. And I don't just mean from this life cycle. I think we might be able to unlock memories from past cycles, too. I can show you the MRIs I did after each hypnosis treatment with the last patient, and you'll see the transformation in the brain as we got him closer to his family."

"But how can I be alive in two different worlds?"

"Time isn't linear, Maria." He gathered the salt and pepper shakers, righting the ones that had been flipped and setting them up around the plate again. "And our life cycles aren't, either. They're constantly overlapping each other and crossing at various points. And there's no way for me to know for sure, but I imagine the way time moves is different in each cycle as well. For example, you've been here for a couple of weeks now." He started to spin one of the salt shakers in a slow circle around its own axis. "But who knows how long it's been since you left your last life? It could be hours or days or even years." The pepper shaker next to it was spinning at twice the speed before he finally let it fall to the table and come to rest. "Time is elusive."

She didn't need any more explanations, and she had no intention of trying to interpret the meaning of his words, for fear her family would move on without her. Would they do that? If months turned into years, would they eventually give up on her? She had to get home. She had a singular focus to get back to her family, a road to take her there, and nothing was going to stand in her way.

"I'll do it."

CHAPTER TWENTY-FIVE

ER SHOULDERS BURNED AS SHE HELD her arms straight
out before her and trained her eyes on Dr. Johnstone's finger
floating between them. Her parents had given their consent, just
like Maria knew they would, and she had pleaded with Dr. Johnstone to get started immediately. He tried to warn her that their
first session wouldn't be their last, that he first needed to deter-
mine if she was even hypnotizable, but she couldn't hear reason.
She was convinced she would be home by nightfall, even though
she couldn't provide him with the kind of memory he needed to
take her there.

Give me a day you would love to repeat with your family, he'd said,
and Maria had nothing but the dream on the beach to offer him.
It was a regrettable admission, an eye-opening moment when she
thought of all the missed opportunities to make memories with
her family. She wouldn't let it happen again. If he could send her
home, she would be a better wife and a better mother. A better
person.

"Block out everything but the sound of my voice," he said, as
they began the session. "And keep your eyes on my finger."

Despite forbidding her mind to overthink it, Maria was convinced she would be unhypnotizable. She wanted so desperately
for it to work that she was certain it wouldn't, that she would
somehow sabotage it.

"Your arms are light and airy, like feathers on a breeze, drifting into the sky." As his voice reached her, the tension in her shoulders dissolved and her hands drifted above her head. "When I move my finger away, you will continue to stare at the same spot between your hands. Focus only on that spot."

Her eyes didn't falter, they didn't blink or twitch or waver, but the air could not hold her attention. She couldn't help but see the window on the far wall in front of her, which led to a world she was desperate to leave. She forced her posture straight and pressed her back into the stiff cushion of her hospital room chair, fighting to see the air bouncing between her two out-stretched arms. A searing pain bit through her wrist as he turned her hands so her palms were facing each other. She tried to force it away, but the ache was deep and tangible, and the more she fought to feel nothing but the air between her arms, the more intense the pain grew.

"Shut your eyes, Maria, and allow the pull between your hands to take over. Your arms are being forced together by your palms, as if each is a magnet. Soon they will come together and meet in the middle."

The heaviness set in again, her arms weighted down with fatigue, but it wasn't the pain that pulled at them now; it was a steady, ensnaring tug that forced them together, like a rubber band constricting around her wrists.

"The closer together they get, the stronger the pull. They're very close now, Maria. In fact, even if you tried to separate them, it would be impossible, because the attraction is too strong." The force was overwhelming, and the instinctive tug she gave against it did nothing but enforce the pull.

"They're getting closer now, Maria. And soon, when they touch, your whole body will go limp and you will hear only the sound of my voice. You will experience nothing—no sounds, no sights, no smells—unless my voice gives you permission. Your hands are even closer now . . . and now . . . they touch."

She could no longer feel her back against the chair, she couldn't hear the birds singing outside the window, and she couldn't smell the scent of Dr. Johnstone's aftershave. All the senses she didn't even know were a part of her were gone, and the world in her head was vast and barren.

"I want you to meet your family at the beach. That beautiful dream you told me about with your husband and your daughters. The sun is shining, you can smell the salt in the air, and the wind is caressing your skin. I give you permission to experience all of that. Watch your children as long as you'd like. Feel the waves between your toes."

The sun beat down on her face as the waves lapped over her feet, forcing her toes to curl under the icy water. She didn't remember it being so cold in her dream. Was this how it happened?

"Enjoy your family, Maria. Build sand castles with your daughters, throw a Frisbee with your husband, just soak it all up and *experience* them."

She kneeled beside her daughters, absorbed in their giggles, while she tried to burn every image into her memory. Her hands ran over her swollen belly and her mind fought to suppress logic, but her movements were too effortless, and she was certain this wasn't how it would happen.

"Good, Maria. I can see you're having a wonderful time with your family, but the sun is setting now, and soon it will be time to go."

The wind forced its way through her, and as the clouds rolled in around her, the sky darkened. She searched the beach for her daughters and her husband, but they were gone. The waves, the surf, the sun, they were all gone. And when the darkness closed in on her, nearly suffocating her, she stood frozen with terror.

There was something in her hand, something she hadn't realized was there. It was cold and hard, and as her fingers ran over its jagged edges, its identity was unmistakable. 307. The white block numbers painted on the metal door in front of her jumped out from the darkness, and the lock that sealed it in place was waiting to be paired with the key in her hand. It was the key that Detective Andrews had wanted. Had he already been here?

Maria fumbled with the lock. She would just take a quick peek—

Whack!

A thunderous clap split through her ears, sending a vibration through her jaw.

Whack!

A blinding flash of light threw her off balance.

Whack!

A distant voice was calling for her. ". . . Maria."

Whack!

"When I clap my hands, you will awaken."

Whack!

Dr. Johnstone hovered above her, his face tense with worry as he clapped like a madman.

Whack!

"Maria, wake up!"

Sweat dripped from her forehead as she leaped from the chair, her heart pounding against her chest. "Stop!" she yelled, her head ringing from the echoes of his deafening claps. "Stop clapping."

"I couldn't get you out," he said, his eyes darting back and forth from Maria to the door. "You weren't listening to my voice anymore, and I didn't know where you were."

"It was the storage unit," she said, her pulse normalizing as the moisture from her shirt chilled the skin beneath. "I was there. I must have gone there before I came back."

"What storage unit?" A hush settled over them, each watching the other, neither sure how to proceed.

"I have to go back," she said, easing herself onto the chair, the familiar ache in her head throbbing to the same beat as the pain in her arm. "You have to take me back there, so I can see what's in that unit."

"Let's give it a rest for today. I'd like to get another MRI to see if your brain has changed at all, but I think we should wait for a day or so before we go back there."

"I have to go back." She laid her hand over his arm, and through the gripping pain that shot up her left wrist, her fingers tightened. "Please," she said. "I'll do as many MRIs as you want. I'll do anything. Just take me back."

"I don't even know what could happen to you if we did that again. You weren't even under my guidance anymore. It was almost like you took over the hypnosis."

"I promise," she begged. "This time I'll do everything you tell me to do. I'll listen to your voice and I'll come back the second you clap your hands."

"I don't know, Maria." He glanced toward the door to her room again before he turned back to her. "I can't believe no one came in here with all that screaming."

"Please, Dr. Johnstone. You of all people should understand my desperation."

"I do. But we can't mess this up."

"Mess *what* up?" She loosened her grip on his arm. "I was there. I could feel it. It's working."

"There's one condition." He raised his finger between them, just like Will had done on that fateful night when Maria promised she'd stay away from the storage unit. "You go where I take you," he said. "And this time I'm taking you to the hospital where you saw your husband. To see if your family is there waiting for you."

Maria nodded. Her instinct was pulling her back to the storage unit, the last place she could remember going before she came back, but the lure of her family was too great. It was too much to resist.

"We'll use the same technique as last time," he said, positioning his finger between her arms and talking her out of the ache in her shoulders. By the time her hands were forced together like magnets and she could see only the air bouncing before her, her mind was quick to void itself of sensation.

"Good, Maria," he said, his voice echoing in the abyss of her mind. "When I allow you to see, you will find yourself surrounded by the people you love. Your husband will be sitting by your bedside, holding your hand. Your daughters will be coloring pictures for you and taping them to the wall by your bed." He paused briefly, taking in a sharp influx of air before sighing it away. "You see them now."

From above her body, Maria watched as machines and tubes pumped air into her lungs and fluid through her veins. Will stroked her hand, kissing each of her knuckles, while her daughters held colorful pictures over her seemingly lifeless body, begging her to awaken.

Dr. Johnstone's voice boomed through her mind, and despite her promises, she fought to block out his words, which pounded through her head. It was her family she wanted to hear; it was their touches she longed to feel.

"Stay with me, Maria," he commanded. "You're surrounded by the love of your family, and if you listen closely, you'll hear the voices of your children."

That's not what Mommy looks like.

Emily's laughter filled the air as Charlotte held the picture up for Will to see. His mouth opened and spilled out laughter that her ears couldn't hear.

Here, Daddy. You draw a picture of Mommy.

Will took the crayons, a smile dancing through his eyes as he glanced up at Maria from time to time, creating an image of her on the paper in his lap. She had forgotten what a beautiful father he was. A scholar for Charlotte's incessant thirst for knowledge and a comedian for Emily's insatiable hunger for laughter. He was a fatherless boy who had turned into the most intuitive and nurturing father Maria had ever known. Why hadn't she ever told him that? Why did it take this tragedy for her to see it?

"Good, Maria." Dr. Johnstone's voice reverberated through the room like an uninvited guest. "If you concentrate hard enough, you'll feel the touch of your husband's skin on your own."

With the picture complete, Will held it up for the girls to see, their giggles at their father's drawing ringing through the air. He set the crayons aside before he reached for Maria's hand, her skin prickling with anticipation. His touch was softer than any she had ever felt, and if Dr. Johnstone had given her permission to cry, she would have wept. Her eyes drifted shut, blocking out the image of her family so she could focus only on the sensation of Will's skin upon her own. His hands swept through her hair and over her face, down her arms and into her fingertips.

Mommy, look!

Charlotte was standing before her when she forced her eyes open, Will's picture in her hand.

This is what Daddy thinks you look like.

It was a crayon sketch of a woman with black hair, lying in a hospital bed, with her eyes shut and her family by her side. The covers draped over her body were flat against her stomach, with no signs of a baby in her belly.

Where is he?

Her voice pounded through her own ears, drowning out Dr. Johnstone's and the racket he was making as he tried to force her back to him.

Whack!

An agonizing pain shot through her left arm as she grabbed at the covers, ripping them away.

"Where is he?" she screamed.

Whack!

"Maria!" Her eyes opened to Dr. Johnstone's arms shaking her wildly as his attention bounced back and forth from her to the door. "Maria, wake up!"

"Where is he?" she yelled, and as her hands tore at her shirt, ripping it from her body, a nurse barged into the room, calling for Haldol. "Where's my baby?"

CHAPTER TWENTY-SIX

THE ACHE IN MARIA'S WRIST CREPT up her arm and settled into her shoulder. The splint was back, and the solitary lightbulb that stared down at her from the ceiling blanketed the room in a strange glow. She pulled her head from the barren mattress and her eyes skimmed over the padded walls of the room. A sealed door with a tiny barred window offered the only view to the outside world. It was called a quiet room, or a seclusion room, and though she'd never been in that particular one, they were all the same.

We're not doing this to punish you.

It's for your own safety.

That's what she used to say to her patients who found the rules of the psych unit too restricting, but it sure felt like punishment.

Her head throbbed as she walked her hands across the walls, the padding cool beneath her fingers. "Can I have some water, please?" She choked on the words, her throat parched and swollen, before a Dixie cup with a swallow of water found its way through the bars and into her hands. She pushed it back empty. "More. Please."

After five more gulps of water, she dropped the cup on the other side of the door and mumbled a thank-you, to which there was no reply. The Haldol, though diluted, continued to trickle through her veins, casting a haze over her thoughts that clouded her memory.

She'd been at the storage unit. That she could remember. She'd wanted to go back, but Dr. Johnstone wouldn't let her, instead taking her to her family, where she'd realized that whatever happened to her in that storage unit had also taken her son.

"Did you get some sleep last night?" Dr. Johnstone's voice floated through the bars before reaching her ears. A gray stubble had sprouted from his face, and his eyes were weary and bleak beneath the dark shadows that encircled them. Maria could almost pity him.

"Probably too much, with that Haldol," she replied.

"Can I come in?" He fumbled with the lock until the door swung wide into the tiny cubicle of a room, and Maria shrugged, stepping over the sheetless mattress and sliding to the floor. The pain that pulsed through her head was intractable, and the light that gushed through the gaping door of her cell, merciless. Dr. Johnstone slid onto the concrete floor beside her. They were a ragged pair, unshaven and filthy, their lives veiled in secrecy and lies.

"Bet you never thought you'd be locked up in one of these," Dr. Johnstone said, his hyena-like laughter ringing through her aching head. Somehow, he'd managed to navigate with finesse this world that was waiting to devour her, this world she had no interest in surviving.

"You did really well yesterday with the hypnosis," he continued. "I don't think it will take many more sessions to get you home, but I'll have to get Dr. Anderson to agree to back off on the psychotropic medications she's prescribing to you, because they can sometimes block the mind from traveling freely."

Maria nodded, her eyes landing on the newly placed bandage on her arm. It was white and tidy, a stark contrast to the cyanotic and swollen fingers that protruded from it. They were fingers that belonged on a cadaver, not a seventeen-year-old girl, and as she studied the bluish tint of her skin, she couldn't shake the image of

Beth's lifeless body lying in the grave. It was the fifth of May, and the little girl had only four more days to live.

"What kind of a person would let a little girl die?"

She could see Dr. Johnstone nodding out of the corner of her eye. They hadn't talked about her purpose, other than to acknowledge that she had one, and Maria was ashamed to bring it up, like a vulnerable part of her was being exposed.

"You're having second thoughts," he said matter-of-factly. "Do you want to talk about it?"

"My husband's little sister is going to die in four days if I don't do something," she said. "And yesterday I was so consumed with getting back to my family that I was willing to just let that happen. What kind of person does that make me?"

"The kind of person who wants her family back," he said. "I don't judge anyone anymore. Not when I've seen the decisions that some of us have had to make."

"But she's just a child."

"People die every day." He held his hands up before dropping them into his lap. "People of every age and sex and religion. You can't save the world."

"But she's not just some person. I was sent here to prevent her death, and I almost let her die. I have to go to Ohio and find my husband before you send me back. I have to warn him."

"You can't."

"What do you mean?" she said. "Why not?"

"It's either your family or the little girl. You can't do both. Changing just one person's destiny will change the lives of hundreds of people around them, maybe even thousands, and it will rewrite a new destiny for you, too. If you make this change, if you do what you were sent here to do, you're letting your other life go forever."

It took her a minute to hear his words, to really understand the implications of them and to comprehend what he was telling her, and while she didn't want to believe him, she couldn't stop her mind from seeing the truth. If she unwound the tangled threads of Will's life that had landed him in her arms, she could see that her husband had faced one series of unfortunate events after another, all stemming from the death of his little sister. But it was those catastrophes that had led him to a life that included Maria. The death of his sister meant one fewer mouth to feed and allowed him to quit his job at the factory and focus on school. The suicide of his mother, a direct result of his sister's murder, took him to a childless uncle who insisted that a college education was his only ticket to freedom. The death of that uncle gave him the motivation and the financial resources to make his dreams of medical school a reality.

"It doesn't seem fair, does it?" Dr. Johnstone said. "Having to make this kind of decision?"

He sighed into his hands, which were folded together before him as if in prayer. He didn't seem the praying type, but if someone had walked in at that moment, they would have mistaken him for a pious man. Maria wondered, for the first time in years, if perhaps there was a God listening and she should have been saying her own prayers all along. But why was He punishing her? What kind of a God would force her to make a choice like this? And in the end, who would she sacrifice, her family or Beth? She was a monster, either way.

CHAPTER TWENTY-SEVEN

I CAN TEACH YOU HOW TO crochet."

Maria pulled her eyes from the window and followed the voice to the little girl sitting in the corner of the dayroom with her. Dr. Johnstone had promised to return before noon so they could discuss the hypnosis treatments with her parents, but so far there were no signs of him. Her outburst during the last session, and her stint in the quiet room, had put everyone on high alert, and there was talk about putting the treatments on hold. Dr. Johnstone said he would take care of it, get everyone back on board, and Maria was ashamed to admit, even to herself, that she hoped he'd be successful. She wanted to go home. She didn't want to grapple with right versus wrong, and she was thankful that Henry was no longer beside her in the hospital to judge her for it.

"I can teach you how to crochet," the little girl repeated, an unidentifiable mess of knotted yarn resting in her lap. "It's really not hard, and my doctor says it's therapeutic."

She couldn't have been more than ten, with tufts of orange frizz sprouting from her head like weeds and skin so pale it defied nature. The silver braces on her teeth gleamed in the sunlight when she smiled. One day she would be beautiful, but adolescence would undoubtedly be cruel.

"That's wonderful." Maria nodded to the project in her lap. "Is it a scarf?"

"You can tell?" She held up the misshapen rows of uneven stitches, her eyes unable to hide her delight. "You're the first person to figure out what it is."

Maria winked at her. "Of course it's a scarf," she said. "Anyone can see that."

The little girl went back to work with a newfound determination, her hands delicate and deft, as Maria looked on, her heart breaking for all the things she had yet to teach her children: to crochet, and to read, and to ride bikes, and to do all the things she was always too busy to do. If it was a lesson someone was trying to teach her, she had learned it. She was ready to go home. She would be better. She would promise, swear on her life, to do whatever she was commanded to do, just to get home. She was so lost in her thoughts that she didn't notice the nurse standing above her until she spoke.

"Maria?" she said. "You have a visitor in your room. Your grandfather."

While the complexity of the news begged an explanation, Maria somehow had the prudence to bite her tongue. Even as she rose from her chair and followed the nurse down the corridor and back to her room, she knew better than to open her mouth. There was no way this woman could have known that Maria had no living grandfathers.

The old man who was propped on the edge of her bed and staring out the window sat unmoving. The thin strands of white, downy hair that fashioned a halo around the crown of his head created a stark contrast to the mottled skin on his scalp, and the gathers of wrinkled skin that sagged off his bones looked like they had been folded and stitched into place. The bones themselves were so brittle, Maria wondered if they might break under the weight of a heavy gaze. When his eyes landed on her, though, she had no doubt that his mind was sharp.

"Grandpa." Maria draped an arm over his shoulder as she eased onto the bed beside him, her fingers running over the jutting edges of his scapula. The old man pulled her into an embrace with the strength of a man half his age.

"Maria, my dear." He breathed in her image as he held her at arm's length. "Look at you."

In silence, they measured each other, the old man with the deceptively frail body and the middle-aged woman with the deceptively young one. The nurse paused at the door before she glanced back at the pair and smiled. "I'll be just down the hall if you need me," she said, pulling the door shut behind her and leaving the room to silence.

Maria shifted her weight away from the man, rising from the bed and slipping onto the wooden chair across from him, neither whispering a word until they heard the *click* of the shutting door.

"So," she said, when she finally heard it. "Who are you?"

His dentures glistened between them as his smile spread to his eyes, which were trained on Maria as if they were etching the details of her onto a canvas in his mind.

"I'm George."

The chair creaked in the silence that followed, as Maria scooted herself forward on it. The man she'd written off as a mistake or a misunderstanding on the part of Dr. Johnstone was pretending to be her grandfather and was wearing an expression that could almost convince her they'd known each other forever.

"How did you know I was here?" she asked.

"You don't remember me?"

Her mind reeled with the explanation Dr. Johnstone had given her of the man named George who'd known where to find her. A man who was too sick to visit. A man he'd brushed aside as an afterthought. "Have we met?" she asked.

"Once upon a time," George replied.

"Then why don't I remember you?"

"Give yourself time," he said. "You will."

His eyes were the same deep brown as her daughter Emily's, but rimmed with the blue halos of age, and as she sank into the depths of them, she could almost see her daughter sitting before her. Did this man know her daughter? Did he know the family she left behind? Had he come from the same world she'd been stolen from?

"But why are you pretending to be my grandfather?"

"No visitors allowed, per Dr. Johnstone's orders. Except family. He told me when he came to visit me the other day."

The deceptions were stacking up in a precarious heap, threatening to topple like a house of cards built on sand, and warning Maria to back off. This was the man Dr. Johnstone was asking about when he wanted to know if she'd had any visitors. It wasn't Henry, after all.

"He doesn't want me talking to you, does he?" Maria asked.

"No," George replied. "He doesn't. He's afraid I'll convince you to do the right thing."

The right thing.

There was a certain amount of shame to those words, and the guilt was suffocating. Did this man already know she was going to let a little girl die? She didn't need to ask him what he meant by "the right thing." She already knew. If Dr. Johnstone was trying to convince her to go home, then George was there to save a little girl's life. She could feel the tug between the two men, the yin and the yang, each certain that his path was the one she should follow.

"Dr. Johnstone said you were the one to tell him I was here," Maria said. "Why would you do that if you didn't want me to listen to him?"

"Would you have believed an old man wandering in off the street if he hadn't been here first?"

Maria shrugged. She couldn't imagine what she would have believed or not believed had George shown up in her hospital room instead of Dr. Johnstone, if he'd tried to convince her to save Beth. After everything she'd been through in the past couple of weeks, hypotheticals were impossible.

"How do you know each other?" she asked. "Is he a friend of yours?"

"Dr. Johnstone was a lost soul when I found him almost thirty years ago, drifting in and out of homeless shelters, hooked on drugs, rambling on to anyone who'd listen about coming back from the future. About how he failed to do what he'd been sent back here to do. He's come a long way, and he's not a bad man. In fact, he's helped many people over the years. But he's so blinded by his research and the guilt he feels over his own choices that he sometimes forgets why we're all here."

"You mean our purpose?"

"No one comes back without a purpose," George said. "He told me you didn't die, which is one of the reasons he's so interested in you. He wants to send you back. He thinks if he can figure out how to manipulate this loophole, he'll somehow be able to manage voluntary time travel in the future."

"Maybe he's right. Maybe there's a reason I didn't die, and I'm supposed to go back."

"You were supposed to die, Maria. But sometimes . . ." He paused and glanced out the window, almost regretful to continue. "Some people just don't know how to let go."

With shaking hands, George pulled a necklace from beneath the collar of his shirt and slid it over his head, running his fingers over the engraving. The silver disk was tarnished with age and wear, and before he placed it in the palm of Maria's hand, he wound the chain around it and kissed it gently.

"I've carried this with me for over six decades now."

Maria read and reread the engraving.

FOSTER, PHILIP V.

PVT.

38 REG. 3 INF.

U.S.A.

It was an old military dog tag, the likes of which she was sure she'd never seen, but the memory of it pulsed through her synapses and fired into her brain, the image flashing over and over in her mind. "How do I know this?"

"You were just a child at the fair, with your mom," he said. "My wife and I were sitting on the bench across from you, watching you lick the last of the cotton candy off your fingers. I'll never forget how you cried when your mom dumped that mess in the garbage." The creases running through his face deepened with his smile as his thoughts took him back to a well-loved and often-played memory. "You stopped crying the second you saw me, and then you marched right up to me and my wife like you'd known us forever."

"Are you sure it was me?"

"I'm sure," he said, and as she held the dog tag in the palm of her hand, the heat from George's skin still radiating from it, Maria could hear the words she'd said all those years ago.

"'Can I see your brother's necklace?'" As the memory materialized before her, she closed her fingers around the metal disk. "That's what I said to you."

"My brother." George smiled. "You were right. He was more of a brother to me than my own flesh and blood, but our brotherhood was formed by the blood we *spilled*, not the blood we *shared*."

The distant gaze of his eyes had taken him far away from the prison-barred window of Maria's hospital room, and though he appeared to be taking in the Alabama spring sky just outside that window, she knew he was seeing people and places and choices that must have lingered in his memory for far too long.

"I want you to keep that," he said, pointing to the chain in her hand.

"I can't take this. This should go to your family."

"That dog tag is the reason I knew you would come back, Maria. The reason I kept an eye on you all these years, waiting for something to happen to let me know that you'd returned."

"But kids say crazy things all the time," Maria replied. "How could you be so sure?"

"When you've seen the things I've seen, you listen to what the universe is telling you. There are no coincidences." The nature of his smile changed before her eyes, and even though she'd never had one in life, Maria felt certain she understood the love of a grandfather.

"How did you figure out that I'd made it back?"

"I knew when you didn't show up to school that morning something was wrong. You were never one to miss school, and when you didn't pass me on the bench where I'd sit and feed the birds every morning, I started calling the hospitals. And then I called Dr. Johnstone."

He nodded to the dog tag, and their eyes met on Maria's clenched fingers. "Philip was my best friend, but I didn't wear that necklace all this time just for him. I wore it for you, too. Knowing you'd need a friend when you came back."

"What happened to him?" Maria asked, nosing her way into a past that the man beside her had likely spent years trying to forget.

"He died," George said. "The second time we fought through World War One, he died." His eyes darkened and the tremor in his hands worsened as his memories dragged him back to a place that should have been reserved for nightmares. "You'd be surprised how different the map of Europe looked back then, and how difficult life was. It's amazing what people can endure. But at least I had the woman I loved and my best friend by my side every day of my life."

He paused, and with a heavy sigh, his body seemed to deflate into the bed.

"But then I came back," he said, "and it was all gone. Philip died on July 15, 1918, along the Marne River in France. It was the second time we fought through World War One, although he never remembered the first. I could have saved him, like I did the first time, but his death was the reason I'd been sent back. My purpose."

"What do you mean?"

"The Second Battle of the Marne. The fight that led to the end of the war. His death was all that was needed to change the course of that battle and ultimately the course of the war. He saved hundreds of thousands of lives. And since I was the one who'd saved him the first time, I was the one who had to let him go."

Maria sat speechless, a thousand questions running through her mind, but deference forced her to keep her mouth shut. Hadn't he suffered enough?

"You're the only person besides my wife who's heard that story. And that's yours to keep." He pointed a crooked finger toward the dog tag still resting in Maria's clenched fist. "I always knew we'd meet again. I knew we were brought together for a reason that day at the fair, so I've been holding on to it to remind you that there's a greater purpose to all of this and that you're not alone in your suffering. This is all connected, Maria. The reason you found me at the fair. The reason you were sent back. It's your purpose."

She opened her mouth to speak, but no words came out. She

could only see the little girl with the marble-like eyes staring back at her and the dirt falling over her face. Beth was waiting to be saved, and George was here to convince her to do it. She picked at the frayed edges of her bandage as she tried to stop the images from spinning through her mind, but her head pounded with the effort.

"My purpose seems so much less significant than yours," she finally said.

"No purpose is insignificant. The choices we make every day are not just about us. They impact everyone around us in ways that you can't even imagine."

Maria had been so focused on her own circumstances and misfortunes, she hadn't stopped to consider the incredible gifts she might offer the world. Diverting catastrophes like 9/11 and the floods from Hurricane Katrina. She'd already decided to leave a note for her mother, to warn her about the cancer that was lurking around the corner, but could she make an even greater impact on society? Would someone listen to her and change the outcomes of those tragedies that were lying in wait down the road?

"Is that what you've been doing since coming back?" she asked. "Saving people from disasters that you knew were going to happen?"

"Unfortunately, there's no changing someone's destiny when it's their turn to die. Unless you were sent back to change their fate, there's nothing you can do. Wars, floods, fires, assassinations. As much as I've tried, I've never once been able to save a life when fate was coming for it."

Maria had already composed the letter to her mother in her mind, the words that would save her from cancer, and while she knew George was right, she also knew she wouldn't be leaving her mother without penning that letter. The life that fate had sent her back to save, the life of the little girl in Ohio, was the one she wasn't ready to spare.

"I was sent back to save a life," she said. "But Dr. Johnstone says he can't send me home if I do it. That I can't have both. But I'm not so sure."

"Once you've changed your destiny here, you'll let go of the life you left behind. I've seen repeaters like you. People who couldn't let go of that other world. But it will slip away when you fulfill your purpose. You'll go through the in-between, and then there won't be any going back."

"The in-between," Maria whispered, remembering the words Henry had used and wishing he was there with her, so they could travel this road together. "What is that?"

"The most beautiful gift you'll ever receive, Maria." The furrows of regret that lined George's face softened before her eyes, years melting away as the story of his life was momentarily forgotten. "The in-between world is where you learn for sure what your purpose is, and it's where you get to see everyone from every life you've ever lived."

"How is that possible?"

"We don't have the words in our human vocabulary to describe it. You see everyone you've ever known, but not with your eyes. And you speak and hear, but not with words or voices or ears. You don't even really feel with your body, but you understand so completely who every single soul is, and you love them, and they love you, and no one needs to be told. And you finally understand what eternity is."

Maria could almost feel herself slipping into this in-between world, seeing the four people she had been longing for since her return—her husband and her three children, one of whom she hadn't even met. But she didn't have to go through that to see them. She didn't have to limit herself to an in-between world, even if it would feel like an eternity, because she had the option of returning to them in real life. They were just waiting for her to wake up.

"Only in death can you go through that in-between world and

be reborn," George continued. "You have to let go of that other world."

"But if I don't do what I was sent here to do, will I stay alive in that other world?"

"I suppose you would. But most likely you're in a coma back there and you won't wake up until you leave this world."

Maria could hear her children's laughter from the recent hypnosis with Dr. Johnstone, as they held the picture Will had sketched of her. The vibrant colors from the thick and clumsy crayons that had shown so clearly a woman lying seemingly lifeless in a hospital bed, with no baby in her belly.

"This life cycle you're living right now is an extension of the one you left behind," George continued. "And you were chosen to come back and change it. It makes you different. The rules have changed for you, and you can no longer have a conscious existence in both worlds simultaneously."

"But it's possible that I could linger on in a coma back there and continue to relive my life here? As long as I don't do what I was sent back here to do?"

The implications of that were astounding, and as Maria thought of the many comatose patients she'd seen during her medical school training and residency, she couldn't help but wonder if those people had been trapped in another world, if they had also just been too stubborn to let go. When they woke up, did they know where they'd been? Did they remember the purposes they'd chosen to ignore?

"You're a scientist, like Dr. Johnstone," he said, interrupting her thoughts as if she'd spoken them aloud. "That's another reason he likes you so much. He thinks you'll be easier to convince. But I hope he's wrong. It's time to let your past go, let your family have new lives."

"New lives?"

"Your children will be born, with or without you, Maria. Whether they enter this world through your body or someone else's, they will always be a part of it. Their energy can never be destroyed. Our spirits are constantly being recycled and evolving, and you were sent here to help with that evolution. Your children have been a part of every world that has come and gone, and they will be a part of every world that has yet to come, just like you and me and everyone else. But they won't always be a part of *your* life. And sometimes, when they do cross your path, they'll do so in different roles."

The jealousy that hit her as she considered the significance of his words was so unsettling that she was embarrassed to even acknowledge it. Thinking of another woman cradling her children and wiping away their tears and hearing their first words was almost too devastating to imagine.

"Please don't say that. I could never let someone else raise my children."

"There's no ownership in this universe, Maria. We all belong to each other. We all take care of each other. You'll see that, when you let go of that other world. Only the strongest from among us are sent back and asked to make the changes that need to be made."

"I don't want to be chosen," Maria said. "I don't want to be strong. I just want my family back."

"I know you do, and I don't envy the decision you have before you." He pulled himself from the bed with surprising ease and fetched a folded piece of yellow paper from his pocket. "You've been entrusted with something that feels too overwhelming to even consider right now. A task that would break most people. But you were chosen for a reason." He placed the yellow paper into her hand and folded his fingers around hers. "Keep this somewhere safe, and get yourself out of this hospital. I'll do whatever I can to walk you through this nightmare, Maria. But you must be the one to fulfill your purpose."

George was gone by the time Maria found her voice. The gifts he'd left for her were heavy in her hands, their weight a burden she didn't think she'd ever have the strength to shoulder, and as she thought about her husband's little sister in Ohio, the image of her family began to fade from her mind.

CHAPTER TWENTY-EIGHT

W HY IS THERE A WHEELCHAIR IN here?"
Maria's mother shimmied around the chair and pointed
back at it as she took the spot opposite Maria on the bed, the spot
George had just vacated. "That wasn't for you, was it?"

Maria shook her head, still clutching the dog tag and the
folded yellow paper with George's phone number and address
scratched onto it.

"I had a visitor," she said. "Turns out he didn't need it."

The afternoon sunlight poured through the window onto her
mother's face, highlighting the shadows under her eyes, which
hadn't been there a week earlier. "Who was your visitor?" she
asked.

"George." Maria opened her fingers from around the silver
necklace in the palm of her hand. "I guess you'd call him an old
friend."

Her mother lifted the tarnished silver disk from Maria's hand
and draped the chain over her fingers, tilting her head to read the
inscription.

"The man from the fair," she whispered, her words floating
through the air in a fine mist and evaporating into nothingness
before Maria was certain she'd heard them. "Was he here?" She
stumbled past the wheelchair that still blocked the doorway and
scanned the hall before returning. "Where is he?"

"He went home," Maria replied, handing her mother the yellow paper, not bothering to tell her why George had come, or that he'd suffered more than anyone she'd ever known, or that he'd cast upon her a burden too great to bear. She wanted to share it all, to shrug off all the lies and secrecy that had been draped over her shoulders like a heavy cloak. The battle in her mind was exhausting, like she was fighting a duel between two sides that were perfectly matched rivals.

On the one hand was George, principled and self-sacrificing, confident that she would look out for the child and do "the right thing." On the other hand was Dr. Johnstone, dishonest and self-interested, but equally confident that she would look out for her own best interest and do the sensible thing. She wondered where Henry would stand in all of this. Maybe he would be the voice of reason.

"Why was he here?" her mother asked as she read over the yellow paper with George's name and address and refolded it.

"It's a long story, but he's the one who told Dr. Johnstone that I'd be here."

"That can't be right. It was so long ago, and it was just one of those strange things . . ." Her mother's words trailed off as she struggled to comprehend what she'd just stumbled into, as if time had wrapped around itself and pulled the past forward. "Did Dr. Johnstone ask him to come?"

"No," Maria replied. "Dr. Johnstone didn't *want* George to visit me. They have different agendas."

"What is going on here, Maria? What agenda are you talking about? I think we need stop with the hypnosis. I don't trust this doctor from Iowa."

"I need to get out of this hospital, Mom. I need to get off these medicines and out of these pajamas and away from all these people." She'd worked so hard to convince her parents that she'd recovered from her recent psychosis and that the medicines and therapy were working, and now she was about to undo it all. She was about to put the truth out there again and attempt to convince her mother of the impossible.

"Remember that night I came into your bedroom and woke you up?" she asked, but her mother didn't respond, and Maria didn't look to see if she'd even heard. She was too busy trying to formulate words to go with the thoughts in her head, but the past and present and future were twisting together in a tangled mess of memories, with no beginning and no end, and she didn't quite know how to proceed.

"The children I told you about," she continued, picking at the frayed and unraveling bandage on her arm. "Your grandchildren. They're real. And I really did come back from the future. And I really am married to a man named Will, who was like a son to you. And I really am pregnant with my third child."

There were tears in her mother's eyes when she finally looked up, the tears of a woman who would do anything to protect her daughter but instead had to watch her spiral out of control, unable to be saved by the increasing number of medicines and specialists and therapies around them. Unable to be saved by her. In the world Maria left behind, she was about her mother's age now, struggling to balance life, just like the woman beside her, struggling to do the right thing by her children.

"We're going to figure this out, Maria." Her mother wiped the tears from her cheeks and laced her fingers through Maria's before pulling in a deep breath and sighing it out between them. "I don't want you to worry about this. We'll get the best specialist in the country if we have to, but we're going to help you. We're going to make this better."

"I don't blame you for not believing me, Mom. I wouldn't believe my daughter, either, if she came to me with a story like this.

But I have to make you see the truth, and I don't know any other way to do it than to break a promise I made to you a long time ago. So, I'm sorry for what I'm about to do."

She had somehow known it would play out this way. From the beginning, she'd known that she would have to share this story to make her mother believe her, but that knowledge didn't lessen the shame. It was a story she'd vowed to keep secret, two years earlier, but today she would break that vow and reveal something that she was certain her mother would soon wish she'd taken to her grave.

"When I was a baby, barely even a year old, you got pregnant again." The words covered her mother like a thick coat of ice as she sat frozen by Maria's side, unable to pull air into her lungs. "You and Dad weren't getting along so well at the time. The stress of a new baby, his long hours at work, your loneliness. You were even talking about divorce."

"Stop." Her mother pushed herself from the bed and backed away from Maria with unsteady steps that carried her to the wheelchair by the door.

"I have to make you see the truth, Mom. You never told anyone about that baby. Not Dad, not your mom, no one. Until you told me, just days before you died." She'd never been able to shake that image: her mother, sedated on morphine, rambling on with a story that she'd begged her to stop telling, playing the role of an unwilling priest at a last confession.

"Stop it," her mother said, stumbling over George's wheelchair. "It's not true. Who told you this?"

"You did. On your deathbed, two years ago. I sat by your side every hour of every day as cancer ate you away. Metastatic, stage four breast cancer. You were sixty-two years old."

Her mother clutched the arm of the wheelchair for balance, unable to hold herself steady. "That's impossible. I never told anyone."

"Not yet. But you will. And I'll promise to carry it to my own grave, but obviously that won't happen, because here I am." Maria held her arms wide, feeling smaller than she ever could have imagined for breaking her mother's trust and backing her into a corner. "I promise I won't breathe a word of it to anyone. Ever. But I didn't know how else to make you see the truth."

"What truth?" Her mother leaned against the wall, fear holding her in place as she watched her daughter from the other side of the room. "What happened to you?"

"I don't know," Maria said. "I'm just as confused as you are. And as grateful as I am to see you again, I just want to go home."

"This *is* your home, Maria." Her mother stepped cautiously toward the bed, the need to comfort her daughter outweighing the senselessness of the words that were being spoken to her. "Why do you keep saying that?"

She slid onto the bed beside Maria, placing her hand over the bandage on her daughter's mangled wrist. There was only so much proof Maria could provide to her. She would have had to walk the journey beside her to fully appreciate it.

"This *was* my home," she said. "But I've left a family behind to be here, and all I want is to be with them again. But I was sent here to do something that will cost me my way back."

Her mother had once been her closest confidante, but that wouldn't happen for almost another decade. She couldn't remember the moment their relationship changed, the moment her mother's role shifted from disciplinarian to mentor to friend. There probably wasn't one moment; it was probably like most mother–daughter relationships: eventually, when your children start careers and get married and have children of their own, your job as a parent seems so unimportant.

She wished she could tell her mother how untrue that was, how she'd needed her every single day since her death and had spoken to her as if she hadn't already been buried. How she needed her now. How she wasn't prepared to make this choice. She wanted someone to tell her what to do, to make it right. But how could she ask the woman sitting by her side to do that for her?

"Good afternoon, ladies." Dr. Johnstone's voice thundered through the room, catching both Maria and her mother off guard. "What is this doing here?" he mumbled, as he pushed the wheelchair into the hallway and shut the door on his way back into the room. "Thanks for meeting me here, Mrs. Bethe. I wanted to discuss Maria's hypnotherapy before we started her next session."

The silver chain hanging from her mother's hand glistened in the sunlight as she tried to slip it into her purse, catching Dr. Johnstone's attention. He stepped forward to examine it.

"Is that a dog tag?"

"Yes, it's . . . it belongs to . . ." She cleared her throat as she clutched the metal necklace, her eyes darting between Maria and Dr. Johnstone. "It belongs to Maria's grandfather."

"Her grandfather?" It wasn't the usual fumbling hand that caught Dr. Johnstone's glasses when they slipped from his nose but a dexterous index finger, which settled the glasses back into place before he reached out for the necklace. "May I?"

"Of course." Maria's mother dropped the dog tag into his outstretched hand. "You just missed him."

"I didn't realize Maria had a visitor." He peered through the bottom half of his bifocals at the inscription on the metal disk. "No one mentioned it to me."

"I didn't realize you were keeping tabs on my visitors," Maria said.

"No, of course not." He handed the necklace back to her mother. "Was that your father or your husband's, Mrs. Bethe?"

"Mine." The words passed her lips without pause or hesitation as she buried the dog tag and the yellow paper deep within her purse. Maria would never have guessed that her mother could be such a proficient liar.

"I see." Dr. Johnstone slid onto the edge of the bed, a good distance from them both. The springs creaked under his weight, but the familiar restless shifting of his body was noticeably absent. He was smoother than Maria thought he could be, this hyperexcitable, bumbling man who'd sat in the cafeteria with her just a couple of days earlier, blabbing on about the theory of relativity and how it related to reincarnation.

"As I was saying," he continued, "I think before the next hypnosis treatment we should discontinue the medications that Dr. Anderson started. She's agreed to this, so Maria won't be getting her evening meds, starting tonight."

"I think maybe it's time for her to come home." Maria hadn't realized she'd been holding her breath until her mother's words silenced Dr. Johnstone, and she finally exhaled into the space between them. "My husband and I will keep her safe. In fact, we'd be more comfortable doing it that way."

Dr. Johnstone hesitated, his eyes searching Maria's face as he tried to reconcile what he'd just stumbled in upon. "I can certainly understand how you'd feel that way," he said. "And if you think she's ready for it, we can do the hypnosis treatments as an outpatient."

"I'm not sure I even want to do the treatments anymore," Maria said, and as Dr. Johnstone's eyebrows shot up and his attention went back and forth from mother to daughter, she could almost pity him for the effort it was taking to keep his mouth shut.

"You don't want the hypnosis?"

"I don't know," Maria replied. "I don't want to give up on it completely, but I need some time to think. If I could just get out of this hospital and off these medications, maybe I could figure out what I need to do."

If it weren't for Maria's mother, Dr. Johnstone would have been able to undo all of George's work. It wouldn't have been difficult. Distracting Maria from her purpose with promises and glimpses of her family was a talent of his. But circumstance had landed him in a tough spot, one that didn't lend itself well to frank conversation.

"You said it was your grandfather that visited you?" He leaned back and peered over the top rim of his glasses.

"Yes," Maria replied. "My grandfather. We discussed the importance of always doing the right thing and fulfilling our purposes in life. Things like that."

He nodded as he sighed into the space between them, conceding defeat to the man who hadn't needed the wheelchair, the man who'd once been his own mentor of sorts, and jotted down a local number on the back of his business card before handing it to Maria's mother.

"I'll be in town for a couple more days, but I have to get back home soon, so if you decide you'd like to continue with the hypnosis, we would need to get started in the next day or two." He rose from the bed and walked to the door, hesitating before opening it and turning back to face them. "And Maria," he said, "the 'right thing' means different things to different people. Unless someone has walked in your shoes throughout your entire life, and shared each of those experiences with you, how can they possibly know what is right for you?"

jenny

THE OTHER WIVES SAID THEY KNEW the moment it happened. They could feel it in their cores, startled awake in the middle of the night, the essences of them forever changed. Jenny didn't feel anything at the moment the rig exploded, the moment Hank died. There was no premonition, no nightmare, no sense of doom. She learned her husband was dead when she turned on the news the morning after the explosion, five days after he left their home for the last time.

Footage of the accident reeled twenty-four hours a day as rescue crews turned into recovery crews and experts briefed the press about possible causes of the disaster. Hank's body was never found and none of his belonging were ever returned.

For weeks, neighbors, friends, and distant relatives tried to nose their way into Jenny's sorrow, thinking they could own a portion of her grief, but while the incessant ringing of the phone followed her into sleep every night, she never thought to answer it. She clung to her misery, unwilling to share it, fearing the pain would dull and she would forget that she deserved it and that she was not worthy of forgiveness.

But it was the guilt, more than the grief, that consumed her.

It gnawed at her soul, feeding like a half-crazed, insatiable rat, devouring what was left of her and ripping her from sleep every night. The secrets that she and Hank had shared in those final moments were secrets that should have followed them both to their graves.

Her son stayed by her side for days, offering the only solace Jenny would accept, but Dean's pity couldn't quell the agony; it just made it worse. She had nothing to offer him in return, and the longer he stayed by her side, the more deeply the consequences of her ineptitude sliced through her. She was incapable of walking her son through the loss of his father, because she didn't know how to grieve. The relief she'd felt upon her own mother's death should have been a warning that something was lacking within her, something grievous, but it wasn't until Hank's death that Jenny realized her husband had filled that void. He'd taught her son not only how to love but also how to *be* loved, a lesson she'd never learned.

It wasn't Dean, though, or the premade meals and cards that found their way to her doorstep each evening, that brought her back to the living. It was the woman in the shed. It was the fact that, for once, she could do something that might offer some justice and hope to someone in need. It was the knowledge that when fate frowns upon certain people, it is the responsibility of others to step forward.

Rachel didn't know the plan. She'd put her complete trust in Jenny to take care of the details and agreed that she wouldn't ask questions. She didn't know that she'd soon be given a new identity, a new passport, a new life. She didn't know that someone would be finding her blue sleeveless shirt and her canvas shoes washed up on the Mississippi shore near the border of Louisiana, or that investigators would soon call off the search when she was presumed dead. She didn't know that Jenny had spent half her life savings to secure the documents that would grant Rachel a new start. Not to mention the cost of confidentiality. Jenny wasn't proud of the connections she had from her days in New Orleans, but they had their benefits.

Jenny couldn't think straight. The details were starting to blend together, and as she sat at the table listening to the ticking of the clock above the door, pounding into her head like a throbbing pulse, she couldn't focus.

It was one of the few things she'd brought to her marriage all those years ago, and as if to remind her that they were alone, it seemed to grow louder by the day. Stupid clock. It didn't know that Hank was gone and that it should have been conserving its *ticks* because no one would ever wind it again. She wrapped her fingers around the glass of water on the table in front of her, the sides slick with condensation and cold beneath her fingers.

Before she could fathom what she was about to do, the glass was hurtling through the air and crashing into the clock face, dust scattering in every direction when it hit the floor. The relentless ticking wouldn't cease, though. Even when she stood above it, her foot poised and ready to smash it to pieces, it refused to surrender. It wasn't until the full weight of her body crashed down onto it that it fell silent.

"Jenny? Are you okay?" Rachel's voice floated through the kitchen as Jenny picked her foot up to examine the remnants of the clock. When she finally looked up, the light was fading through the kitchen window, highlighting the changes that had turned Rachel into a new woman.

She'd been staying in the shed for almost a month and had put on some weight. Her hair was finally starting to grow out and the auburn roots looked shiny and healthy. She was turning a corner, starting a new life, while Jenny was wrapping up her old one.

"Do I look like I'm doing okay?" Jenny asked, and when they

both surveyed the mess of broken glass surrounding them on the floor and the crumpled clock face stuck to the bottom of Jenny's shoe, there was nothing they could do but laugh. It felt good to laugh. Life was hard and messy and heartbreaking, but in that moment shared between two friends, it was also beautiful.

They stayed up late into the night, drinking wine, reliving memories, and telling secrets as the sounds of the bayou enveloped them in a familiar chorus. The night air was cool as they dragged log after log to the fire pit and doused them with kerosene, watching the flames dance into the sky and rain down embers and ashes.

It was Rachel's idea, but it was Jenny who dragged the red bin from the guest bedroom closet. It banged against the ground with the protests of the condemned. As Jenny propped the photo of David on a nearby rock so he could witness the scene, the two women topped off their wineglasses and clinked them together one last time.

"To new beginnings."

Rachel retreated to the shed for her final night on the bayou, leaving Jenny to do what should have been done years earlier. A photo album swollen with memories of one-time lovers was the first to go, swallowed by the flames as the plastic sheaths around the pictures melted away, leaving distorted images of half-burned faces with ghoulish smiles staring back at her. The flames shot high into the sky, as if they were pleased with the sacrifice but hungry for more, so Jenny fed them, memory by memory, until the singed residue of her former life was all that remained.

When the ash had settled and the bin was empty, she held the last photo of David she would ever see, the one her husband had left for her, and ran her fingers over it, kissing it softly. He was as dead to her as her husband was, and when the photo slipped from her fingers and drifted into the flames, her hand drifted to her belly, where a heart had recently begun to beat.

PART III

CHAPTER THIRTY

maria

THE PHOTO HAD MADE ITS WAY back to the corkboard and the bathroom had been scrubbed, but try as she might, Maria couldn't block out the image of her mother on her hands and knees, sobbing as she rinsed the blood from the bathroom walls and watched it swirl down the drain.

The girl in the mirror was scowling at Maria for ruining her life and destroying her future. Her hair was a greasy, tangled mess, her skin sunken on her cheeks, and the dark circles that shadowed her eyes were macabre and dreadful. She wasn't so striking anymore. The thick, pink scar that wound its way up her wrist like a knotted rope was angry against her pale skin. It was the kind of scar that would define her throughout her life, and Maria was heavy with guilt for branding herself with it.

Sylvia would have been disappointed. Whatever insight she had offered to Maria hadn't helped. The words spoken in the privacy of her office, the pictures and warnings from the dream, and the letter that never found Maria's hands had been powerless to help. Even being out of the hospital had offered little clarity. Instead, it had sent her into a sort of depression, making her unable to eat or sleep or focus. She spent most of her time staring at the calendar and counting down the hours until Beth's murder. She had forty-eight hours, plus or minus.

A light rap on the door, another safety check from her parents, snuffed out the thoughts that had been frequenting her mind since she had returned from the hospital. By instinct, Maria pulled her sleeve down to cover her wrist.

"I'm fine," she yelled toward the door. "Just going to the bathroom."

"Maria?" Her mother peeked her head into the bedroom before stepping inside. "I wanted to return these to you," she said, before reaching out and dropping the dog tag and the yellow paper into Maria's hand. Maria closed her fingers around them, wishing she could give voice to the thoughts that were haunting her mind and the decision she was being forced to make. "What you told me in the hospital . . ." her mother continued. "I would appreciate it if you wouldn't say anything to your father."

"Of course not," Maria replied. "I would never do that. And I don't judge you. I hope you know that I would never judge you for that."

"You don't have to," her mother whispered. "I've judged myself every hour of every day since I made that decision."

"Don't, Mom." Maria's hand drifted across her belly. She longed for the touch of the child she had almost let go, the child she had kept only because the memory of her mother's grief had never deserted her. "That choice changed me in ways you can't even imagine."

"That man from the fair," her mother said, glancing down at the dog tag and the paper in Maria's hand. "What did he say to you? What did he want you to do?"

Maria thought about George's unfaltering belief that she was supposed to have died the day she came back. She thought about the sacrifices he'd made in his life, the years he'd spent watching over her, the support he was willing to offer. She thought about what it would mean to her mother to hear that George was urging her to stay, that he was imploring her to make a decision that would bind her to this life forever.

"He wanted me to give up my life back home," Maria said. "My husband and kids."

She could only watch as her mother tried to balance her emotions, the weight of her sorrow like an anchor strong enough to drag them both under, and when the tears finally came, she didn't try to stop them. She let them carry her back to her home in Mississippi, where she'd stood nine months pregnant and overwhelmed with life, unable to allow herself five minutes to cry, as if that would have made her weak. If she'd only known.

"I'm sorry, Mom," she said. "I'm so sorry to put this on you." Their sobs were silent as they held each other, mother and daughter, each fighting her own battle, neither wanting to let the other go. Who else could understand the tragedy and the beauty of Maria's journey if not her mother?

Maria stared at the yellow paper in her hand long after her mother had gone. She sat on the pink bedspread and listened to the birds chirping outside her window as if they had no idea how cruel the world around them could be. She'd been fighting for her release from the hospital for so long, but she hadn't considered how overwhelming freedom would be. As she finally uncurled her fingers from around the dog tag and the yellow paper and watched them fall into the bottom drawer of her nightstand, the chime of the doorbell rang through the house.

Henry looked out of place standing on her front doorstep, wearing street clothes instead of pajamas, and boots instead of slippers, and Maria instinctively ran a hand through her hair, wishing she was dressed in something other than sweatpants and a sweatshirt. At least she'd brushed her teeth and put on a bra, an improvement from their last meeting.

"I wasn't sure I'd ever see you again," she said, tugging her sweatshirt sleeve over her scarred wrist.

"You can't get rid of me that easily," Henry laughed. "I got your name and number for a reason."

Maria could feel the heat spreading through her face, and she knew the blush that went with it was betraying her. There was an unexpected easiness to their company, a familiarity that had belonged only to her husband for the past fifteen years, and it didn't seem to go unnoticed by Henry. When his eyes caught hold of hers, she couldn't seem to pry them away.

"I really wanted to see you again," he continued. "I was worried about you after our last conversation, and I never really got to say good-bye."

So much had happened since that last conversation, hopeful revelations about where she'd come back from and a string of complexities about where she was going. She wondered if Henry would even believe her when she told him.

"Would you like to come inside?" she asked. "I have a lot to tell you."

"I was hoping we could go for a walk. Maybe head over to Mulberry Park?"

The park was closer than she remembered. After promising her mother she'd be back before dinner, she and Henry strolled down to one of Maria's favorite childhood parks. Like most things from her childhood, though, the picture was not as grand as her fading memory had painted it. She would have sworn the path they were walking, the one where she raced her banana-seat bicycle over thirty years earlier, had been paved when she was a child, but the gravel beneath their feet crunched as she and Henry ambled beside the sludge-filled pond. And hadn't there once been ducks in that pond?

"I used to come here when I was child," she said, as they approached a bench on the far side of the pond. Henry cleared off some leaves and dirt with his hand before offering the seat to her. Someone had raised him to be a gentleman. "It seemed so much bigger back then," she continued. "Have you noticed that, since coming back? How things are not quite as impressive as they once seemed?"

"I think that happens when you get older," he replied, sliding onto the bench beside her. "The world loses its magic."

He was probably right. Age had a way of diminishing grandeur. She wondered at what point this park had lost its magic for her. If she'd visited it ten years ago, would it have looked the same? At what point would she have stopped seeing the flower-lined bicycle path and the ducks swimming in the pond?

"I've never been to this park," Henry continued. "My dad and I moved here when I was seventeen. It was so many years ago now, and I feel like I've spent my life trying to forget this place."

"Why did you want to forget it?"

"Bad memories. We moved here after my dad married my stepmom, and then he died of a heart attack less than a year later. I drove out of this town twenty-two years ago and swore I'd never come back."

"I'm sorry," Maria said. "Has that already happened? I mean, is your dad . . ."

"Yeah." Henry didn't make her finish the question. "He died a couple of weeks before I came back."

"Is that why you were in the hospital?"

"I didn't take it so well," he said, scratching at his chin like a man who wore a beard. Maria tried to picture that man, scruffy and unshaven, maybe a baseball cap to cover his messy hair. She couldn't see him in the clean-shaven boy with the close-cropped hair who sat by her side. "After the funeral, I broke into my dad's liquor cabinet and almost died of alcohol poisoning. That's when my stepmom had me committed."

"So, you live with your stepmom?"

"For now," he said. "She's a good woman, and she'd let me stay if I needed to, but I'm going back home to the country soon. My dad left me his house and some money that he'd saved up. The last time I was here, I burned through all of it on drugs and booze and anything else I could get my hands on, in a matter of months."

As Maria listened to his story, the blandness of her sheltered life sat like a flavorless bite of an unseasoned dish on her tongue. Besides some of her patients, she'd never known anyone who had a wild and self-destructive streak. Will had certainly never binged on drugs. He barely even drank alcohol, making Maria's evening cocktails look indulgent.

"That sounds like a heck of a party," she said. "Will I be invited this time?"

"You're too late," Henry laughed. "Party's over. The money's spoken for this time. It's the reason I was sent back."

The echoes of their laughter faded over the pond, as the burdens they carried elbowed their way back in and choked out the energy around them. They were always lingering in the periphery, those constant reminders that their lives were not entirely their own. Henry was already resigned to it, confident in what needed to be done and willing to make whatever sacrifice needed to be made. Maria's burden was hovering like an unbalanced seesaw: on one side was a family who was waiting for their mother's return and on the other was a little girl who was waiting for death. It was an unfair game.

"You seem so comfortable here," she said. "Like you've already accepted everything that you've been asked to do."

"What other choice do I have? It's not like I can go back home."

"But what if you could? What if going back home was still an option?"

"What do you mean?"

It surprised her that he hadn't considered it. Even if she'd died, Maria had to believe that getting herself back to her family would still be in the forefront of her mind. She envied Henry's contentment. She'd never been one to play the hand she was dealt, even though life tended to give her the advantage of a stacked deck at every turn.

What if? What if? What if?

Always the same drive, followed by the same questions. What if I could be better? What if I could have more? What if I could do it my own way? All those questions had led her to a successful career, financial stability, and a four-bedroom, three-bath house in a beautiful neighborhood, with equally successful neighbors. But time was all that mattered now. Time she'd spent so focused on climbing the ladder that she'd forgotten the people who were waiting for her at the bottom: her family.

"I didn't die," Maria said. "My family is back there waiting for me, and that doctor from Iowa that I told you about says he can send me back to them."

"But how could you come back if you didn't die?"

Maria shrugged. She didn't have the courage to repeat George's words, that she was *supposed* to die in that other world but was just too stubborn to let go. On some level, she felt ashamed by that admission, as if she wasn't brave enough or strong enough to do what she'd been sent back here to do.

"Something happened to me," she said, unable to see past the door of the storage unit and unwilling to pry it open. "Maybe something that should have killed me, but I don't know. I don't remember any of it. I just know that I didn't die, and he said he could send me back."

"Then what are you waiting for?"

Maria could feel the little girl from her dreams tugging at her shirt and asking her the same question, wanting to know when she was coming to save her. She was waiting for an answer, too. Everyone around her was waiting for her to make a decision.

"It's not so simple," she said. "I was sent here to save my husband's little sister, but if I go home, then I can't do it. And, on the other hand, if I save her, then I can't go home."

It took Henry a moment to absorb the meaning of her words, and as she sat quietly beside him, she knew he understood their significance. It was a decision that would result not only in great sacrifice but also in the possibility of great reward. By the time he responded, the sun had dropped beneath the limbs of the tallest trees on the far side of the pond and the chill that had whispered through its branches met her on the bench below.

"I'd like to believe that I'd stay and do what I was sent here to do," he said, pulling Maria's attention from the trees. "But in reality, I don't think I could pass up the chance to go back to my family."

She hadn't expected that from him and felt almost saddened by his words. She wanted him to tell her to stay. She wanted to believe that he would have chosen to stay, too, given the choice, which was ridiculous, because she was a married woman. Whatever flirtations had danced between them were sophomoric and meaningless, and getting back to her family was the only goal that should have been occupying her mind. She nodded her head in response, twisting an imaginary wedding band around her left ring finger. She no longer had a tan line around that finger or concerns about how she was ever going to get it off, with all the pregnancy weight she'd gained. All the foolish things she had worried about, and now she was almost willing to give up the life of a little girl to get them back.

"I feel selfish for saying this," Henry said, interrupting her thoughts, "but I don't want you to go back home."

Maria could almost feel the warmth of his breath brushing across her skin when she turned to face him, to tell him that he shouldn't say those things or feel those things, but as the distance between them closed, she wanted nothing more than to feel his lips against hers.

"I know you, Maria. I know you were there when I came back, because I feel like I've known you forever."

As he leaned into her, the memory of her husband barreled over her with the crushing weight of a thousand elephants, and the vise that clamped around her head wasn't too far behind, forcing her to pull herself from the bench.

"You don't know me, Henry. I'm not this person you see here in front of you." With her hands held wide, Maria glanced down at her seventeen-year-old body and stiffened with guilt for wanting to feel the touch of another man. "I'm a wife and a mother of two beautiful little girls, and I'm pregnant with a son who I hope will get the chance to be born." She sank back down onto the bench beside him, dropping her hands into her lap and focusing on the scar that was peeking out from her sweatshirt. "And I'm a psychiatrist, of all things," she said, holding up the grisly wound on her wrist for him to see. "A psychiatrist who somehow got locked up on a psych unit in a town that I haven't lived in for over twenty years."

Henry pulled himself to the edge of the bench, a response on the tip of his tongue as he distanced himself from her and studied her face like it was changing in front of his eyes. He glanced at his wrist as if he had somewhere to be, but there was no watch there to tell him if he was late. "You're a psychiatrist?"

"It's sad, isn't it?" she said. "For a psychiatrist, I'm really not handling things too well."

Henry didn't respond. He watched her as the sun crept farther behind the trees across from the pond and night began to leach into the scenery around them, and for the first time, Maria wondered what her life might look like if Henry were the man beside her instead of Will. What would she become if she had to start all over again with a different man? Would she do it all the same? Would she choose such a demanding career? Would she choose to be a wife or a mother?

"I should probably get you home," Henry said, taking another glance at his naked wrist. "I don't want your parents to worry about you."

They walked back mostly in silence, a few questions and comments thrown in to fill the void, while Maria bristled at Henry's sudden remoteness. They talked about the chilly spring they were having, about her psychiatry practice, and about the town in Mississippi she'd left behind. He seemed very interested in Bienville, although he said he'd never heard of it.

"I'm not surprised," Maria mumbled. "There's really nothing there."

Something had changed between them, something significant that she had somehow missed, and whatever warmth had enveloped them on the park bench by the pond had dissipated into the chilled air around them. By the time they got back to her front door, the sun had almost set.

"What will you do now?" he asked, walking her up the steps.

"I don't know," she replied, thinking about the little girl in Ohio whose life was ticking away minute by minute. "But I have to make a decision soon."

Henry nodded before he held out his hand to her, and Maria reluctantly reached out to shake it, wondering what she'd done to deserve his sudden indifference. There was no good-bye hug, no promise to call or stop by in a few days. Before he turned to head back to the truck that was parked at the end of the walkway, Henry simply smiled and left her with three words that hung in the air around them and whose meaning was both ominous and vague.

"I'm sorry, Maria."

CHAPTER THIRTY-ONE

THE AMBER LIQUID CLUNG TO THE walls of the crystal decanter as Maria swirled it in gentle circles. She tilted the top back enough to catch the aroma—woody, pungent, and sweet. She could almost hear the ice cubes clanking together in her glass and feel the breeze on her skin as a rush of memories flooded her mind. She had acquired the taste for whiskey over endless evenings on the back patio of her home in Bienville, when her life was mundane and predictable, when she took for granted that her husband would always return.

She didn't need to turn around to know that her father was standing at the doorway of the study. It was, after all, *his* study, and she'd been expecting him. Perhaps even waiting for him. She'd spent so little time in that room as a child, never expressly forbidden from entering but certainly not invited in. With its dark paneled walls and deep-cushioned leather sofas, it was the least familiar room in the house to her. It smelled of her father—woody, pungent, and sweet.

"The smell of whiskey always reminded me of you," she said, not bothering to turn around, placing the decanter back on the mirrored tray beside the tumblers. "I didn't realize it was whiskey until I was older, of course."

When she faced her father, she was both surprised and comforted by his smile. She could see the man who would one day replace him beneath the facade of the man who stood before her. "I suppose that's why I took a liking to it."

"I don't know whether to be proud or worried about a comment like that from my teenage daughter." He stepped up next to her and glanced down at the decanter. "I guess I should have known better than to leave alcohol so easily available around the house."

Their eyes met over the crystal bottle before Maria placed a gentle hand on her father's back. "I never broke into your liquor cabinet, Dad. I was never that kind of teenager."

Her father nodded absently beside her, his features more pained than she felt able to bear witness to. She carried misery with her everywhere she went these days, doling it out to everyone she loved, bit by bit breaking down those whose resilience had once stood unfaltering. She'd never really known her father in her youth. He wasn't the sort of man who doted on babies, and his discomfort with children was more evident to her when he became a grandfather. The scarcity of pictures she had of him with her daughters was not because he didn't love them. He just didn't know what to do with them. Tom Bethe was an academic man. A professor of literature at a local liberal arts college who could spend hours dissecting the literary conventions of various poets and playwrights and novelists, all the while sipping on whiskey. She imagined he'd have partaken in pipe smoking, too, if her mother had allowed it. He was an interesting man, just not to a child, which was why Maria didn't really get to know him until she was an adult.

"I need your help with something, Dad." She sank down into the plushness of the leather sofa nearest the door while she watched her father pour a skosh of whiskey into one of his tumblers. He eased onto the sofa across from her, crossed his legs, and rested his glass on the armrest beside him. It was a well-rehearsed position for him, and Maria was comforted by the familiarity of it. "I have a decision to make. An impossible decision, really, and I don't know what to do."

"There are no impossible decisions, Maria. Difficult ones, yes. And perhaps even agonizing ones, but none that are impossible."

When he sipped the whiskey, she could almost feel it sliding down her throat, the warmth spreading through her chest before landing in her belly.

"This would definitely be categorized as agonizing then."

Her father simply nodded, expecting her to continue. But how could she continue? How could she explain the unexplainable and then ask him to help her make a choice between life and death when one of the deaths could be her own?

"I can't tell you the specifics," she continued. "You wouldn't believe me, anyway."

He didn't respond immediately. He waited to see whether Maria might continue. When she didn't, he turned his attention to the tumbler in his hand, which he twirled softly against the worn armrest of the leather sofa. She could almost believe he was listening to it, the way his concentration didn't falter as he watched the remnants of his drink finally still at the bottom of the glass.

"Well then," he said, startling her with the suddenness of his words. "The first thing I do when I have an important decision to make is to list my options. And remember, of course, that not doing anything is also an option. It must constitute one of your potential choices."

Maria nodded, acutely aware of the choices that were looming in front of her as they spun through her mind, but not so confident that she could peel them apart, layer by layer, and present them in a tidy list. "It's complicated," she said, drawing in a deep breath before exhaling and holding up one finger. "But I'll try."

One: let Beth die and go back to her family through Dr. Johnstone's hypnosis. She held up another finger. Two: let Beth die and try to relive her previous life. Three: save Beth and try to relive her previous life. Four: save Beth and lose her family.

By the time she'd weeded out her options, she sat with four fingers raised but was no closer to a decision. When her father asked her if she was done, she simply nodded.

"Now," he said. "Would you consider any of your choices less moral than the others?" She nodded as she thought about the choices that involved letting a little girl die, and left two of her fingers up. "Then take those two off your list."

"I can't do that. It's complicated."

"Of course it's complicated. What you're going through is a moral dilemma of sorts, but you *can* take those two options off your list, and you *should*, since you'll have to live with the consequences of whatever decision you make."

"But what if it makes no difference? I could argue that, on some level, all of these choices are immoral. And what if these choices aren't really even mine? What if everything's already predestined to happen the way it's going to happen? In fact, one of those immoral choices that I could pick is to do nothing. And if I do nothing, aren't I just leaving everything up to fate? To God's will?"

"God is a cop out, Maria."

He gulped down the remainder of the whiskey in the tumbler before he stood up for a refill, hesitating at the bar as if he wanted to offer her a drink. She waited for him to get repositioned on the couch before proceeding, noticing that his glass was filled a bit higher this time. They'd had this conversation before, but her father didn't know that and was therefore ill-prepared for her next words.

"*It matters not how strait the gate, how charged with punishments the scroll, I am the master of my fate, I am the captain of my soul.*"

Tom Bethe watched his daughter as she recited the last stanza to one of his favorite poems, and Maria couldn't help but feel a tinge of guilt for the deception. She already knew why he had left the church all those years ago. He'd already explained to her his struggles with the idea of a predestined life, the idea that God would ask us to seek Him out in prayer for wisdom when He already knew the choices we would make; that if we prayed hard enough, and begged for forgiveness, our depravities would go unpunished; that the consequences of our choices didn't fall upon our own shoulders because the outcome was always God's will.

"I didn't know you were familiar with Henley," he said, coughing into his fist when his voice got caught in his throat. "'Invictus' is one of my favorite poems."

"I know. You told me once."

He took a large gulp of whiskey before he uncrossed his legs and leaned back into the sofa. His face was flushed. "I don't remember that," he mumbled.

"It was a while ago."

She could see so clearly the two of them sitting on the deck of his condo in Clearwater Beach, sharing drinks and stories long into the night, toasting the memory of the wife and mother they both dearly missed. He'd retired to Florida when he became a widower. He couldn't handle the memories. Or maybe it was the ghosts. Maria had shown up with a bottle of Talisker single malt scotch and two Cuban cigars that had been gifted to her by one of her patients, and when he'd had enough scotch in him to loosen up his tongue, he held out the cigar admiringly and admitted he'd once been audience to a Che Guevara rally. Apparently, he'd been trying to impress a girl but had made an early exit when he realized half the men there were trying to impress that same girl.

She missed that man. She'd never been his equal when it came to knowledge about philosophy or religion or politics, but she missed those frustrating and provoking conversations out on his deck, just like she missed her all-night conversations with Will. Those obstinate traits that ran through her father's blood were the same ones that had endeared her to her husband. In many ways, they had been polar opposites. Will was social, charismatic, and spiritual. Her father, reclusive, rigid, and devoutly atheistic. But just like her father, Will was stubborn and defensive in his beliefs. Unlike most of the men she'd dated, he never surrendered his morals to impress her. While other men coddled her and tried to impress her with compliments and roses, Will challenged her. It made him interesting.

"You look so much like your mother right now." Maria looked up to see her father watching her, studying her face. "I met her when she was just a few years older than you are now," he said, sighing into his drink before tilting it back and finishing it off. "That was a long time ago."

"Would you do it all over?" Under the glow of lamplight, she watched him contemplate the question. She wasn't sure she wanted to know the truth, but she knew that Tom Bethe would give it to her. "If you had a choice, would you choose this life again?"

"Absolutely."

"What if it meant doing something horrible? Something you never imagined you could do?"

"Under the right circumstances, Maria, we are all capable of committing atrocities. Some of us just refuse to admit it."

Until that moment, she hadn't realized that it wasn't her father's advice she was seeking. She wasn't looking for his permission, wasn't even open to his suggestions. She'd already made up her mind. She just needed to hear that she wasn't a monster.

CHAPTER THIRTY-TWO

W ILL I DIE?"
Dr. Johnstone watched her from the other side of
the desk and offered no response. The diplomas and awards that
hung on the wall behind him had Dr. Anderson's name on them,
but if not for that, it could have been any psychiatrist's office.
Her mother had reluctantly allowed her to meet with him again,
and Maria had been able, with a last-minute phone call, to stop
him from returning to Iowa. He looked like a different man. His
face was clean-shaven, his shirt wrinkle-free, and his hair freshly
trimmed. She almost didn't recognize him.

"Will I die?" she asked again. "When you send me back home
with the hypnosis, will my parents have to bury me?"

"Yes," he finally replied. "They will."

"And what will you tell people about the dead girl on the
couch? How will you defend yourself after two hypnosis deaths?"

"The coroner will do an autopsy and find a bleed in your brain.
And then I'll write a research paper on it. How schizophrenics
with prospective hallucinations have a propensity for brain aneu-
rysms."

"Is that what happened to the other person you sent home? A
brain aneurysm?" He nodded in response. "And you think that
will happen to me, too?"

"I think so."

It seemed like such an important question, something they would have discussed before now. Leaving loved ones to deal with the aftermath certainly raised the stakes, but she couldn't fault Dr. Johnstone for it entirely. There must have been some part of her that already knew the answer.

"Why didn't you tell me?" she asked.

"I just assumed you'd figured it out. I thought you knew that your death here would be your ticket home."

"So I could die in a car crash and I'd go back home?"

"Or a suicide," he replied, nodding toward her wrist. "But why would you want to do that when I can send you home so peacefully?"

Death didn't scare her anymore. It was strange, walking through life without the fear of death, perhaps even welcoming it. It didn't matter to her how she died, whether it was painful or peaceful or violent. Leaving behind her parents was what haunted her now. If she had to lose her own daughter, how would she want her to go? A car accident? Suicide? Hypnosis?

"What about the other repeaters?" she said. "The ones who died before they came back? Did you ever try to send them back with hypnosis?"

"Unfortunately, it doesn't work that way. Not yet, anyway. But I'm working on it. And not all of us are meant to go home. Think about some of the repeaters throughout history who have gone on to accomplish extraordinary feats with the gifts they were given. Mozart, Picasso, Bobby Fischer."

"Then what makes me so special?" she said. "Why are you so interested in sending me back, if I'll just die here and you'll never see me again?"

"Because I *will* see you again. You'll find me when you go back and convince whatever version of me exists that you were here and that I was the one to send you back. And we'll start to build a network. People from different lives, all working toward the same goals."

"How do you know I'll do that?"

"Of course you will, Maria. Think about the implications of this. Imagine being able to send people back and forth to different lives they've already lived, with all the knowledge they've learned along the way. Look at Bobby Fischer. We call him a child prodigy because by fourteen years of age he became the youngest U.S. chess champion, and by fifteen years of age was the youngest *international* grandmaster in history. But what if he came back with that knowledge? What if seventy years of chess experience and world-class competition followed him back from death and took root in a ten-year-old kid from a broken home in Chicago, who then went on to become a legend?" The flurry of Dr. Johnstone's excitement was ricocheting off the walls of the office, bringing life to the stale air around them. "And Mozart," he continued. "He started composing music when he was five and wrote his first symphony when he was just eight years old. Can you imagine?"

"But what makes you so sure they were repeaters? They could have just been really talented kids."

"That's an excellent point, Maria. And you're right. I can't be sure they were repeaters, since they both had formal training before they became masters at such young ages. But think about the savants. The people with absolutely no training who wake up one morning able to speak a new language, or crack cyber codes, or solve complex algebraic equations. The arts are one thing. Chess and music are beautiful pursuits, of course. But think about all the other ways this could be used."

George was right. She was a scientist. She was fascinated by the implications of time travel, but she was equally leery of it. She'd seen firsthand the cost of it and wouldn't wish it on anyone. There was a method to the universe. There were rules. And even though Maria was trying to skirt them, she knew there would be consequences. Dr. Johnstone wasn't just skirting the rules, though. He was trying to rewrite the rule book.

"You can't play God," she said. "That's not how this works."

"Sometimes that *is* how it works. You should know that better than anyone, Maria." The air stilled as time seemed to pause between them, two doctors arguing about the line between God and science. It was a line that had never before existed for her. There was never a God, or an alternate universe, or a realm of existence that defied knowledge. There was just science. Facts that could be proven and disproven by experimentation. Theories that existed because of research that could be replicated. Illnesses that could be cured with laboratory-produced medicines. "You called me today to ask me to play God," he said. "Didn't you?"

"I'm not asking you to play God. I'm asking you to send me back to my family because I'm not dead. It's different."

"But didn't God send you here for a purpose? Aren't we playing God by sending you back?"

"I don't even believe in God," she said, flustered by his questions and frustrated with herself for not having the right answers. She was once the kind of person who had an answer for everything, but lately she'd been finding herself confused and inarticulate. It was so foreign to her. "I don't know how I got here."

"*Something* sent you here," Dr. Johnstone replied. "God, Jehovah, Yahweh, Allah, the universe, the wind. Call it whatever you want, but there's a reason you're here, and by asking me to send you back, you're just as complicit as I am."

"Maybe I am," she sighed. "But I'm just one insignificant person trying to go back to her family. What you're talking about doing is entirely different. It's the kind of stuff that starts wars."

"It's also the kind of stuff that *prevents* wars," he said. "It's all in the way you choose to see it."

She supposed he was right. Who was she to point out the dangers implicit in taking advantage of a loophole the universe had missed, when she was first in line to use it? And who would she be when she got home? How would this place have changed her? She wanted to believe she'd be a better wife and mother, the kind who spent lunch hours with her husband and cooked healthy breakfasts for her children. A better doctor to her patients. The kind who listened to their stories and didn't throw diagnoses and labels and drugs at them. But, underneath it all, who would she really be? A wife whose guilt would never allow her to share the awful secret of this journey with her husband. A mother whose anguish would never allow her to look at her own children without seeing the bruises on the little girl she had helped to bury.

"I have a few good-bye letters to write before I can go," Maria said, before standing and making her way toward the door. Her parents deserved something from her, some kind of explanation or apology, but she doubted there were any words in the English language that could come close to doing the job she needed them to do. And George deserved something, too, some kind of excuse for her weakness and gratitude for his strength. He'd be disappointed in her; they'd all be. "I'll be ready tomorrow, if that works for you," she said, and Dr. Johnstone leaned back into the chair and nodded in her direction.

"Tomorrow it is," he said, his lips hinting at a smile. He'd gotten what he wanted, he and Maria both, and while she was confident that shame would accompany her throughout her life for the decision she was making, she was also confident that returning to her family would make it all worth it.

CHAPTER THIRTY-THREE

I KNEW YOU WOULDN'T LISTEN TO me."

The air was cool, but the bite that had cut through her skin the last time she found herself on the back patio of her home in Mississippi with a scotch glass in her hand was noticeably absent. Her husband's voice, as clear as the features on his face, reached her with ease, but Maria could only watch in stunned silence, almost too afraid to breathe. She was home. Will was sitting by her side. Her children were upstairs in their bedrooms. But hope was a thief, and Maria knew how it preyed on its victims with visions of what could be, before ripping it all away.

"You're not real, are you?" she said, pulling herself to the edge of the chair before glancing down at the ice cubes that clinked against the sides of the glass in her hand. She placed the drink on the table between them and wiped the moisture from her fingers. "And that's not really scotch in there, is it?"

"It's whatever you want it to be." Will's crooked smile was almost enough to break her, and the laughter that played through his words hinted at something mischievous. Did he know that she was coming home? Was he waiting for her?

"Will you disappear if I touch you?" Maria leaned in closer to him, cautious of her actions, certain that one wrong move would rip her away from him again.

"I guess you'll just have to find out."

She closed her eyes before she stretched her head toward him. "I'm so sorry I didn't listen to you," she said, breathing out the words and reaching for the feel of his cheek with her lips.

A faint knocking swept through the air around them and severed the connection that was holding them together. Maria never got to feel the warmth of her husband's skin. Instead, when she opened her eyes, they landed on the sliding glass door separating them from the inside of the house.

"Listen to me now, Maria." Will pulled himself forward to the edge of the chair.

"What is that noise?" The knocking continued, growing louder by the moment, until even Will looked back at the glass door.

"Please, Maria. You have to listen to me."

"Who's banging on the glass?" When Maria stood, the maternity dress she wore fell past her knees, and the belly that had once filled it was gone. "What happened to the baby?" she asked, pulling at the baggy dress. "Did I lose him? What happened at the storage unit?"

"We'll have plenty of time to talk about that later." The knocking intensified as Will gestured for her to sit back down. "You have to go now, but there's something I need you to do for me before you come back to us."

"Of course," Maria replied. "Anything."

"I need you to find me in Ohio. There's something you need to see." The urgency in Will's voice was so uncharacteristic of him that it gave Maria pause.

I can't.

Those were the words she wanted to say, but how could she say no to her husband? After everything she'd put him through, how could she deny him this? She didn't want to go to Ohio. She couldn't risk the chance that she might see his little sister and be faced with the brutal truth of what her choice would cost. Did he know Beth was still alive? Did he know that Maria was choosing their family over her?

"Why can't you show me now?" she asked. "Or when I get home?"

"I can't, Maria. I'm so sorry. I know how hard it will be, but I need you to be the strong one."

"But how will I find you," she asked, almost unable to hear her voice over the sound of the banging. "And will you even know who I am?" Maria pulled herself from the chair again and walked to the back door, peering into the darkness. The knocking was relentless, and the more she tried to block it out, the louder it became. "What is that noise?"

Will was gone when she turned back to him, his chair abandoned, as if he'd never even been there. But the banging wouldn't cease.

It didn't stop even after it pulled her from sleep, away from her home and her husband and everything she wanted to go back to. It was just past midnight, and when Maria dragged herself from under the pink comforter and peered out the window, the eyes that penetrated the darkness, watching her from the depths of night, were instantly familiar. She slid the window open to a chilled breeze.

"What are you doing here, Henry?"

"I need to talk to you." His hands gripped the ledge of the windowsill as if he intended to pull himself inside. Maria's eyes worked their way from his hands to the muscles that twitched beneath his T-shirt, and she blushed when he caught her studying the details of his body.

"At midnight?" She stood with her arms crossed, ashamed that she could notice another man just moments after leaving her husband. Henry had a pull on her that she couldn't deny. Maybe it was the trauma that had bonded them, the agonizing sacrifices they'd been asked to make, the unbearable circumstances they'd shared.

"I know," he said. "I'm sorry. But I can explain it to you, if we could talk for a minute."

Before long, Maria found herself in the passenger seat of

Henry's pickup truck, sitting in the gravel lot beside the park with the sludge-filled pond. When he cut the engine, an intrusive silence enveloped them, made more obvious by the blackness of the night. Maria stared into it, listening to the frogs calling to each other and feeling Henry's eyes upon her, curious as to what he saw. Was she beautiful to him? Was she broken? Was she hopeless? It shouldn't have mattered, but for some reason it did, and when he reached his hand over the center console and laid it on her arm, the intimacy of it urged her to pull away. It was the warmth of his skin that stopped her, though. Or maybe it was the sorrow in his eyes. They were so honest. They were beautiful and penetrating but sad, and when he turned his body to face her and pressed his hand gently into her arm, she could almost feel his loss.

"My husband visited me tonight," Maria finally said. "In a dream."

"Was it a good visit?"

"I guess." Maria shrugged, her gaze stuck on the insects buzzing around the light of the lamppost, as if they couldn't see what happened to their friends who ventured too close. "But he asked me to do something that I don't think I can do."

Henry didn't press her for details. He didn't ask her to elaborate or explain what she meant. He knew she would continue when she was ready. He was living his own nightmare and facing his own ghosts, and he understood the worth of patience.

"He wants me to find him here in this life. He says he has something to show me."

"Did he say what it was?"

"No," she replied. "But I'm afraid to find him, because I might end up seeing his sister."

"The one you're supposed to save?"

Maria nodded. She didn't want to elaborate. She didn't want to explain to Henry how she'd lied to her husband when he'd asked her to stay away from the storage unit, and how she was already considering lying to him again.

"She only has a couple of days to live," she said. "And I'm going home tomorrow."

"You can't, Maria." She'd forgotten Henry's hand was still draped across her arm, until his fingers gently brushed across her skin. "You're not supposed to go home."

"Why not?"

"I know who you are," he continued. "I figured it out yesterday when we were at the park and you told me about your family in Bienville, and your job as a psychiatrist, and your son who hadn't been born . . ." He paused, and she could see that he was struggling to continue, that he wasn't sure how to force the next words out. "You're Maria Forssmann."

"How do you . . ." As her two worlds collided, Maria couldn't still her mind. It was spinning with people and places and names, and she couldn't remember which Maria she was supposed to be. When she finally found her voice, it sounded distant and hollow. "How do you know that name?"

"The whole country knew that name," he said. "They held all-night vigils and sent hand-drawn cards to your family and watched your story on the news, night after night. I prayed for you. And Rachel, too."

"What are you talking about?"

"You were right. You didn't die. You're stuck in a coma because Rachel shot you."

His words spiraled through the air before they hit her, the blow crushing and unyielding, and the deafening blast from the hypnosis ricocheted through her ears until she could no longer hear the words that fell from her mouth.

"No, she didn't . . . She wouldn't . . ." Her voice rose until it pierced through her own ears and she was screaming at Henry. "Why would you say something like that? You're a liar!"

"I'm not lying to you," he said. "Rachel Tillman shot you at some kind of storage unit, and then she ran."

Maria couldn't still her mind. It jumped from image to image, flashing back to the hypnosis with Dr. Johnstone. 307. Her storage unit number. The key in her hand.

"I'm so sorry." Henry reached for her, but she pushed him away, desperate to distance herself from him and frantic to escape his message.

"Don't touch me!"

She managed to get the door open just moments before she vomited on the ground below, then stumbled from the car on legs that could barely hold her. She ran, as fast and as far as those legs could take her, but Henry was close behind, and when his arms wrapped around her waist, she gave up her fight. She sank to the ground and sobbed, begging him to take it back. But Henry could no more take back her past than he could change her future, and while she had no memory of the events that he swore took place, she somehow knew they were true.

"You can't be right," she sobbed. "Rachel would never do something like that, and she didn't even have a gun. She hated guns."

I'm sorry, Maria. I thought it would end differently.

Sylvia had tried to save her, but Maria wasn't her purpose. She'd done everything she could to keep her away from Rachel and the storage unit, but nothing was going to change Maria's fate. Henry was right. She could feel it. The image was hazy, but the smells and the sounds were a part of her, so visceral and real that it was futile to deny any of it. Rachel shot her, but even as she knew that to be true, she also knew that Rachel *wouldn't* have shot her. Not Rachel.

"I have to go back," she said, pulling herself up from the ground. "I have to take care of this."

"You can't." Henry stood up beside her, shaking his head and trying to reach out for the hand she kept pulling away. "You weren't supposed to survive that, Maria. You can't go back there."

"You said you would do the same thing if you had the choice, that you'd go back to your family, too."

"I didn't know what I was saying. I didn't realize that you were supposed to die that day."

"But I didn't die," she said. "And there must be a reason for that." George was trying to force his way into her thoughts, but she was doing her best to block him out: *Some people just don't know how to let go.*

The image of the flat sheets tucked around her body from the hypnosis session and the baggy maternity dress she'd worn in the dream just moments earlier were fresh in her mind, forcing her to confront the constant fear for her unborn son that she'd carried throughout her entire pregnancy. And now this: a gunshot wound. He couldn't possibly have survived it. "My son," she whispered.

"Blaise."

The name hung in the darkness between them, and Maria was certain she'd misheard Henry, until he continued. "Blaise Forssmann."

"How could you know that name? I never told anyone."

The grief stabbed at her like a thousand pointed daggers as she thought about the journal in her nightstand drawer and the way her husband must have wept as he sat on the edge of their bed, reading through its pages of hopes and dreams and fears that she held for their children—Charlotte and Emily and Blaise. The two daughters who were already living and thriving and the son who had yet to be born. She should have been there with him. Did he have to bury their son alone?

"They saved him," Henry said, and when she reached out to

steady herself, certain she was about to hit the ground, his arms were there waiting to catch her.

"My son survived? Are you sure?"

"Yes," he said. "I'm sure. The whole country was cheering for your miracle baby."

"He's alive," she whispered, thankful that someone with the power to spare her son had been listening that day as she'd been wheeled down the hospital corridor, begging for his life. She was grateful for that mercy. Of all the people her husband had buried in his life, at least his son wouldn't be one of them.

"I have to go back," she said. "My son needs his mother."

"He'll have a mother, Maria. This time he'll be born to a family that will love him just like you do."

She could only hear George's words as Henry tried to convince her of all the things the old man couldn't: that her children would be born with or without her, that there was no ownership in the universe, that it was time for her to let them go. But he would have no better luck than George, because she didn't have the strength or the courage to close the loophole that had been left open for her.

"I can't do it," she said. "I won't let them be torn apart like that."

"There's a reason things happened the way they did, a reason Rachel shot you, and as difficult as this is to hear, it was your fate to die in that storage unit."

"That might be true," Maria said. "And there might come a time when Rachel shoots me in a life where I can't hang on, but it doesn't have to be this one."

"This isn't just about you dying there, Maria. This is about you making the decision to do what you were sent here to do. About fulfilling your purpose. If you let that little girl die, whether you return to your family or not, you'll have to live with those consequences for eternity."

"Why do you care about my eternity? What difference does it make to you if I stay or go back to my family? I'm not seventeen-year-old Maria Bethe. I'm thirty-nine-year-old Maria Forssmann. I'm a wife and a mother, and that will never change."

"I didn't just come here to tell you about Rachel." His eyes danced between shades of green as Maria watched him beneath the glow of a streetlight. A stillness settled between them, comfortable and familiar, as if they'd done this before. As if they'd once stood beneath a darkened sky, seeing each other so clearly that they could anticipate every thought and word and movement. "I remembered your story from seeing you on the news, but that's not how I really know you. You were there with me, Maria, when I came back. I know you were."

She was surprised at the comfort she took from his words, surprised that she didn't want their story to end there, and while she didn't know who she would see in eternity when she eventually came back from death, she hoped Henry would be there. She would miss him when she left. She'd miss the way he checked his wrist even though he never wore a watch, the way he scratched at his chin but couldn't grow a beard, and the way he comforted her with his touch even though his hands were rough and calloused.

"I'm sorry, Henry. But I can't choose you over my family."

"I'm not asking you to choose me. I'm asking you to do what you were sent here to do, because I care about you and I know how much you'll suffer if you don't."

She was defenseless against his words. She'd been ready to argue with him about how she couldn't abandon her family over some juvenile flirtations and butterflies, but Henry wasn't the kind of boy who would ask that of her. He may have felt the butterflies, but he wasn't an eighteen-year-old boy who was tasting love for the first time. He was a man, who understood the enormity of what he was asking, and he was a man who cared about her eternity.

"You're probably right," she said. "I probably *am* destined to suffer for the choices I'm making today. But I'm okay with that if I can get my family back, and you shouldn't feel guilty about not being able to stop me. You're a good man, Henry, and I hope you're right. I hope we do have a life together someday."

CHAPTER THIRTY-FOUR

MARIA'S FINGERS FUMBLED OVER THE COUNTERTOP in the darkness of the kitchen until she found what she was looking for. She pulled the keys from her mother's purse, along with two twenty-dollar bills and a notepad, then left a mostly rambling letter for her parents with no indication of where she was headed or when she might return. In the top right corner, she wrote the date—May 8, 1988—and laid it by the coffeemaker, in full view, before she slipped out the back door and into the night.

Red sky at night, sailor's delight; red sky in morning, sailor's warning.

The dawn light was breaking by the time Maria hit Interstate 65, and the sun was illuminating the clouds, giving the sky a red hue. She could almost hear the old adage in her mother's voice as she drove on in a thick silence under an omen-filled sky through the middle of landlocked Tennessee. She was going to see her husband. She didn't know if she'd even get out of the car, but she'd at least drive to Ohio so she could tell him she tried.

7:30 A.M.

Her parents would have read the letter by now, and they were probably out looking for her. Every car she passed worsened her anxiety as she reminded herself that her picture was not being disseminated across the internet on Facebook or Twitter. No one around her could possibly know who she was, or even that she was missing. She'd call her parents from Ohio, reschedule her appointment with

Dr. Johnstone for the following morning, and be home with her husband and children by the afternoon, on the same day her husband's sister would be murdered.

With a nearly empty fuel tank and no GPS navigation system to guide her through Louisville, she pulled off at the closest exit and into a gas station. A rack of maps sat next to the checkout counter, and after a quick scan through them she picked out one that covered Ohio and the surrounding states. She placed it on the counter with a twenty-dollar bill. "Whatever's left, just put it on pump three," she said, motioning toward her car.

"You got it." The cashier's smile faded as she glimpsed the horrendous scar snaking up the inside of Maria's arm. It was so grossly obvious, this angry line of thick pink tissue that had been carved into her flesh. She tugged her sleeve down to hide it, embarrassed and ashamed and angry.

The route to Toledo was familiar, even without the map, and Maria somehow managed to find her way to her husband's old neighborhood. Will had driven her by the abandoned trailer park many times when they were in medical school, particularly on the days when his past would come back to haunt him. He'd even taken her back to the exact spot where his trailer had once stood, or so he said. She remembered questioning him as they looked over the pile of trash and rubble before them and wondering how he could be so sure. But he insisted he was right. He said he could feel it.

They were mostly a blur now, those secondhand memories of her husband's childhood, but there was one particular autumn night that stood out from the others. A night when she waited impatiently with her arms crossed in front of her chest, shivering in the cool air, desperate for Will to finish his reminiscing so they could return to the warmth of their apartment. If only she could go back to that day and ask him what he felt as he stood there. Was

Beth with him that night, and was he comforted by her presence? Or did that place bring only sadness because of the evil that had ripped her away?

They'd never returned to Ohio after the girls were born. Will had asked many times, but Maria had always found an excuse to get out of it. She'd been so selfish. It would have meant so much to him to take his daughters to see the gravestone of his mother and sister, the grandmother and aunt they would never get to meet. She'd add it to the list of deeds she'd promise to keep when she made it back to them.

The entrance to the trailer park was different now. It greeted Maria with a scattering of sad, faded tulips, remnants of years gone by, when a manager once considered sprucing up the place. Row upon row of trailers, distinguishable only by the extent of their dilapidation, lined the litter-filled dead-end streets. Maria eased the car to a stop beside a block of mailboxes, her mind spinning through plans and strategies. Twelve hours and eight hundred miles had brought her to that moment, but there she sat, exhausted, helpless, and out of ideas. How could she find her husband if she didn't even know where to look?

3:24 P.M.

She'd been sitting by the mailboxes for over an hour when a pack of after-school kids started making its way across the parking lot. With backpacks slung over their shoulders and jackets dragging the ground, they passed by her car like a swarm of bees, far too busy to notice the strange girl with slouched shoulders sitting in the driver's seat. They were a sea of unfamiliar faces, and while she'd never even seen a photo of her husband in his youth, she knew he was not among them.

The crowd thinned to a trickle as one or two lone students crossed her path, and by the time she could see the last boy approaching, her confidence was waning. There was something familiar about that last boy, though, and while she couldn't see his face from the distance, there was no doubt in her mind it was Will. It was something about the way he walked. The way his shoulders were pulled back and his head held high, the unmistakable confidence he carried, which was reserved for so few teenagers, Maria couldn't remember any from her own childhood.

Will had once described himself as a loner in high school, but she'd never really understood the meaning of his words before that moment. He wasn't the picture of the awkward, ostracized kid his words had painted for her. He was the independent, self-assured teenager who would transition seamlessly into adulthood well before his time. Maria watched her husband in awe, grateful to have been given this gift, never before understanding the boy that had made him into the man she loved.

Her pulse quickened as he neared, her grip on the door handle slipping from the moisture of her palm as she sat in restless anticipation. He didn't notice her as he walked in front of the car. He didn't smile or wave or even nod in her direction. In one swift movement, he unlocked his mailbox, removed the contents, and turned to pass by her again, not an ounce of recognition on his face.

Maria's fingers trembled as she slid them from the handle and watched her husband walk away from the car and toward a fate that would bring him back to her. She'd come all this way to see him, but the devil on her shoulder wouldn't allow her to move. It held her to the seat, knowing her weaknesses and whispering into her ear that she didn't have to do it. She didn't have to face her husband today, because he didn't have to know whether she'd made the trip or not. All she had to do was drive away.

CHAPTER THIRTY-FIVE

W ILL."

The name passed over her lips with an aching familiarity as Maria pulled herself from the car. The boy standing before her had the same cobalt blue eyes she'd spent the past fifteen years gazing into, but when he smiled, it was the cordial smile of a stranger.

"You don't remember me, do you?" she said, but Will only laughed. It was an uncomfortable, on-the-spot laugh that she'd never been audience to, and as they watched each other through the silence, it was clear that he wasn't expecting her.

"Do we go to school together?" he said, but Maria just shook her head, unable to speak, for fear her words would reduce her to tears.

"Is there somewhere we can talk?" she finally said, and Will hesitated before pointing to a row of trailers behind them.

"I have to take the mail home and drop off my backpack, but you can come with me if you want."

Over the background noise of dribbling basketballs and screaming children, Maria walked by Will's side, the urge to take his hand and touch his skin so great that she had to force her own hands into her pockets. She'd never imagined her husband as the boy who walked beside her now. He'd never told her about the earring that was poking out from his earlobe or the mop of hair that fell to his shoulders or the gold chain that hung around his neck. They were immaterial things, but pieces of a history she'd never been a part of. Was this what he wanted her to see? This version of him?

"So how do I know you if you're not from here?" When he sneaked a sideways glance in Maria's direction, she blushed under his gaze.

"We used to go to school together."

Her words drifted away as they arrived at a weed-lined walkway that led to the front door of a run-down trailer. With tentative steps, she followed him past a lawn of thistles, where neglected and rusted-out toys from seasons past lay scattered like the bones of half-buried skeletons. They both ducked their heads beneath the shredded awning over the porch, where a pair of mismatched and corroded chairs were balanced beside each other. Maria was overwhelmed with guilt as she thought of the azaleas in her mother's garden, and of the beautiful home she'd left just that morning, and of all the luxuries she'd been afforded in life. She'd never imagined her husband had grown up in a home with so few.

"You can come in," he said, easing the front door open and casting a hesitant glance back at her before stepping through the doorway. "I don't think anyone's home."

It was a cavernous box of a house, the inside blanketed by a darkness so thick that her movements were arduous and slow. It was no place for a child.

"Shut the damn door."

The voice that rumbled from the man on the couch was coarse and gruff, and the baseball hat that covered his face was stained with sweat and dirt, but it was him. It was the stepfather she'd never met, the man who'd ruined her husband's life, the man who'd been rotting in prison for almost a decade before she and Will met. Her mind was telling her to run, compelling her to make her escape, but she couldn't seem to force her legs to move. Instead, she watched with a sick fascination as he slithered from the couch and slicked his grease-caked hair back.

"Well," he said to Maria, sliding his cap onto his head. "Who do we have here?"

His breath was rancid and stale from the combination of cheap whiskey and cigarettes, and as she waited to be rescued from the man her husband had despised his entire adult life, reality delivered a blow she was ill-prepared to handle.

"Dad, this is . . ." Will's words drifted away as he stared at Maria, not even knowing her name, ignorant of the fact that she was once his wife and the mother of his children and that they had once loved more deeply than most couples do in a lifetime.

"Maria," she whispered. "I'm Maria."

The sticky warmth of his stepfather's hand as he pressed it into hers stirred up the memories of a nightmare that was now becoming her reality, and she couldn't shake the image of the bruises that had covered Beth's pallid skin. She glanced down at his hands, the same hands that had wrapped themselves around Beth's neck as they stole her last breath.

"Maria's a friend from school," Will said.

"I see," the man replied, squeezing her hand with a wink. "She's prettier than the other one you've been bringing around."

His eyes swept over her body like a predator sizing up his prey, and through her nausea, Maria forced herself to smile. She forced herself to pretend that she didn't know what he was doing to his eight-year-old daughter behind the doors of that wretched trailer.

"It's not like that, Dad. We're just friends." Will set the mail on the kitchen counter and dropped his backpack onto the floor, motioning for Maria to join him as he headed toward the door. "I'll be back in a little bit."

The screen door slammed behind them, and the glare of the

sun burned into her eyes as they made their way across the porch. The pressure in her chest finally lifted, but nothing could quell the nausea in her gut. There was a monster in the trailer, and Maria would have to rely on him, that child molester and murderer, if she was to return to her husband and children.

"Can you wait for me here?" Will was standing at the edge of the stairs, checking his watch before glancing down the street. "I have to run to the bus stop, but I'll be back in less than five minutes."

Maria's eyes flashed to the door separating her from the man inside, but she turned back just in time to see Will bounding down the stairs, two at a time, and abandoning her beside the rusted chairs on the front porch. His stepfather's presence burned into her back like a searing flame, and she was almost too afraid to move. She stood motionless, like an awkward statue, her breaths shallow and her eyes unmoving as she struggled to blend in with the scenery around her. The psychiatrist in her yearned to know the hows and whys of that man's actions, but the mother in her was far too angry to approach him rationally.

It could have been a minute or it could have been an hour before Will finally turned the corner at the end of the street. It took her a moment to recognize the little girl from the faded snapshot, skipping toward the trailer, edging closer to her destiny. Maria had never pictured her so alive. She'd never imagined that Beth would be so real, that her hair would bounce when she ran, or that she wouldn't bother tying her shoelaces when they came undone. What would Will do if he knew the real danger his little sister was facing? Did he know that stumbling over untied shoelaces couldn't compare to the horror lurking behind their door?

The stairs creaked as Maria took them one by one, watching the pair approach hand in hand. She met them at the edge of the ragged lawn and knelt down in front of the little girl, oblivious to the gravel that was driving into her knees. The cobalt eyes that stared back at her were more vibrant and alive than she ever could have imagined, and as she wrapped her arms around the little girl's delicate shoulders, Beth leaned in with a hug that almost knocked her off balance. The scent of bubblegum shampoo wafted through the air around them as Maria pulled her close.

"Beth," she said. "It's so good to finally meet you."

The little girl smiled up at her, her laughter floating through the air around them, and hugged her back as if she'd been waiting for her to show up, as if she'd known all along that Maria would never let her down.

CHAPTER THIRTY-SIX

B ETH SPUN OUT OF CONTROL ON the old, rickety roundabout, her hair defying gravity as shrieks of joy hit them like
the wails of a siren. They'd done this before, Will and Maria—
sat on a park bench and watched a little girl lose herself in fun. It
was a beautiful and agonizing memory, and when she looked at
Will's face, she could almost believe he was sharing it with her.
He hadn't questioned her about who she was, or what she was doing there, or why she was so insistent that Beth join them. He just
seemed to be enjoying her company.

"There are so many things I'd like to talk to you about, Will."
When she looked over at him, she was thrown off by the smile on
his face. It was the same smile he'd worn over the course of their
fifteen-year marriage, likely the same one he'd be wearing twenty
years from now. "I can tell you're trying not to laugh about something," she said. "What's so funny?"

"Nothing." He shook his head and turned away, unable to
mask the crooked smile.

"Come on. I know that look. Just tell me."

"It's nothing," he laughed. "I just think it's funny that you call
me Will."

"What do you mean? That's your name."

"Nobody calls me Will. I go by William."

It was such a trivial thing, Will or William, but hearing that piece of her husband's history cut more deeply than seemed possible. What else didn't she know? What other bits of her husband's life had she been too busy to learn about him? "I thought you'd always gone by Will."

"It's okay. I kind of like it that you call me Will." He shrugged and kicked at the stones beneath his feet. "So how do you really know me? I have a feeling we never went to school together."

"Not yet." Her eyes followed Beth as the little girl ran from the roundabout to the swing set. "But I know a lot of things about you. And your sister." She hesitated before she continued. "I had a dream about her, not too long ago."

"A dream?" Will glanced at his sister, who was draped over a swing on her belly, her hair hanging between her dangling arms as she dragged her feet over the gravel. "What do you mean?"

"Do you believe that people visit us in our dreams?"

"Not really," he mumbled. "But I guess I've never really thought about it."

In all the years she had spent with her husband, she never could have imagined the words that were coming from his mouth. She couldn't have imagined there was ever a version of him that didn't believe with every fiber of his being that the people we love visit us in our dreams, and as she thought about the man he would be in twenty years or thirty years, she wondered what he would say to her. If Maria could give him the option, would he let his sister die to keep his family together? Who would he choose?

I know how hard it will be, but I need you to be the strong one.

The words hit her like a wave she hadn't been expecting, sending her tumbling through the surf, not knowing up from down and wondering if she would ever come up for breath again. Will couldn't choose. He'd sent Maria to Ohio to see the little girl whose life was in the balance, because she deserved a fair fight, too. But he couldn't be the one to choose. He would love her either way, she was sure of it, but could she ever love herself again if she let Beth die? Could she even live with herself?

Maria watched her flying through the air and waving from the swings. Beth deserved more than she'd been given in life. She deserved to be a child and to be protected. She deserved the same things that Maria wanted for her own children: safety and laughter and love. And as she thought about all the reasons she wanted to let that little girl go, she knew she could never do it. She knew she was there to save her. On some level, she must have known what she would do when she got to that point. She must have known that she would free her husband from the nightmares that haunted his sleep, that she would allow her children to grow up with a mother who wouldn't have to leave, and that she would say good-bye.

But how could she do it? There was no amount of finesse that could make it easier to bear. The words she was about to say would change Will's life forever, and once she voiced them, there was no taking them back. She fidgeted with the sleeve of her shirt, trying to pull it over her scar as she worked up the courage.

"Beth's father is doing things to her," she said, blurting out the words before she lost her courage. "Sexual things. And if you don't stop him, he's going to end up killing her. Tomorrow."

And there it was, like falling through the air, like the moment twelve-year-old Maria first jumped off Chimney Rock into the frigid lake below. One minute she'd been standing on the side of the cliff, her stomach churning as she peered over the edge and willed herself to take the plunge. And the next minute she'd been shrouded in weightlessness as time stood still, her decision behind her but the consequences still to come. There was no going back. Once you were falling through the air, it couldn't be undone.

Maria watched the boy beside her through the silence. It was one of the few times in her life when she couldn't read his emotions. His eyes were too full of sorrow for it to be anger, but his words, when they finally came out, were venomous.

"Who do you think you are? I don't even know you, and you show up at my house and accuse my dad of molesting my little sister?"

"He's not your dad," Maria said. "He's just a guy who moved in with your mom when he was down on his luck and stayed because no one else would take him. And you've hated him for it since the moment he showed up. The only good thing he ever did was bring your sister into the world, but there's a part of you that knows the truth about him and Beth. What he's been doing to her for the past year."

"That's enough." Will's hand shot up between them as he sprang from the bench, his patience pushed to the limit. "I think you should go."

"You have to listen to me," she pleaded. "I can't tell you how I know this. I'm not even sure I understand it. But I know things about you and your family that are impossible for anyone to know."

He stepped over the worn grass in front of the bench, his feet pacing restlessly as he glared back at her. She was about to lose him. She'd had fifteen years to learn every success, every failure, and every secret her husband ever had, yet there she sat, unable to remember even one, and she was about to lose him.

"Wait," she said, reaching for his arm before he could walk away. "When you were four years old you overheard your mom tell a friend that she wished she'd never had you." His feet stilled, but the suspicion in his eyes didn't fade, and as he stood above her, staring at her fingers pressing into the skin of his arm, she could see that her words were reaching him. "She said it would have made her life so much easier if she'd just had an abortion, and you could never forgive her for that." When he stepped forward, Maria released the grip on his arm and let her hand fall away. "And then, a few years later, when Beth was born and your stepdad didn't want you around anymore, she sent you to live with your grandmother. But you knew you had to get back to Beth because, in your mind, it had always been your job to protect her. You were only ten."

"How could you know that?" He eased back onto the bench beside her, cautious of her words and putting some distance between them. "Who told you this?"

"That was when you started acting up and getting into trouble," she continued. "It was so unlike you. And when your grandmother finally couldn't take it anymore, she brought you back home. Things settled into place for a while, and because you followed your stepfather's rules, he let you stay. But on the day of Beth's eighth birthday, you and your mom went out to get her a present."

"Stop." He dropped his head into his hands, his elbows resting on the tops of his legs. He didn't need to hear more, but Maria continued, determined to make him face the truth.

"When you got back from the store, you found your stepfather giving her a bath. She was crying, and when you asked her what happened she wouldn't speak. She wouldn't say a word. And even though you refused to believe it, you knew that something was horribly wrong."

"This is impossible." Will's focus drifted to his sister, who was sailing through the air on the swing, her arms stretched out to the sides and her face turned up toward the sun. Maria wondered if he was capable of doing it. Was he capable of writing a new ending? She knew the man he'd once been would have acted without hesitation, but this boy beside her with the earring in his ear and hair down his back wasn't her husband, and there was no road that would lead to the man she loved without the trauma of his childhood. The circumstances of his life would turn him into someone else this time, and there was nothing she could do to rescue him the way his uncle had, to make him the man she'd wanted to spend her life with. And why would he want to spend his life with her—a woman who was always wanting something different, something more from him, always wanting him to be someone he could never be.

"There are pictures of your sister, ones I know you won't want to see, as well as some other evidence that he's hiding in the locked cabinet in his bedroom. Call the police and tell them. He'll kill her tomorrow if you don't."

Will didn't respond, but his sorrow weighed heavily on her. She'd never seen him suffer so deeply, and though she knew he had, it was only because he'd told her. She'd never had to witness the fresh, devastating wounds of his loss, and whatever pain he was bearing in that moment, on that bench beside her, must have paled in comparison to what he went through when he lost his sister, and his mother, and his wife. She'd been so consumed with returning to her family, she hadn't considered that letting them go might be the one thing that could save them.

"How do you know?" Will asked, his voice pulling her back from the void. Fighting through his words was a resolve that she was certain would carry him and his sister to a better place. It was a place where Beth's father wouldn't strangle her just to hide the evidence, where his mother wouldn't overdose on sleeping pills and narcotics to escape the guilt, and where his uncle wouldn't be the surrogate father he needed to guide him through all of life's tragedies. It was a place that didn't include Maria.

"Another dream," she said. "Well, I guess it was more of a premonition. We were a bit older then, and we had met and fallen in love." She laughed under her breath and swallowed back her tears. "You had already lost Beth by then, in the dream, and I swore that if I could bring her back for you, I would do it."

"But you didn't even know me. How can you dream about real people you don't even know?"

"I know you, Will."

She reached out and took his hand, her heart breaking as the end loomed. His hands were so achingly familiar, so perfect for what he had once been, and as she ran her fingers over his skin, she wondered what they were destined to become now, who they were destined to hold. It was almost too painful to imagine.

"Thank you," he said. "She's the most important thing in the world to me."

"I know she is," Maria replied. "And I want to thank you, too. For so many things I can't even begin to tell you."

She could sit there forever, taking in every nuance of him, and it wouldn't be long enough: the sapphire eyes that followed her as she walked down the aisle at their wedding, the delicate fingers that caressed her skin when they made love, and the beautiful mind that challenged her to be a better person in everything she ever did. In another time and another place, she would have her husband back, this man she would love for eternity. In another life, she wouldn't have to let him go.

"Someday," she whispered, as she pulled him into a final embrace, "we'll be together again."

CHAPTER THIRTY-SEVEN

IT WAS THE SMELL OF BLOOD that Maria remembered most from that day, the coppery thickness that blended seamlessly with the acrid scent of gunpowder, grotesque and warm and soupy. There were other memories, too: Rachel's sleeveless blue shirt, the shock in her eyes, the gun in her hand. She'd heard the footsteps as they approached, the clicking of Rachel's shoes echoing off the concrete walls of the storage unit, but it was still a shock to see her standing there, gun in hand, as the weight of the laptop grew heavy in her arms. There were no greetings between them, no formalities, as Maria's eyes homed in on the metal barrel of the .22 in Rachel's hand. The seconds stretched into an uncomfortable silence before Maria spoke.

"Why do you have a gun?"

Rachel held the pistol with trembling hands that were unaccustomed to the weight and feel of a gun. Her movements were slow and cautious, like the weapon was a snake that could strike out and bite her at any moment. "I didn't know how else to get in here," she said. "I lost my key and I tried bolt cutters yesterday, but they didn't work. And I looked online and read that I could shoot off the lock."

"Why didn't you just ask me for the key?" Maria's eyes went to the gun, and as she wondered whether her secretary even knew how to use it, another contraction started to grip at her belly. "Were you really going to shoot the lock off?"

"I don't know," Rachel said, sighing and dropping her hand to her side, the gun pointing toward her feet. She looked defeated, the way Maria remembered her from her son's funeral. "I don't know what I'm doing, Maria. I just wanted to get my laptop and I didn't know what else to do."

Maria dropped her gaze to the computer in her arms, the one Sylvia had told her about, the one Detective Andrews would be looking for in a couple of days. She didn't know what she was doing with it, or what she expected to find on it. After all the warnings and questions and investigations, she couldn't understand what had compelled her to sneak out of her house on the day her son would be born to take something that didn't even belong to her.

"I'm sorry," she said. "Sylvia told me before she died that I should get this to the police. I should have just stayed out of it. I don't even know what she was talking about."

"She was talking about the letters that I wrote to Nick," Rachel said. "When I was grieving for our son and heartbroken, I told him that maybe our relationship would be better without Jonathan, maybe we could start over. But I never meant it. They were just stupid, rambling words that I typed out one night because I was lonely and heartbroken."

"What are you talking about?" Maria said.

"Sylvia thought I killed Jonathan. She left me a note before she died, too. And I don't know how she knew about those letters that I wrote to Nick, because I never even sent them, but she did. And she was convinced that it was proof I killed my son. But I could never have hurt Jonathan. You know that, don't you, Maria?"

"Of course," Maria replied. "Is that what this is all about? Letters you wrote?"

Rachel nodded, her hands fidgeting with the gun and her feet shifting restlessly on the concrete floor, a wildness dancing through her eyes.

"The detective will understand." Maria paused as a contraction brewed in her belly, her eyes still focused on the gun in Rachel's hand. "Don't worry. Nothing bad will happen to you."

"No," Rachel said, a franticness darting through her eyes. "It's not fair for people to be questioning me about my son's death. Haven't I been through enough?"

"But what do I say if he asks me about it? I don't know that I can lie to him."

"We'll just say we haven't been here. I'll get rid of the computer and it'll be the end of it. Please, Maria. Please do this for me."

Maria would never know if it was something she would have done for Rachel or not, if she would have let her friend have her peace. The pain dropped her to her knees, a relentless and excruciating contraction that gripped her belly with iron claws as the computer slipped from her fingers and crashed to the ground. "Hospital . . ." she panted. "Baby's . . . coming."

"It's okay, Maria." Rachel locked her arms under Maria's from behind and eased her to the ground. "Come on," she said. "I've got you."

It was a beautiful day. The sky was blue, the birds were singing, and it was the day her son would be born. Maria never felt the bullet that pierced her chest. It was the noise that hit her first, followed by a flash of light that faded into Rachel's horror-stricken face.

"Oh God, Maria! No!" Rachel's words tumbled through the tunnel of Maria's mind. "No! Please, Maria! It was an accident! It just went off!"

Every breath was an insurmountable effort, riddled with a burning pain where the bullet had torn through her flesh and lungs.

". . . please send an ambulance . . . I shot my friend . . . It was an accident . . . Come quickly . . ."

Rachel faded away, her face and her words and the terror that went with them, and when Maria opened her eyes again, Will had taken Rachel's place. The lights of the hospital corridor flashed behind his head as he hovered over the stretcher that whisked her through the hall.

"Please . . ." They were Maria's last words, whispered to him in the fading blackness. "Please don't let him die."

CHAPTER THIRTY-EIGHT

Six months later

SHE WAS JUST A WOMAN IN a park, it was just an ordinary winter day, and he was just a man holding his infant son on a bench beneath a shedding oak tree. There was no reason for anyone to suspect she had followed him there or that she had planned their encounter.

"He's beautiful," the woman said, sliding onto the bench beside him, peering into the bundle of blue resting in his arms. The man's wedding band glistened in the late afternoon sun.

"Thank you," he said. His child's eyes flickered beneath their lids, and his tiny hands, looking like they'd been stitched together by an expert seamstress, twitched as he chased a dream through his own little wonderland. "He's seven months old today."

The woman caressed the hidden bulge beneath her coat and laughed. "Me too."

"Congratulations." A fleeting glimpse of sorrow flashed through the man's eyes. "Your first?"

"No," the woman laughed. "But surely my last."

The man laughed too, his smile unveiling a boyish charm. "You never know," he said. "This one here was our surprise baby."

"This one too," the woman said, rubbing her belly.

They sat in a comfortable silence as leaves swirled around them and floated on the wind, landing in gentle heaps on the ground. The woman reached down and picked one up, her eyes drifting from it to the baby in the man's arms, powerless to pull her gaze from the child. The whorls of his hair wove a pattern through her memory as if she had once known him, as if her lips had once caressed the downy hair on his head and the soft lids of his eyes.

"We just never know what life has in store for us," the man said. "But things happen for a reason. Of that I'm sure."

"Are you?" The woman could see his words before her like a mirage, so full of hope in one moment, then slipping through her fingers in the next. "After everything you've been through, how can you say that?"

"After everything I've been through?" The man's gaze was steady on his son's face, no shock or scorn permeating his words. "I take it we're not meeting by chance today. Did you see me on the news?"

"Yes," the woman said. "I saw the interview you gave last week. And no, we're not meeting by chance. I followed you here."

The man's lips brushed over his son's forehead, his head nodding pensively. "I suppose it makes no difference how you found me." She could feel the moment his eyes landed on her, that steely gaze that had penetrated the television screen, into her living room, not two weeks earlier. "The fact that you're sitting here beside me means that we were meant to meet today. That we must have something to learn from each other."

She shifted her weight on the bench, craving distance from the rawness of his gaze. "But what if we don't have anything to learn from each other?" she said. "What if this meeting wasn't a part of our destinies and I just made it happen because I needed to tell you something? What if everything you said in that interview about seeing our lost loved ones again is wrong, and when we die, we just disappear? Vanish? What if you never get to see your wife again?" Her eyes jumped frantically from the man's face to his son's as she tempered her impulse to reach out for the child, to feel his weight and warmth in her arms. "What if you're wrong?"

"I take it you lost someone too," the man said.

The woman nodded, a hefty sigh escaping her lips. "Yes," she said. "I lost someone too." She didn't weigh him down with the details. She didn't need to. Her loss was written into her face as much as it had been written into her life. She was a widow, but unlike the man beside her, she had been condemned to silence when her husband left. There was no rendezvous in her dreams, no whispers through the wind, no painted skies at dawn. Did they not love each other enough? Did this man and his wife love each other more? Did they call themselves soul mates and promise to stay together in this life and forever after?

"Give him some time," the man said, his face pressed against the baby's cheeks. "And be willing to see him in the places you'd least expect."

She wanted to believe him; she yearned for his words to bear truth. But as she dropped her eyes to her belly and let the leaf slip from her fingers, she knew she had made a mistake by following him there. She was a keeper of secrets, and the one she'd come to share didn't want to be told. None of her secrets did. She'd held on to most of them for so long that time was turning them into vines that were more difficult to contain by the day, twisting and climbing and choking out everything around them. If only they'd been clipped sooner, maybe they wouldn't be devouring her.

"I wish I had your optimism," she said, rising from the bench and stealing one last glance at the baby in the man's arms before turning to leave. "I'm sorry I bothered you."

"Wait," the man said, halting the woman's footsteps. "I never got your name."

"Jenny," she replied, turning to face him. "My name is Jenny."

"Please." He nodded toward the empty spot on the bench

beside him. "Don't leave. I'm Will, and this here is Blaise." He bounced the baby in his arms and laughed. "But I guess you already knew that."

Jenny hesitated before stepping over the discarded carpet of leaves that had fallen to the ground and easing herself back down onto the bench beside them. Didn't the man beside her deserve to know about the woman who had killed his wife? She'd gone over this moment so many times in her mind, but she'd never settled on a strategy. She'd thought that, when the time came, her words would start flowing and she'd instinctively know how to steer them, but as she sat there beside him, she could think of nothing but the bare and brutal truth.

I helped the woman who killed your wife escape.

Her exhaustion from countless sleepless nights was wearing on her, and the decision to confess felt suddenly reckless and irresponsible. What if he went to the police? What if she was arrested and her child was taken from her? But consequences were a part of life, a part of every choice and action and reaction, and the consequence of not telling this man about the woman who killed his wife would be her own undoing. She would carry it as a burden until it became too heavy to ignore, and then she would balance the enormity of it on her shoulders until it was all she could feel, and finally she would succumb to the massive weight of it until it crushed her.

"Rachel is still alive."

The man on the bench beside her didn't move at her words. He didn't yell or gasp or even flinch. He gave himself a minute to hear Jenny's message and then took in a deep breath that he exhaled into the air around them. He kissed the top of his son's head before he breathed out his next words.

"How do you know Rachel?"

"The father of her son, the little boy who died last year, is my cousin." Jenny couldn't pull her eyes up to meet his gaze, her focus landing instead on the pile of leaves at her feet. "She came to me for help after she shot your wife. She was devastated. She wanted me to tell you that it was an accident. Maria had a contraction, and she was trying to help her onto the floor when the gun went off, and . . ."

Jenny didn't continue with the details. She couldn't bring herself to voice them out loud, the intimate details about the last minutes of Maria's life. His wife didn't die that day, but the life that she and her family knew ended in that moment.

"Rachel's death was staged," Jenny continued. "But she won't be coming back."

"Where is she?"

"I don't know." Jenny could feel the heat from Will's stare burning into the side of her face, but she couldn't force herself to look at him. She sat under his gaze like a cowering and guilty dog waiting for its owner to release it from shame, waiting for forgiveness. "I swear to God I don't know where she is. But I don't think you'll find her if you go looking."

Jenny couldn't breathe. She couldn't focus on the leaves that were dancing at her feet or the wind that was biting at her skin. Her life was dependent on the man beside her, like he was an antidote. She'd already swallowed the poison, and only he could save her. But would he do it? And did she even deserve to be saved? She'd do it all again if she had to. Rachel's crime was desperation, and she didn't deserve to rot in prison for that.

"It's better for all of us if Rachel stays dead," Will finally said, and Jenny could feel the moment his words reached her, like the chains had been severed. The air rushed back into her lungs and her blurred senses started to sharpen. Life would go on.

"I'm grateful that you're the kind of man who understands forgiveness," she said. "I'm not sure I could do the same thing if I was in your situation."

"I don't forgive Rachel," he replied. "But Maria would have, and she would want me to do the same."

"I still don't know if I could do it. Sometimes I can't even get myself out of bed in the morning." When she finally forced herself to look up at the man beside her, Jenny could see why his wife had fallen in love with him. She could see how Maria had chosen to spend her life with him, this man who was willing to let love rule over anger and desperation and spite. "How do you do it every day?" she asked. "How do you wake up and get your children fed and dressed and get yourself through work?"

"Again," he said, "I do it because my wife would have wanted me to."

"Do you really see her in your dreams? Because I don't see my husband anywhere. I want to, but he never shows up. Do you think it's because we didn't love each other enough?"

"The fact that you're sad about not seeing your husband in your dreams leads me to believe that you loved each other plenty," he said. "And, yes. I really do see my wife in my dreams."

"I thought maybe you were just saying those things for your kids." Her eyes landed on the baby in his arms. He had woken from his nap and was gazing up at her with the indigo eyes of his father, stirring an instinct inside of her to pull him into her chest and wrap him in her own cloak of protection. She'd never felt that yearning for any child but her own.

"Maybe you're just not listening."

"Maybe," Jenny muttered, hesitant to pull her eyes from the baby. "Or maybe I'm just too angry to hear him."

She was surprised when the words left her mouth. Until that moment, she hadn't realized how much anger she was harboring. She was angry that she was being left behind, angry that she would have to pick up all the pieces of their life, and angry that she would have to forge ahead on her own.

"Maybe that anger you're feeling is really just grief," Will said. "I felt the same way when Maria left, but now I choose to see what I've been given as a gift. To be able to see my children grow. To hold my newborn baby. How can I scorn my wife for leaving me behind, when I've been given these beautiful moments that were ripped away from her?" The wind whistled through the branches above their heads, sending a shower of leaves over them. A lone, flawless oak leaf landed on the baby's chest. "Maria would never have chosen to leave," he continued, as he watched Jenny pick up the leaf from his son's chest and hold it between her fingers, turning it over in her hand, wondering at the randomness of it all.

Maybe he was right. She missed her husband. In the beginning, she thought it was just the loneliness of an empty house that made her long for him, but as time went on and the intimate details of their life started surfacing at random moments, she knew it was *him* that she missed—the scent of his cologne, the rumble of his laughter, the flash of his smile. They never lingered. They were just flickers of memories, reminders that he wasn't coming back, reminders that she was on her own this time. No one was coming to save her, and whatever dreams she had for an education or a career or a new start would again have to wait, because life had a way of rearranging priorities and motherhood would always come first.

If he hadn't died on that oil rig, Hank would have come home. Despite the lies and deceptions, she was certain he would have returned. They would have celebrated the birth of their new child and started over with diapers and day care and school bus schedules. They would have grown old together, sitting on the porch swing and watching the bayou, enduring the years that chipped away at their youth. They would have taken care of each other, and the regret that Jenny felt over the failures in her life, the undone tasks, would finally die with her in the bayou, even if it was some other woman's home.

"Hank wouldn't have chosen to leave, either," she whispered, before pulling herself from the bench and tugging her sweater over her belly. "Thank you." She tucked the leaf into her pocket and captured in her mind the image of the man with the sapphire eyes, holding the baby who would stay in her memory forever. "I'll listen more closely," she said. "Maybe he's been here all along."

maria

"Y OU'RE A HARD MAN TO FIND."

Maria's words knocked the fishing pole from Henry's hands. It fell to the pier at his feet and almost bounced into the murky water below.

"You're here," he said, cautious steps carrying him toward her, like she might vanish if his movements were too sudden. Maria watched him from the grass as the leaves of impossibly thick oak trees rustled above her head in the wind.

"I'm here," she said. Spanish moss draped from arching limbs in sheets of soft white, framing her into the scenery. If she'd dressed the part, she might have believed she'd just breezed into an antebellum fairy tale. "I didn't know a swamp could be so beautiful."

"We'll lose this tree in Hurricane Katrina." Henry's eyes followed her gaze up the trunk of the massive oak beside her. "And it's a bayou," he said with a wink, "not a swamp."

Maria shrugged her shoulders and smiled, watching Henry as he crossed the pier and stepped onto the grass.

"I was hoping you'd show up one day," he continued, joining Maria beneath the canopy of leaves. "How'd you find me?"

"Google," she joked.

Henry laughed, the green of his eyes almost translucent against the glare of the sun. She hadn't seen him since the spring, not since she'd said good-bye to her husband, but as the winter chill swirled around them, a spark of hope pricked at her skin. The wind whispered through the trees that dotted the bayou beyond the pier, and the waters, dark and mysterious, seemed to call to her as her feet padded over the uneven wooden planks.

"I know this place," she whispered, her memory coming through in flashes she couldn't quite grasp, as her words floated away with the wind through the leaves. "I've been here before. I can feel it."

Henry stood beside her, his expression a mixture of delight and wonder as his T-shirt fluttered in the breeze, hinting at the hardened muscles beneath it.

"Maybe you're the woman in the bayou," he said, edging closer to her. The slight tilt of his head softened the lines of his jaw as he studied her face. There was a secret dancing through his eyes.

"The what?"

"I've heard stories about you," he said.

"What are you talking about?"

"Once upon a time, Maria, this was your home." She reached out to steady herself, suddenly dizzy as she stared down at the four-foot drop off the edge of the pier and wondered what was lurking in the depths of darkness below. Henry wrapped his arm around her waist, pressing his fingers into the small of her back as she gripped his shoulder.

"Come here," he said, taking her other hand in his and guiding her like a ballroom dancer to the other side of the pier. "This is the best seat in the house."

He eased her down onto the planks, where they sat side by side, their feet dangling over the water. Maria blushed when she felt his eyes on her.

"I've missed you," he said. "I've been wanting to call or visit and find out how everything went in Ohio, but I also wanted to give you some time."

"It was awful," she said. "It was devastating and heartbreaking. But probably the most beautiful thing I've ever done."

"I'm proud of you. I know how hard that was."

"I know you do," she said, and though she knew he'd suffered as much as anyone, she couldn't talk about her family with him, because every time she thought about Will and her daughters and everything she'd lost, it was a battle just to keep going. There were times she had to remind herself to breathe and force herself to eat, not because she wanted to but because there were people around her begging her not to leave.

The fishing pole that Henry had dropped when she arrived lay beside her, and if the sun's glare hadn't glinted on the metal plate fastened to its handle, Maria might have missed it. "Who's Hank Fontaine?" she said, reading the words etched into the metal.

"You're looking at him," he laughed, holding his arms out wide and winking back at her. "Henry James Fontaine the third. Otherwise known as Hank."

She leaned back and eyed him from head to toe, trying the word out in her mind. "You are *so* not a Hank."

"I so *am* a Hank," he said. "You're the only person who calls me Henry."

"But I don't think I could ever call you Hank."

"It's okay. I kind of like it that you call me Henry."

Those words, so familiar and painful, belonged to her husband. But this man was not Will. His smile was different; his hands were different; his mind was different. Everything about him was different, and as she watched him watching her, she knew there would never come a time when she wouldn't compare him with her husband. It wasn't fair. Every moment of her life would be spent trying to create new memories that could never compete with the ones she couldn't leave behind.

"I can't stop thinking about them," she said.

"It'll get better. I promise. Time will heal this."

"Will it?"

"There will come a day when you'll think about your family, Maria, and you'll actually smile, because it won't be the loss that you remember but the love. And you'll tell me all about them. How you met your husband, how you fell in love, and how it felt to hold your children for the first time. I want to hear all of that."

"I don't want to think about them," she said. But everywhere she turned, they were there. Her daughters' laughter. Her husband's voice. It was constant and agonizing. Sometimes she would swear she could feel his hand on her back or his fingers in her hair, but when she turned around, he was never there. She couldn't escape it. Every night they were waiting for her in her dreams.

"You don't have to keep running from them. You can live this life without them and still let their memories be a part of it." Henry nodded to the water below their feet. "I can't tell you how many hours I spent fishing out here with my son. When I came back last spring, I thought this spot would be too painful to visit, but it turns out I hardly ever leave it, because he's almost always here with me. Sometimes I swear I can hear his voice when the wind blows just right through the trees."

"I'm glad that you have this," Maria said, acutely aware that there was no going home for her, no seeing her children in flashes running through their home or hearing her husband's voice floating in from the screened door of the back porch. "This was the house your father left you?"

"My grandfather and his brothers built it over fifty years ago." Henry kicked at the air beneath their feet. "Needs a little fixing up."

"Is that your plan for the spring? A fixer-upper?"

"No." He laughed as he glanced down at his hands and stilled his feet. "I'm going to college."

"Is that right?"

"I never thought of college as being practical for someone like me," he said. "But I think I understand it now. How an education can free up your life. Give you more options. I may not be able to get into one of those fancy schools that *you'll* go to, but I can hit a community college nearby."

"That's great, Henry."

"Well, you don't seem like the kind of girl who'd marry an un-educated man."

Maria turned her face away from him as she laughed, trying to hide the blush that was sneaking into her cheeks. "We're talking marriage already? You don't think we're moving a little fast? I never pictured myself being a teenage bride."

"I guess we can wait until you're twenty. But we can't move in together until we're married."

"Really?" She laughed.

"I'm an old-fashioned kind of guy, Maria. In fact, you don't have to work at all, if you don't want to. I mean, I don't get the feeling you'd be happy without a career, but . . ."

As he struggled to find the right words, Maria reached out for his hand and slipped her fingers between his. She'd never dated a man like Henry. She'd known men like him, of course, but she'd always considered them a threat to her independence, an obstacle to her becoming the woman she'd always envisioned herself to be.

"I just want you to know that I'll always take care of you, Maria."

She could feel the weight of his stare following the scar that wound its way out from beneath her shirt, and before she could pull her sleeve down to cover it, he eased it up and ran his fingers over the thick and angry skin. His touch was tender, and her skin tingled beneath it.

"You don't ever have to hide this from me." The green of his eyes was like a beacon, a lighthouse illuminating her way home. "This is what made you who you are, and it will always remind me of your strength and the sacrifices you made." His fingers followed the path of her arm, over her shoulder and around her jaw, before he brushed them across her cheek. "You're beautiful, Maria."

"Beauty fades, though, doesn't it?"

"Not your kind of beauty," he said, and though she ached to feel the warmth of his breath on her face and the heat of his skin against her own, when he pressed his lips into hers, she pushed him away.

"I can't." She pulled herself to her feet, her eyes clenched, her husband and children refusing to abandon her thoughts. "I can't get them out of my head."

"I understand," he said, standing before her, patient and composed. "And I'll wait as long as it takes, because you belong here, Maria."

She closed her eyes and tilted her head back to let the sun splash over her face, the music of the bayou blending together in a beautiful chorus that washed through her. "But I didn't even know your name. How could I be your wife?"

"This is your home," he replied, and as Maria gazed out over the bayou, she wondered if he was right. It was certainly a place she could love, an ageless place where life meandered in stride with nature and time was of no concern. Sunlight sprinkled over his body as it filtered through the leaves, washing over his skin like a light rain. "And names aren't important, Maria. It's about our spirits, and yours has always been a part of this bayou."

She didn't flinch when he reached his hand toward her face and gently ran his fingers over the side of her cheek. She leaned her head into the palm of his hand, embracing the warmth of his skin upon hers and learning the intricacies of his touch. It was nothing like her husband's touch, nothing like the hands that had once held her, but there was a gentleness to them, despite the calluses and the graceless fingers. They were hands that had experienced life, had cradled a baby and caressed a woman, and as his fingers swept over Maria's skin, gently traveling down the front of her neck, she knew that she would also become a part of their story.

epilogue

Please join us as we celebrate the life of Dr. Maria (Bethe) Fontaine, of Calebasse, Louisiana, formerly of Pine Creek, Alabama, who passed away on April 19, 2066, at the age of 95, surrounded by her loving family. She is preceded in death by her faithful husband, Dr. Henry James Fontaine III, and is survived by her two daughters, Elizabeth (Fontaine) Collins and Georgia (Fontaine) Bruce, her sons-in-law, Anthony Collins and Samuel Bruce, her 5 grandchildren, and her 13 great-grandchildren. Dr. Fontaine and her husband founded the Fontaine Institute, a research and treatment center credited with advancing the diagnostic capabilities and scope of treatment for people with schizophrenia. She will be greatly missed by her family, friends, and community.

ELIZABETH READ OVER THE NOTICE THAT she had cut from the newspaper two days earlier and sipped on a steaming mug of coffee. She was running late, as usual, but she couldn't resist another flip through the keepsake trunk with her mother's possessions. A faded snapshot of two young women was tucked into one of the sheaths, riddled with thumbtack holes and frayed around the edges. When she slipped her reading glasses on to get a better look, she saw that it was her mother and grandmother, young and beautiful, their arms draped around each other. They both wore beaming smiles and held old-fashioned tennis rackets in their hands.

She tucked it back into the album before riffling through the rest of the pages. Near the end, she found a weathered envelope, yellowed with age, stamped with a return address of Toledo, Ohio. If only she weren't so pressed for time. When she slid it back into the album, a tarnished silver necklace fell to the floor. It was a dog tag, one of the old necklaces soldiers used to wear before they were chipped. The engraving read "Foster, Philip V." An old flame?

With a quick glance at her watch, Elizabeth headed to the shower with her lukewarm cup of coffee. It was the day of her mother's funeral, and while she repeated the eulogy in her head, she couldn't help but remember her father's funeral, five years earlier. The words her mother had spoken about him were far more eloquent than any she'd ever heard, and Elizabeth was certain hers would not compare.

"You coming, Beth?" Tony's voice boomed over the din of the shower. Her husband was the only reason she ever made it anywhere on time, though it was still a rare occurrence. As had been true of her mother, time had little meaning to Elizabeth. With her coffee gone and her shower done, she dressed in the new black pantsuit she'd bought just for the occasion. She knew she'd never wear it again; the memory of her mother's death would be stitched into its fabric, impossible to wash away.

She snatched her coat from the chair in the kitchen but stopped in the doorway of the den and watched her husband as he surfed through channels on the television, thinking about the fortune she'd been granted in life. *You've been lucky in love*, her mother used to say, and she was right.

"You ready?" he said, switching off the television. Elizabeth nodded as she placed her hand in his and examined the wrinkles that folded together over their skin, wondering what people would say about them when it was their time.

The service hall was almost full by the time Elizabeth got there, and her sister, Georgia, was dutifully shaking hands and doling out hugs in the welcoming line, not angered by Elizabeth's tardiness. In fact, she had expected nothing less.

"Sorry I'm a little late," Elizabeth said, leaning in for a quick hug.

"It's okay," Georgia replied. "She's not going anywhere."

Elizabeth laughed. "That was morbid and tasteless. Mom would have loved it."

"Just as much as she would have loved the fact that you were late for her funeral." Georgia winked at her sister before continuing. "You got your speech ready?"

"It's all in here," Elizabeth said, tapping her forehead with her finger.

The greeting line was unending as the sisters exchanged words and hugs with family and friends, most of whom they'd never met, and before long an elderly woman, well into her eighties, stopped in front of them. She had thinning white hair and deep blue eyes, and though Elizabeth didn't recognize her, the woman wore a beaming smile. "You look just like your mother," she said, slipping her hands into Elizabeth's.

"Thank you," Elizabeth said. "I'll take that as a compliment. And how did you know my mother?"

"She saved my life," the woman replied. "Many years ago, well before you were even born."

"Were you a patient of hers?"

"Oh, no." The smile faded from the woman's lips, but her eyes still shined as she recalled her past with Maria Fontaine. "She visited me once in Ohio, when I was a very young girl. It was such a long time ago, but it still feels like yesterday. She was so beautiful. For a while after she left, I wasn't even sure she had been real. We wrote to each other a couple of times over the years, but I guess life and time just got in the way. Your mom and my brother, they had such a special connection. They lost touch not too long after that visit, but William used to talk about her all the time."

Elizabeth's mind flashed back to the letter she didn't have time to read that morning, the one postmarked from Ohio. "Is your brother here?" she asked.

"Oh, no," the woman said. "William passed away many years ago, shortly after his wife died."

"I'm sorry to hear that."

"Don't be, my dear. He had a wonderful life. In part because of sacrifices your mother made for him. *We may never fully understand our purpose, but there's a reason for everything.* Your mom wrote that to me once. I've never forgotten it."

It wasn't until the woman squeezed Elizabeth's fingers that she realized they were still holding hands, and when the woman finally let go and disappeared into the crowd, a blanket of peace surrounded Elizabeth.

"Are you ready?"

Elizabeth jumped at her sister's voice. The guests had been seated, and as a hush spread over the crowd, she made her way to the front.

"Yes," she whispered to herself. "I'm ready."

"Thank you all for coming today to remember my mother, Maria Fontaine, and to celebrate her life. My sister, Georgia, and I have spent a lot of time together over the past few days, reliving events that we hadn't thought of in decades. There was a lot of laughing, a lot of crying, and a lot of wine. Ninety-five years is a long time to live, so, as I'm sure you can imagine, there were a lot of memories. Some of them we weren't even alive for, but when you hear your parents repeat the same stories year after year at the dinner table, those memories somehow take shape in your head as if they were your own.

"I thought I would come up here today and relate one of those memories with you, a story that stuck out in my mind and got to the essence of who my mother was, but there were so many that it was too hard to pick just one. And who the essence of my mother was, or *is*, is impossible to pin down. She was a mom when I needed nurturing, a comedian when I needed cheering up, a confidante when I needed support. She was everything to me. So, instead of narrowing her down to one story, today I'm going to talk about what it was like to be the daughter of Maria Fontaine.

"No regrets. Yesterday, while Georgia and I were going through my mom's stuff, we decided that if Maria Fontaine was ever to get a tattoo, it would have read, 'No regrets.' Not that she skated through life without ever looking back and shaking her head, because there was a lot of head shaking in her life, but if you knew my mother, then you know she wasn't the one sitting on the sidelines letting life pass her by. She once told me, 'Elizabeth, if you must have regrets in life, let them be for the things you've done and not the things you wish you'd done.' I was thirteen when she told me that, having second thoughts about auditioning for the dance team at school. I didn't make the team. I was a horrible dancer. But I never regretted that audition, because the only dancer there with worse rhythm than me ended up being one of my dearest friends for life.

"She was always full of sage advice like that, and never too busy to spare a moment. It didn't matter what was going on, if I brought her a book or a game or a problem, she'd drop whatever she was doing just to spend time with me. The people my mother loved in life always came first, and she was quick to remind me that it's not the *things* we remember in our lives, and sometimes it's not even the places we go, it's the way those things and places and people make us feel. It's the emotions that are attached to them that make us remember them.

"I don't remember much about my prom dress from high school, but I kept a torn-up swatch of it in a keepsake trunk for years because I couldn't bear to part with it. I don't know if it had spaghetti straps or sequins or bows, but I do remember how it made me feel when I danced in the rain with my parents, on the pier behind our house, when I got home from prom that night. I was crying when my date dropped me off, about God knows what, but what stuck with me most from that night was my parents coaxing me out the back door and through the soggy grass, in our bare feet. The stereo blaring country music from my dad's old pickup truck. My parents laughing hysterically as they pulled me onto the pier with them and tried to teach me the Macarena.

"I didn't realize then what a gift it was to have my parents. How their relationship taught me to love my husband, and be loved in return. How the respect they had for each other would carry into my own marriage and help forge it into something that could stand for eternity. How their friendship demonstrated that a life shared, even with its struggles, is more beautiful than one lived alone.

"But it wasn't just their dedication to each other and their family that made them special. It was also the thousands of people they helped throughout their lives. I know many of you here today were coworkers or even patients of my mother's, and you've probably heard this before, but in case you haven't, her advice to you would be this: Wear your scars proudly. Let them be a testament to where you've been and what you've survived. They are the road map of your life. They are what made you who you are.

"I'm so thankful and immensely proud to have had Maria Fontaine as my mother, and I know Georgia is, too. We learned so many lessons from her, but one of the most important, and the one that will stay even if all the others leave me, is this: Not only should we lead our lives with moral integrity, but we should hold that integrity unfaltering, even when the stakes are high. *Especially* when the stakes are high.

"My mother used to tell me that my name, Elizabeth, was a constant reminder to her that the most difficult choices in life, the ones that involve the most sacrifice, would bring the greatest rewards. I never met the woman I was named after, and my mother didn't like to talk about her too much, but I'm grateful for the lesson she passed on to us.

"I'm grateful, too, for the life I was granted and the family I was blessed with. I couldn't have asked for more. But the greater the love, the greater the loss, and the end is always hard. When she left us, she was ready to go. She had no fear of death, promising we'd meet again. I'm taking her word for that, and if you're watching from heaven, Mom, standing with Dad by your side, I hope you can see how loved you are. Not only by me, but by everyone in this room and everyone you have ever touched."

Despite the sniffles spreading through the crowd when the clapping ceased, Elizabeth managed to slip out of the service hall with her composure intact. She wound her way into the lobby, where drinks and appetizers were being served. Her mouth was parched and her hands were trembling before she swallowed down a cup of orange juice and nibbled on a turkey sandwich. The stragglers rushing through the door nodded in her direction, and when she'd finished her sandwich and tossed the plate in the trash, the door to the service hall opened behind her. The man who entered was tall and lean and about her age. The suit he wore was made of fine Italian wool, and his eyes were the most beautiful cobalt blue she'd ever seen.

"That was a wonderful tribute to your mother," he said. "Thank you for sharing it."

"Thank you," she replied. "And thanks for coming."

"I wouldn't miss this for anything."

There was a familiarity to the man that nagged at her like a persistent itch, as if their lives had once been stitched together but the seams had since been torn. "And how did you know my mother?" Elizabeth asked.

"I never actually got to meet her," the man replied, pulling an envelope from the breast pocket of his suit. "But my mother made me promise to deliver this to you upon her death."

"Your mother?"

"Jennifer Fuller. She was the founder and CEO of Fuller Industries. We're an organization that invests in companies that harness natural energy. But our philanthropy work mostly involves women's rights issues throughout the world."

"Everyone knows what Fuller Industries is. I saw the news of your mother's death on the television a couple years ago. I'm sorry."

"Thank you," he said, handing her the envelope. "This is for the Fontaine Institute. It's a donation that we hope will keep the doors open now that your parents are both gone."

Elizabeth took the envelope with tentative hands. "Why would she donate to us?"

"Your parents were pivotal to her success," he said. "I don't imagine they ever shared this with you, but when my mother was in college in New Orleans, back in the late eighties and early nineties, there was an anonymous donor who paid for her tuition. As well as her room and board. It took me years—and quite a bit of

bribing, I'm ashamed to admit—to uncover the identity of the do-
nors. But I did it."

His words drummed through the air as Elizabeth sat transfixed by the blue of his eyes. They were so penetrating and familiar
that she couldn't quite focus on his words. "What do you mean?"
she said. "Are you saying that my parents paid for her college
education?"

"I know it doesn't make any sense, but I'm sure it was your parents. And they went to such great lengths to conceal their identi-
ties that my mother didn't think it right to out them. Before she
died, though, she put it in her will that upon your mother's death,
the Fontaine Institute would receive this donation."

Elizabeth eased her finger beneath the seal of the envelope and
sliced it open, careful not to tear the check inside. She gasped when
she saw the amount and had to reread it a few times before she
could speak. "I can't take this," she said. It was more than the foun-
dation had made in its entire existence, and more than they would
need to keep it running for twenty years. "This is too much."

"It's not enough, Elizabeth. There's not enough money in the
world to repay your parents for what they did." Applause spilled
through the service hall doors as another speaker finished his eulogy. "You better get back to your guests," he said, holding his
hand out to her. "It was an honor to meet you."

"I'm sorry," she said, "but I never got your name." His hand was
soft in hers, his fingers long and deft like those of a concert pianist,
and when the warmth of his skin reached her, she felt certain she
had known him forever.

"Blaise," he said, a boyish smile breaking across his face. "My
name is Blaise."

ACKNOWLEDGMENTS

I'd be remiss if I did not start with my agent, Stephanie Rostan. Thank you, Steph, for taking a chance on me all those years ago, for your kindness and grace and patience. This story wouldn't have made its way out into the world without you, and I still don't know what I did to deserve you. To Sarah Bedingfield and Courtney Paganelli at LGR. Thank you for being champions of this story and for seeing its promise long before it was polished. Your insights and recommendations contributed not only to this book but also to my abilities as a writer.

To my editor, Kristin Sevick, I don't know how you do it. Thank you for always being on and available, even during a global pandemic, and somehow keeping me on track through it all. You are a treasure, and I am so thankful to have you in my corner. Bess Cozby, I adore you. Thank you for your tireless pursuit in turning my novel into the best version of itself. I wish our time together wasn't so brief. To the rest of the Tor/Forge publishing team, thank-you isn't enough. I see each and every one of you, and I will forever be thankful that I am a part of this family.

Katie Klimowicz, you are a genius. Your cover design captured Maria so perfectly and left me breathless the first time I saw it. Thank you for that.

To my early readers—Carrie Niolet, Katy Roberts, and Damon

Denaburg—thank you for slogging through draft after draft with me. I hope you're all well rested and ready for another go-around.

To my two biggest cheerleaders, Phil and Anne Festoso, whose opinions of me are completely inflated and biased, thank you for your love and support and confidence. I am honored to be your daughter.

To my own daughters, I can't tell you how many times the mere act of writing this novel left me in tears at the thought of ever losing you. Mari, I cherish your beautiful mind and your sensitive nature. Late-night hugs from you are the best. Keep sneaking out of your room for midnight snacks; you know I'll be there typing away. Vidy, I am in awe of you every day. Your work ethic and your drive and your commitment to your dreams are rivaled by no one. I treasure our time together at the barn, and I hope you always know that your dreams are my dreams, too. Jiya, my darling, thank you for teaching me that love is limitless, that bleak beginnings can have beautiful endings, and that there is truly no ownership in this universe. I still can't figure out how that little body holds all that laughter and joy. You are a blessing to the world.

And, finally, to the love of my life, my confidant, my partner in crime: Where would I be without you, Sati Adlakha? Thank you for your overconfidence in me and for all the times you said yes to my crazy ideas. You deserve some kind of participation trophy for sticking it out with me. Maybe for your birthday; we'll see. The world is a more beautiful place with you in it, and anyone who has ever known you can attest to that. I can't imagine doing this life with anyone else. I would never have the strength to let you go.

Turn the page for a sneak peek at
Sarah Adlakha's next novel

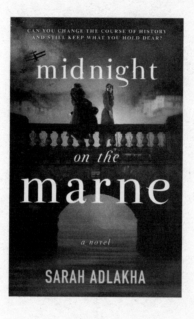

Available Summer 2022

Marcelle

Soissons, France
May 1991

THE DIARY ARRIVED ON A MONDAY. It was old, the pages worn, and the words faded. Even with her strongest reading glasses, Marcelle couldn't pick out more than a phrase or two. English was a language she rarely read, though it was one of many she spoke.

The package had come from America, bound in a roll of tape that had barely managed to hold it together as it had traveled across the ocean to reach her. The author, a man Marcelle hadn't seen in over seventy years, was dead, and while she had often thought they would meet again one day, life had other plans for them both.

There were other treasures in the box: newspaper clippings, photos, letters. If she'd been ten years younger, Marcelle would have already pored over them, but ninety-four years had taken a toll on her eyes, and, like everything else in her life, reading was something she couldn't do for herself. Instead, she waited patiently for five days, for Friday, for the day her daughter would arrive from Paris.

Liliane had offered to read the diary to her, but this was not something Marcelle wanted to share with her caregiver. Not an hour of Marcelle's day passed without company. Daytime caregivers. Nighttime nurses. Doctors. Therapists. Dietitians. Gabriel had secured only the best for his mother, the guilt he felt over his absence in her life softened only by the level of care he could provide for her.

Juliette, on the other hand, didn't have the financial means to help with caregivers and specialists. When she had finally given up trying to move Marcelle in with her, she had insisted they at least spend the weekends together. Marcelle's only daughter divided her time between a Paris apartment during the week, where her days were spent with her daughter and her grandchildren, and Soissons during the weekends with her mother. It wasn't an easy commute, especially for a woman nearing seventy, the ninety-minute drive taking her over roads that were starting to resemble the speedways they had heard about in Germany. But Marcelle had refused to abandon her home in Soissons. She wouldn't do that until it was time to join her husband and her sister and her parents in the cemetery behind the cathedral square.

"Bonjour, Maman." Juliette leaned in and planted a kiss on Marcelle's cheek before she sank down onto the sofa beside her. She was right on time, as usual. "What are you doing inside? It is such a lovely day; I expected to find you in the garden."

Marcelle nodded toward the box on the table before them. "I got a package on Monday. I thought you could help me with it. My eyes, you know."

"A package?" Juliette pulled the box on the table closer, her eyes scanning over the shipping label. "America? Who do you know in America?"

"An old friend," Marcelle replied, not sure how to explain to her daughter who George had been to her, not even sure how to explain it to herself. She had met him on only two occasions, but what he had done for her, and what she had felt for him, was nothing she could put into words.

"A man friend?" Juliette pulled an aged photograph from inside the box before turning it over to read the inscription on the back. "George Mountcastle," she said. "He was a very handsome soldier. I did not know you had an American boyfriend before Papa."

The tremor in Marcelle's hands worsened as she took the photo from her daughter and squinted at the image. It was no use. The face staring back at her was as blurred as the one that had lived inside her memory for over seven decades. "He was not a boyfriend."

Juliette rifled through the box, past the newspaper clippings, and the letters, and the keepsakes. "This one looks like a movie star," she said, pulling out another photograph and reading from the back of it. "Philip Foster. Was he a boyfriend, too?"

"My goodness, Juliette." Marcelle shook her head and sighed. "There were no boyfriends. And I do not remember any Philip."

Juliette laughed as she tucked the photo back into the box before pulling out a yellowed newspaper clipping. "How about this one?" she asked, scanning over the article. "Max Neumann. He was a German. Do you remember him?"

"No . . . I do not think so . . . but maybe . . ." Marcelle shook her head again, frustrated. Her memory had started failing her years ago. Names she couldn't put with faces. Places that seemed both familiar and foreign at once. The term *Alzheimer's* had been tossed around lately, but Marcelle refused to listen. She would not allow her mind to be taken by a disease that had been named after a German. She was simply old; her mind was tired.

"It was a long time ago, Maman." Juliette refolded the article and placed it back in the box before closing the top. She was a perceptive woman, always in tune with the people around her and sensitive to their emotions. Nothing like her brother. "How about a cup of tea in the garden?"

Marcelle's rose garden was almost as famous as her mother's had once been. Her mother had lost interest in gardening after the first war with the Germans, upon returning home to Soissons from Paris and finding nothing but rubble and weeds. Marcelle had planted a new garden to go with the home they had rebuilt when the Germans had surrendered, a place where her mother could spend the rest of her days surrounded by a symphony of colors and the budding of new life. It was a mercy that her mother had passed before the Second World War, before the color had been drained from their lives once more. It would have destroyed her.

Marcelle's teacup rattled against the saucer as she tried to place it onto the table beside her wheelchair. The garden was in full bloom, and as she watched a plump bumblebee bounce from bud to bud, she found herself defenseless against the memories that washed over her.

"It was the summer of 1918," she said, as Juliette took the cup from her hands. "That was when I met him."

"Maman, you don't have to do this." Juliette waved away her mother's words. "There is no reason for you to go back there."

Marcelle's daughter was no stranger to war, or to German occupation. They rarely spoke of the war they had lived through together, and Marcelle had never shared her experiences of the first war with her daughter. The Forgotten War. It was hard to believe a war that had toppled four imperial dynasties could be forgotten.

"You should know what happened," Marcelle replied. "Once I am gone, there will be no one left to tell it."

Juliette pulled the diary from beneath her chair and held it up in front of her mother. "It is all in here," she said. "I took a glance through this while I was preparing the tea, and it looks like this man, George, has already told your story."

"What could he know about my story?" Marcelle huffed. "He barely knew me."

"Shall we find out?" Juliette opened the journal and held it up so Marcelle could see that one lone sentence was scrawled across the middle of the front page. She squinted out of habit, but the ink ran together. "It reads, *the real story of The Great War*."

Juliette turned the page, and Marcelle listened as her daughter brought life to the words and awakened memories that had long ago been put to sleep. The night the Germans had bombed Soissons at the start of the war in 1914. The cellar beneath her father's store where they'd taken shelter. The train station in Montmirail where she and her sister had volunteered as nurses.

"How is this possible?" Marcelle whispered, interrupting her daughter's reading. "How could this man know all these things about me? I never told him any of this."

"Do you want me to stop, Maman?"

Marcelle didn't have an answer for her. There were moments in the story of her life that she had fought to erase from her mind, but there were also moments of joy that had escaped her memory unknowingly, gifts that were being given back to her through her daughter's words.

"Maman!" Juliette gasped, as her eyes bounced over the pages before her. "Were you a spy?"

It was a secret she had kept for seventy years, her husband guarding it well for her. He'd understood why they couldn't share it with her sister or her parents after the war. She smiled at her daughter and nodded in response.

"Did Papa know?" Juliette asked, and again, Marcelle nodded. "Why wouldn't you tell us this, Maman? This is remarkable."

"It was a long time ago, Juliette. And it was not as glamorous as it sounds."

As her daughter flipped through the diary, the fog began to lift from Marcelle's clouded memories. She could see George, the man who'd written the words on those pages; she could feel the sun warming her skin on the day they'd first met; she could hear his voice as he'd delivered the message that would save her life. Perhaps it was a mistake giving that journal to her daughter. Perhaps those memories should have been buried with the people who'd made them.

"Maman." Tears glistened in Juliette's eyes when she looked up at Marcelle after skimming through a few more pages, an equal amount of sorrow and disbelief sewn through her features. "How could you keep all of this from us?"

"All of what?"

"That you were a prisoner in a German war camp."

"I was never . . ." Marcelle tripped over her thoughts, trying to find a sliver of truth in her daughter's words. "That is not right," she finally managed. "I was never a prisoner in a war camp."

"But it says right here." Juliette pointed at the page, at a cluster of indecipherable words. "You were captured and taken to a prison in Jaulgonne."

"No, that did not . . . it almost happened . . . but . . ." Marcelle had imagined that scenario so many times in her life, what might have happened if George hadn't stopped her, that it often felt like a real memory. But it wasn't real. Was it?

"It says right here," Juliette continued. "After the Germans won the battle at the Marne River . . . in July 1918 . . ." Juliette skimmed through the pages, reciting disjointed pieces of a story that felt strangely familiar, but one that Marcelle knew was false. ". . . they marched into Paris . . ."

"No. That is not true, Juliette. I was there. It was July of 1918. We had been at war for four years, and the Americans had just joined the fight. We held the Germans back at the Marne River. They never got to Paris. Our troops pushed them back until they surrendered a few months later. I was there." Marcelle pointed to the journal in her daughter's hands, remembering the celebrations in the streets when the Germans had surrendered. The music. The laughter. The dancing. The day George had come back. "It did not happen this way," she whispered, unable to still the worsening tremor in her hands. "The Germans did not take Paris."

"I'm sorry, Maman." Juliette closed the book and returned it to the spot beneath her chair before reaching out to her mother. "Maybe this was not a good idea," she said, pressing her hand into Marcelle's. "I did not realize it was a made-up story."

Was it a made-up story? Was it fabricated by a man who had known things about Marcelle that were impossible for him to know? It didn't happen that way, did it? But if it was made up, why did it feel so true?

"Could you start from the beginning again?" Marcelle asked, before clearing her throat and forcing a calm into her voice. "I would like to hear the entire story."

CHAPTER 1

Marcelle

Soissons, France
September 1914

THE WINDS SHIFTED OUTSIDE THE WINDOW as the light faded, the burdens of the world clawing at Marcelle's beautiful life and trying to rip it to shreds. She was dutiful in her indifference to it, ignoring the empty house around her with a steadfast determination.

She dreamed, instead, of Pierre. She occupied her thoughts with stolen kisses, secret engagements, and romantic wars. Not the kind of war that took place on battlefields and in trenches, not the kind that men wrote of. She dreamed of the war she had envisioned when the Germans had first announced their intentions to invade France: the soldiers in their crisp uniforms; the troops in their perfect formations; the lovers in their final embraces. She would be a soldier's wife soon, and what could be more romantic than that?

Pierre had left for the front just two days earlier, along with Marcelle's brothers, and while the proposal hadn't yet been announced, she was certain that when they all returned for Christmas in a few short months, it would become official. She would be eighteen next year, old enough to be a bride.

Madame Fournier.

The name tasted sweet on her tongue, like the candies her father had brought home from the store last year after Madame Martin's nephew had visited with an armful of goodies from America. He had bartered them for an expensive bottle of Bordeaux from his cellar, and Marcelle had never tasted anything sweeter.

But that was before her father changed, before everything changed. Her brothers had tried to explain the dynamics of the war to them at supper the night before they'd left, but it was a convoluted tale, and Marcelle wasn't certain they'd understood it themselves. From what she had gathered, the archduke of Austria had been assassinated by Serbians two months earlier, leading to a war that pitted one faction of European countries against another. Austria-Hungary, Germany, and Turkey were the aggressors, while France had allied itself with Russia and Great Britain to defend Serbia.

Marcelle's father had said it was a bit like a chess match, but Marcelle thought it sounded more like a schoolyard brawl, just a bunch of bullies taking sides and fighting. What it boiled down to for her was that two days earlier, her fiancé and her brothers had been marched out of town to defend their northeastern border with Belgium, not one hundred kilometers away, because Germany was poised to strike.

Marcelle felt certain that the Germans were in for a devastating defeat. How could they fight a war on two fronts? Russia to their east; France and Great Britain to their west. The boys would be home before Christmas. She was sure of it.

The sun continued to sink outside the window, but Marcelle waited until the sky had almost succumbed to darkness before she wrapped a shawl around her shoulders and walked the short distance from their home to her father's store down the street. The shop was empty when she arrived, so she followed the soft light filtering in from above as it guided her down the stairs to the cellar. The jewelry box was the first thing she noticed. It sat on the wooden table against the far wall of the room looking out of place by the sacks of food that had been tossed down beside it: potatoes, flour, sugar, beans.

"Que faites-vous?" Marcelle asked. *What are you doing?*

From a darkened corner just beyond the light's reach, her mother stepped forward.

"Nothing, dear," she said. "Just tidying up. Doing some rear-ranging."

"Stop lying to her, Eva." The wine bottles clinked as her father stacked them beneath the wooden table, his temper in full bloom. "She is practically a woman. We need everyone's help here. Stop trying to shelter her from this."

"Shelter me from what?" Marcelle stepped forward, eyeing her sister, who was handing the bottles to their father. Rosalie was an obedient girl. Despite sharing their mother's womb and every minute of their lives thereafter, they had so little in common.

Marcelle was five when she had first realized they were special. She had seen her reflection in her mother's mirror at home, so she knew it was the same as her sister's, but it was not until her mother had taken them to the river for a picnic on their fifth birthday, and she'd seen their reflections side by side in the pool of water, that she had really understood what they were: two different versions of the same person.

Marcelle was the achiever. Nothing was beyond her reach. She was one of the few girls in Soissons to complete her second level examinations, and she excelled in her studies, eager to learn every nuance of history and language and mathematics. Her plans had once included making the one-hundred-kilometer trek southwest to Paris upon her eighteenth birthday to find work as a teacher. She had never shared that dream with anyone. Her parents would have discouraged it, and by the time her second level examinations had rolled around, she had already fallen for Pierre.

Rosalie, by contrast, was the pleaser. She was a quiet and serious girl, sullen, to a certain extent, especially since talk of war had arrived at their doorstep. Life was a chore for Rosalie, a tedious undertaking that required following all the rules in all the right order. She would never have dreamed of running off to Paris without their father's permission. She did what was expected of her.

"Come, dear," her mother said, smoothing her hair back and pinning the strays into place before gripping Marcelle's elbow. "Let's get you back home. The air down here is not good for you."

"No." Marcelle pulled her shoulders back and straightened her spine, pressing her heels firmly into the soft earthen floor and standing almost as tall as her mother. "I demand to know what is going on here."

"You demand to know?" Her father almost banged his head on one of the low-hanging beams of the ceiling when he spun around. "You are a little girl with her head in the clouds. Open your eyes if you want to see what is happening here. The Germans are coming. If they have not already killed your brothers or taken them hostage, they will do so tomorrow. And then they will be here. They will destroy our town and take what they want, and we will be at their mercy."

Marcelle stepped back at the assault of his words.

"You want to know what we are doing here?" he continued. "We are trying to survive. We are trying to save our family. And your sister is the only child I have left who is strong enough to help me do that."

"Mon Dieu, Gabriel!" Her mother stepped between them, wrapping an arm around Marcelle and forcing her up the stairs. The light from outside was muted when they crested the final step and entered the store, and it wasn't until Marcelle looked around that she spotted the crisscrossed mesh that had been taped to the windows. She hadn't noticed it when she had entered just moments earlier, or the bare shelves, or the silence.

The streets were empty. The men who spent their afternoons smoking and arguing and laughing outside of the store were missing, the women who shuffled arm in arm from shop to shop were gone, and the children who chased the dogs from one side of the cobblestone street to the other were nowhere to be seen. When had this happened?

"What is that?" Marcelle pointed to the mesh that was taped to the windows.

"It is to prevent glass from shattering and spraying into the store." Her mother hesitated before she continued. "If the Germans shell us, we need to be prepared."

Marcelle simply nodded and followed her mother home in silence. She sat on the mattress she shared with her sister, the one her brothers had once shared, and tried not to imagine where they might be now. She tried not to think about Pierre and the letters she had already written to him. She tried not to hear their voices or see their faces. She tried, but her father's words would not leave her: *if they have not already killed your brothers . . .*

She didn't come out for supper that night. Her mother tried to take her some bread, but Marcelle refused to eat. She refused to speak or change her clothes or acknowledge her sister when she came to bed. Her father was right. She was a naïve little girl with her head in the clouds. She had refused to see the signs all around her. She had sent the men in her life off to war believing they would return safely to her.

But hadn't they deserved that?

For all she knew, her father was mistaken. He was not the Almighty; he could not possibly know their fates. He was a man like any other man, and Marcelle would keep her head bowed in prayer to the heavenly Father who *did* know the fates of all men, the Father who could perform miracles and was the only One who could deliver her brothers and her fiancé from evil.

About the Author

Angela Russo Photography

SARAH ADLAKHA (she/her) is a native of Chicago and a practicing psychiatrist who now lives along the Gulf Coast of Mississippi with her husband and their three daughters. *She Wouldn't Change a Thing* is her first novel.

sarahadlakha.com
Facebook.com/adlakhabooks
Twitter: @SarahAdlakha
Instagram: sarahadlakha